THIS TOWN WON'T TELL

THIS TOWN WON'T TELL

A NOVEL

RHODI HAWK

NEW YORK

Published in the United States by Crooked Lane Books, an imprint of
The Quick Brown Fox & Company LLC.

Crooked Lane Books and its logo are trademarks of The Quick Brown Fox & Company LLC.

Library of Congress Catalog-in-Publication data available upon request.

ISBN (hardcover): 979-8-89242-505-6
ISBN (paperback): 979-8-89242-506-3
ISBN (ebook): 979-8-89242-507-0

Cover design by *the* Book Designers / Ian Koviak

Printed in the United States.

www.crookedlanebooks.com

Crooked Lane Books
34 West 27th St., 10th Floor
New York, NY 10001

First Edition: May 2026

The authorized representative in the EU for product safety and compliance is eucomply OÜPärnu mnt 139b-14, 11317 Tallinn, Estonia, hello@eucompliancepartner.com, +33757690241

10 9 8 7 6 5 4 3 2 1

For those who don't know what they're
doing, but keep trying anyway.
This book is for you.

CHAPTER

1

Keyed Up

I WAS SUPPOSED TO see a shrink as part of my release conditions, but I got a job at a roadhouse instead. My boyfriend said a roadhouse was no place for a girl. Seven years later this girl became a woman, still working at Harvey's Hideout, and my boyfriend became my husband—and then my ex. But, he was still my kid's dad, and family meant everything.

Now, it was Saturday night. My boss rocked the piano, hair flung over his eyes as townsfolk hit the dance floor. We'd run out of firewood, but then my cousin Logan showed up with a truckload of it, and the big stone hearth kept blazing. An hour later, I bounced a policeman for trying to sing with the band.

Who needs a shrink?

As we approached midnight, the band took its break, and that marked the end of my shift. Except then I noticed the line—ladies in leather, suede, or denim, all queued up by the washroom.

I groaned. "Please, not the toilet."

At a mountaintop roadhouse, the waitress pulled double duty as bartender. But also bookkeeper, card dealer, cleaning crew, and maintenance guy. And bouncer—I scanned for another rowdy I could drag out by the ear. Anything but the toilet.

* * *

Someone had posted Out of Order on one of the stalls. I entered with rubber gloves and held my breath.

And yet nothing in there made me want to shriek. The toilet stood clean and dry and smelling of chlorine. I released my breath. I tried flushing, but the handle flapped freely. An internal connection, then. I hoisted the porcelain lid and set it on the toilet seat, then peered inside.

The water sat low in the tank.

Also: There was a gun.

I stared, my mind shooting out thought streamers.

This sort of thing happened in big cities with gangs and dealers and sex traffickers. We were a tiny mountain town. I had returned home to Suspicion, Montana, to escape this. Sure, Harvey's Hideout was a roadhouse, but it was a roadhouse with no road. They rerouted the highway decades ago. People around here brawled over trail cam pranks or failure to knock snow off their boots. They did not stash firearms in toilets.

This gun was tiny.

Its grip stood on the float above the waterline, and the muzzle rested on the arm to the flusher chain. It was a Saturday night special, a Röhm .22 snub-nose revolver with a faux mahogany grip. I recognized it because—

Of all the thought streamers that flew, this was the red one: This gun belonged to my cousin Logan, who'd just saved the night with a delivery of firewood.

* * *

I caught him as he headed out the big wooden doors. "Logan!"

He glanced over his shoulder. "Hey. I'm in a rush."

"Yeah? Who you rushing out to meet this time of night, a wolverine?"

He'd been focused on the double doors, but now his attention lit back on me.

I reached into my pocket. "Need this for your big midnight conference?"

He caught my hand and swung his arm around me, shrouding the gun under his leather jacket, then scooted me into the now-closed dining area.

I said, "Thought you were in a hurry."

"Shh, Janey."

"You wanna fill in some gaps for me?"

"Couldn't you just leave it?"

"No. I need you to get it out of here."

"Janey. Listen. Will you hold it for me?"

I reared back from him. "What, like it's a beer?"

"Please. I got an early morning for a guided trip. I just cannot take this with me. I need you to hang onto it until I get back."

Logan's idea of mixing things up was navigating by moss and bear scat, so I couldn't imagine what he wanted with this little snub nose. I glanced back at the hall where the bikers sat. I always wondered if they ran meth. They kept their outlaw business quiet, and never gave me any trouble. If they're the reason my cousin carried a gun, I'd knock their heads together.

The little revolver weighed as much as a can of Coke, but it imparted more gravity than its heft. Already, with my work shift at an end, I could feel my thoughts trying to pry free. Family was everything. But where family was concerned, my daughter Em ranked highest.

And yet—

With this gun, I had power.

With this gun, I could become a good mother.

"Oh, no. No, no, no." I thrust it into his jacket pocket. "I can't."

He retrieved it, slipped it inside my apron, and closed his hand over mine. "Please. I'm in trouble. I need your help. I promise I'll explain when I get back."

My breath hitched. Logan never asked for my help.

I said, "But I'm keyed up."

He paused, eyeing me. Logan was always the one helping *me.* His needy orphaned cousin Janey. His knocked-up teenage cousin Janey. Now his broke-ass single mom cousin Janey. He never hesitated. He brought over bags of groceries, took Em on hikes, watched her when I had to work.

He said, "Not if you're keyed up," and reached to take it back.

"Wait."

I ran my hand over it inside my apron. "Yeah, sure. Course I'll do it."

* * *

I went home to my log cabin garage apartment and washed that apron. Tonight was Em's night with my ex, and thank God, because my place was freezing.

I sat by my window and polished the gun, then peered inside. A spiral line gleamed down the barrel. I wrapped it in flour sacks—cheap by the dozen but nice enough for embroidery—and bound the parcel with twine. It looked safe, like a diagonal-cut sandwich.

But then the clouds opened above my landlord's cabin.

With this thing, I'd be a better mother.

Between the clouds, the moon bulged against its etchings. I glimpsed the seas of the moon. My thoughts pried free. And then swelled. Thoughts about my ex.

Dangerous thoughts.

I wasn't sure how long I could keep this up.

CHAPTER

2

Kitty Cat

THAT RESTRAINING ORDER stopped me from setting foot inside my own home.

The thing was, I received a disturbing call from Em's school. She was supposed to attend the spring bake sale, and Trent said he'd bring her, along with a tray of brownies. But the school phoned to say Em never showed up.

So now here I sat in my car, in front of the home I paid for but could not enter, keyed up. Someone had better tell me what happened to my daughter.

I was not supposed to be here. Trent would give me a perfectly good explanation for Em's missing the bake sale. He'd accuse me of being up to my nonsense, then he'd call the police. Even though I didn't smoke, and I certainly wasn't a stalker, when I got keyed up I did both of these things.

Twenty-four hours had passed since I pulled the gun from the toilet. I'd made it through last night. Today, waiting tables for the Sunday brunch crowd, I was one person, and tonight after getting that call from the school, I'd become someone else again. I didn't know how to fix this.

I tapped my ring on the steering wheel and gazed across the street. Music poured from the little house, short with yellow shingles, the gaping black hole on the bottom stair emphasized with a rim of snow. I had painted the door red. The house could have been such a cute place for Em to grow up. Trent had taken it from us.

The clouds swallowed the moon, leaving the house in full darkness. Any illumination came from the floodlights in Harvey's backyard, my boss and former neighbor. The mansions of Cable Hill had mushroomed up around older railroad homes like mine. Most of the tiny cottages had been torn down and replaced with behemoths. Mine was the last hold-out.

Was Em here? Unable to get to her bake sale because Trent and his latest squeeze were too busy having sex inside my house? Because I could tell from that music that's what they were up to. They were absolutely having sex in there.

My phone pinged. Photos from Em—from the bake sale. She and Sierra smiled in front of a plate of cream-filled Danishes. I understood at once that Sierra's mother had taken the girls. No one but Sierra's mother would have them baking Danishes instead of the usual cookies or cupcakes or brownies. Probably, Em would stay the night at Sierra's.

I texted her:

The school called wondering where you are.

She replied immediately:

Sorry.

No explanation. It wasn't my night with Em, so no one clued me in. Still, a wave of relief coursed through me to know she was okay.

Would it have killed Trent to answer my messages? I was sure she'd been kidnapped or left stranded somewhere all alone. Even now, I wondered if Trent had forgotten all about the bake sale. Sierra's mother had probably swooped in to save the day.

If Trent was going to share custody, he needed to ensure our daughter was his highest priority.

In the glove box, next to my sunglasses, Logan's revolver was still safely tucked inside its flour sacks.

I can leave now. Em's safe.

Except . . .

Tap, tap, tap, went my ring on the steering wheel. And in greater intervals the snow fell: *pat . . . pat . . . pat . . .* with an undercurrent of Trent's music going *thump—thump*. Gears in a clockwork.

I mashed the cigarette between my lips and fired off a message to Trent: Need to talk.

I clicked Send before I could stop myself.

Trent had no job. He couldn't even afford house payments. He was a reckless parent.

From the house, the song changed on the playlist. This'll be . . .

Wait. He changed it.

I frowned, listened. Took another pull on my cigarette. It burned to the filter and I opened the door and smashed it into the pavement, heard it sizzle on the ice.

"Hrs And Hrs" by Muni Long.

What the hell? I was the one who'd played this song for him, and he'd called it boring. He'd literally pretended to snore. I held my lighter at eye level with the house, flamed it to cover the window. That new girl, two girlfriends beyond the one he'd cheated on me with. The song was for her.

I picked up my cell phone and called him.

It rang and rang, then, "Yo, Trent here. Bummed I missed ya . . ."—in his swingin'est swingin' Richard voice.

I tossed my phone at the console.

No way could I let Em grow up in some wolf den. I'd come up in foster homes, some good, some bad. It felt like I was raised by wolves, and now here I was, a wolf trying to raise a child. If I had my house back, I could give her a structured environment.

With my left hand, I flicked my lighter. With my right hand, I pulled the gun from the glove box.

I could smoke one last cigarette. Or. Or, I could take this gun in there and make him talk to me.

I reached into the change compartment and dug out a quarter. The old Subaru Legacy was a rust bucket, but I kept it neat. No drinking straw papers, no orphaned french fries or crayons or coupons. I cleaned once a week, inside and out, even on my worst days. Even back in my boozed-up days.

My instinct was to jump on the roof and howl at the snow clouds. But for Em, I had to do what was right. If only I knew what the right thing was. Good moms always knew what to do. Good moms didn't have restraining orders. Good moms had warm, safe homes for their daughters.

I hooked my finger into the twine and tugged the flour sacks free. Logan's little snub nose gleamed. Nestled there in my lap atop its flour sack bed, it looked like it had just woken up.

I picked up the quarter. "Heads: the gun. Tails: one last cigarette."

I flipped the coin, caught it, slapped it on the back of my hand.

This was how I took the winding road to luck. A coin flip wasn't luck, it was 50/50 chance. But chance could get me there. Luck was dumb, bold, and bald. Luck had no conscience, though it did play favorites. Sometimes, it favored me.

The dome light didn't work. I had to flame the lighter to see the coin.

Heads: the gun.

Blood surged from my neck to my temples, and my heartbeat crushed all sounds.

I picked up the Röhm. It had heft, and it smelled like oiled metal.

I said, "Game on, Kitty Cat."

CHAPTER 3

Bang

SNOW CRUNCHED BENEATH my boots. I tucked the Saturday night special in the pocket of my leather jacket.

Trent's new chick had made fleeting appearances from inside his F-150. Crunchy hair, Emmie had told me. With the restraining order, I was only allowed to drop her off for custodial visits at the school or the library, never Trent's place (which used to be my place).

Sherry. Her name was Sherry. Like an after-dinner drink. Or was that before? Something cloying.

Harvey's floodlights shone on the right side yard, so I'd risk getting caught down that way. If I walked down the left side, I'd advance under cover of darkness.

I walked to the right because fuck the dark.

A dim glow filtered from the bedroom window above. Sex lighting. I pulled back my hood and gazed up, but the angle revealed only the ceiling.

I realized I was going to look. Because once I got up on that deck, I'd have a view into the bedroom. Better to look first and screw up my courage—desensitize myself to "ex sex"—than to march in and get a shock.

A glance at Harvey's fence confirmed all was quiet.

The deck stairs creaked beneath my boots. Not that anyone could hear me with that slow, thumping music. I inched upward, pulling out the snub nose and holding my arm long. My free hand toppled a track of snow from the railing.

The kitchen lay to my right and to my left, the bedroom.

I breathed in and crossed to the curtains. I peered through.

He had a trick of turning on the closet chain-lamp and pulling the door half closed for mood lighting. It took a moment for my eyes to adjust.

Then: Trent lay face-down in Sherry's muff.

I gave a tiny shriek and spun away, my hand clamped to my mouth.

The snow crackled in the evergreens. My scream had been minimal, but it existed. I waited, listening for the music to stop, the curtains to fly open. My breath puffed, staccato and white, rising against falling snow.

I swallowed and then inched back to the glass. There they were. Too happy to stop and investigate a scream beyond the wall.

Sherry writhed and gripped the pillow. I wondered if it still smelled like my hair.

Slush loosened from the roof and tumbled onto the back of my neck. I eased toward the kitchen door and tried the knob. Locked. As if that could stop me.

The swivel lock hung pitiful at the kitchen window. It broke two summers ago, and in this weather, the wood shrinks. I anchored the revolver against the molding and struck upward with the heel of my hand, timing it with the music beats. It hurt, and it rattled the frame.

They can't hear this?

But then moaning erupted from beyond the walls, escalating to hysterics.

Oh, God, she's a screamer. I dropped my forehead to the glass.

Now or never. Their distraction would wind to an end. I shoved at the window again. It budged half an inch.

A hand grabbed my wrist. Another clamped my mouth before I could scream. Someone gripped me from behind, yanking my snub-nose arm upward, forcing it toward the sky.

Bang! went the revolver—

More like a click. Dry fire.

CHAPTER

4

Harvey Elliot and Frieda Kanjo

HARVEY.

He started dragging me by the hood.

"I wasn't going to shoot him!"

"Shut up!" The snub nose bulged from the pocket of Harvey's plaid flannel pajama pants.

He released me to hike them up. He'd lost weight from whatever cardiac problem he'd been having. And yet he still looked healthy—his thick brown and gray hair swooped in a cowlick, gathering snowflakes as we trekked.

Thank God it was Harvey and not his wife, Frieda Kanjo. She'd drop me in the blender and hit Spin. Then she'd call the cops. I looked back. Trent's house remained dark, music churning.

We entered the shed and Harvey whirled to face me.

"Talk," he whispered.

"Harvey, I wasn't going to shoot anybody—"

He seized me by the elbows and yanked my face up to his, so close and so sudden I thought he meant to kiss me. My bladder nearly split.

He breathed in deeply and then pushed me away. "You're lucky I don't smell booze on you."

I slumped and shook my head.

He said, "Do you have any idea how terrible your timing is? Swear to God, you just—"

Frieda Kanjo's voice called from the house: "Harvey?"

My throat seized to a pinhole. Harvey waved me back, and I shrank into the darkness.

Please, oh, please. Just this one thing, that Frieda never saw me.

Harvey stepped out into the drifting snowflakes. "Yeah?"

Frieda said, "What're you doing in that shed?"

Harvey coughed, brushed snow off the stacked firewood. "Aw, nothing, honey. There was a raccoon getting into the trash and I think it ran in here."

Frieda fell silent. I shifted my weight to my left boot and tucked my hands under my armpits, waiting. Making myself invisible.

Frieda called back, "Those raccoons are always tearing things up around here."

Harvey said, "Yeah, they're always tearing things up."

"While you're getting rid of it, send Janey in here to me. I want to talk to her."

Oh, no.

My hands fluttered to the lava slide that used to be my face. Harvey's shoulders sagged. Frieda turned back inside and shut the door.

* * *

Harvey, Frieda, and I sat around the cherry dining room table. The room looked nice. It smelled like cinnamon apple. The fireplace crackled, and a blanket with a bear motif draped the sofa. Everything tidy and welcoming. Except Frieda. She glared at me with her forehead bent into the shape of a bat in flight.

"I'll take a Dewar's," she said to Harvey.

Frieda's iron-colored hair hung free. She wore a thin robe over a loose T-shirt and no bra, with drawstring pants. Harvey opened a wood-paneled cabinet that separated the dining area from the kitchen, and pulled out a bottle.

Frieda kept glaring at me. I flicked my gaze from Frieda to the bottle to Harvey, now retrieving glasses from the kitchen and filling them with ice. He set two on the table, one for Frieda and one for himself. He placed the Dewar's on the table, too. Then he went back to the fridge and returned with a bottle of soda.

Frieda said, "You forgot her."

Harvey slid his own glass in front of me.

"I don't want any. I gotta go." I rose from my chair.

Frieda said, "Sit down."

I thought to make a run for it, then thought better. Harvey and Frieda eyed me as I sat back down.

Frieda said, "She been drinking?"

Frieda had been staring at me but was clearly addressing Harvey.

Harvey took a swallow of scotch and soda, then released a lion breath. "Nope."

"You sure?"

"Smell her."

Frieda tore her eyes from me long enough to shoot him a scowl. "I don't need to smell her. I asked if you're sure."

"I'm sure."

She paused. "I'm not happy with you either, Harvey Elliot. Did you think you were just going to manage this little attempted murder without my knowing? How'd that make me look in this state? If something got out?"

I said, "I wasn't going to murder anybody."

Frieda said to me, "When was the last time you had a drink?"

"Seven and a half years ago." I felt inclined to lean over and throw up between my knees.

"You haven't faltered since then?"

"I messed up a lot in the beginning. But it's been seven and a half years since I had a drink."

Frieda looked at Harvey. "She lying?"

Harvey had pulled the Röhm from his pajama pocket and was examining it. "I do not know. She is capable of bullshit. But I have not seen her drinking, nor have I seen her drunk around the Hideout or anywhere else for about as long as she says."

Then he said, "This gun's not loaded."

The two of them drilled eyes into me like I was crazier for *not* trying to kill Trent. I longed for that Dewar's, and I wanted a damn cigarette.

I pushed away from the table.

"Sit your ass back down," Frieda said.

I went rigid because I'd never heard an important person like Frieda Kanjo talk that way.

I said, "I need to move. I can't just sit."

"You will sit."

I slumped back into the chair and yanked off my leather jacket.

Harvey said, "If you weren't going to shoot him, why didn't you just get rid of the revolver?"

The fire spat from the hearth. I folded my arms, bounced my leg.

Frieda said, "Because she wanted to *have* it, Harvey. She needed it to scare her baby daddy. Didn't you, girl?"

Heat flooded my cheeks. We used to call each other "girl" and "girlfriend" back in the group home, and it felt like a sisterhood. Frieda used it differently. She wielded it like addressing a servant. Her expression showed a mean kind of pleasure.

Harvey said, "Where'd you get the damn thing?"

I turned away.

"Answer him," Frieda said.

I swallowed and tried to meet my boss's eyes. "At the Hideout. It belongs to my cousin. Logan."

Frieda and Harvey exchanged a weighted glance, then Harvey said, "Go on."

I shrugged. "That's it. A bunch of them were having dinner and I found it after they left."

My lie sucked. It didn't even improve things. If it were just Harvey and me sitting here, I'd have told him about the Out of Order toilet.

"'Found it,'" Frieda sneered, but worse—the surprise and disappointment on Harvey's face.

I said, "No, for real, there's a circle of salt. I wouldn't steal at the Hideout."

Frieda smirked, rolled her eyes.

I dug in. "You want me to just toss a gun in the lost and found with people's mittens?"

I licked my lips, the fireplace and the scent of Dewars scorching them. "I knew it was Logan's, but he's off guiding that fly-fishing trip."

Harvey said, "And you didn't tell me this, why?"

I said, "You've been out with medical appointments! Logan'll get it back, so I didn't think it was a big deal."

Frieda's bat brows turned to stone. "Harvey, I'm going to need you to warm up the Tundra."

I whipped my gaze to Harvey, my legs ready to spring. My heart like a jackrabbit.

Frieda said to him, "Get my purse, too. It's in the back seat of the Audi."

Harvey said, "What do you need the Tundra for?"

"Just do it."

He sighed, gave a meaningful glance to me—and I clung to it, because he was a friend; really, my only friend other than Logan—but he pushed off from his knees and rose. My stomach turned. Harvey trudged to the back door and collected two sets of keys from the hook, then left.

Frieda stared at me. Hard.

Then, she picked up her phone and pointed at me. "You watch. Watch carefully. Because this is the moment you lose your little girl."

CHAPTER

5

Wolves

FRIEDA DIALED THREE numbers: Nine-one-one.

I leaped from my chair and snatched the phone before she could press Send.

Frieda's bat brows flared. "You just added battery to your charges."

"Frieda. Frieda, listen to me. I am willing to do anything. Please don't call the police. I am *begging* you. All I wanted was to scare Trent. I wanted him to take it seriously, being a parent. To get her to school when he's supposed to. I work two jobs, waiting tables at the Hideout and running the card games, just so I can scrape out a living for her. Trent doesn't have a job."

"Give me back my phone."

"My daughter needs a home."

"My phone!"

"You can't let them take her—"

"Now!"

I presented the cell phone, 911 still displayed on the screen.

Frieda snatched it and cuffed me over the ear. I staggered backward, stunned.

She jammed a fist to her hip and turned away, then wheeled back on me. "What drugs you on?"

"I'm not on anything!"

Frieda slapped me hard enough to draw blood. I floundered, my tongue dodging to the gap where I'd lost a molar all those years ago in foster care.

"You lying to me?"

"I don't do drugs! I swear!"

The fireplace blazed hot for me and only me. I started for the door.

Frieda was on me. She grabbed my wrist with surprising strength. "Sit down."

"Stop! Leave me alone!"

She spoke through her teeth, nails digging into my wrist. "Sit down, girl. I have something to show you."

I wanted to rake her cheek. Or bolt. But I sat.

She poured more Dewar's, not bothering with the soda. She remained standing. Had herself a nice long drink.

Then, she pulled something up on her phone and handed it to me. I looked, and the room tilted. Frieda eased behind my chair and watched over my shoulder. On her screen, I recognized the back deck of the house—my old home, now Trent's—as seen from a security camera mounted on the rear of Harvey and Frieda's place. When did they install a security camera?

As if in answer, Frieda said, "Been some break-ins on Cable Hill lately."

In the footage, through a portal of snowflakes, lay Harvey and Frieda's yard. And Trent's. And then me sneaking up the side yard. Me, pulling back the hood of my parka. Me, tilting my face up toward Trent's bedroom. Harvey and Frieda's floodlights clearly rendered my face. Next, the camera showed me climbing the deck stairs, my gun arm long, my free hand releasing snow where I slid it along the railing.

I didn't want to watch what happened next. I closed my eyes and set down the phone.

Frieda said, "Only reason Harvey ever gave you a job is because he felt sorry for you. I heard you gave birth while you were in jail."

It had been juvenile detention, not jail. I had Emmie nine years ago, when I was seventeen and incarcerated for being a runaway. Em didn't know this. Tears coursed down my face, and I wiped them with my sleeve.

Frieda said, "It's a wonder they didn't take that child away before now. That time has come."

"No! She's my daughter."

Horror cleaved my throat. They couldn't separate Emmie and me. What would happen to her?

Frieda waved at Trent's house. "And if you think that fool can hang onto guardianship for more than ten minutes, you're wrong. Know what 'substitute care' means? It means the state figures out what's to become of your child. I will personally see to it. You think your priors are safe because you were a juvenile? I can crack that wide open. I will feed that prosecutor like a deer tick."

"Please, Frieda! I'll do anything. I'll clean your house. Every day."

Frieda swirled her drink, the ice crowding the glass. "I don't want you anywhere near my house."

But then she said, "You lie to me once and I call the police. I'll make sure you never see your little girl outside a prison visiting room. Do you hear me?"

"Yes. I won't lie."

"Are you on drugs?"

"No. I mean, not those kind. I'm supposed to be on meds, but I ran out."

"What kind of medication?"

I swallowed, horrified to talk about this with Frieda. "They're for bipolar disorder."

"Where's your little girl right now?"

"Em's with her—I mean, she's with a friend."

Frieda cuffed me, and pain tore through my tongue. My chair toppled as the door flew open. Harvey burst in.

I scrambled to my feet, rooting myself in front of Frieda, knowing that to fight back, or to run, meant disaster for Em. My mouth tasted like iron. I felt like a caged, cornered animal.

Harvey dashed to Frieda and yanked her away. "Frieda! Christ, get it together."

Frieda pointed at me. "That was for *almost* lying."

I burbled out of my mind—grinning and baring teeth. My chest heaved as though I'd been running. I took two steps toward Frieda. She stiffened.

"Janey!" Harvey barked.

My fingers twitched. I leaned close until she sucked in a fearful breath, then I spat blood onto the oak planks at her feet. I dragged my wrist across my lower lip. Blood on my wrist. Blood on the floor.

Harvey pointed at the chairs. "Both of you, sit down!"

I grimaced at him, eyes bulging.

I knew these people. Not the way a person knew their neighbors. Not the way someone knew their coworkers. I saw them now. I saw them both.

He righted my chair and pointed at it. "Janey. Sit."

I felt my lips quake, but I slumped into the chair. And with that, my brain bit down on practical thought again.

Why?

What would big shot Frieda Kanjo want with *me*? I was nobody. A waitress. I had grown up in the system.

No way could I allow anyone else to raise my daughter, let Em fall to the mercy of chance—good foster parents or bad ones. In the system, it was a roll of the dice.

Harvey picked up Logan's little Saturday night special and pet it.

He said to Frieda, "I couldn't find your purse."

"It's right there." She pointed at the bookshelf where her cow print Burberry handbag perched next to a black cloth hardcover of *The Cincinnati Kid* by Richard Jessup.

A hiss of frustration escaped from Harvey.

Frieda leaned down next to me. The fizzy scotch smell overwhelmed and repulsed, and yet it also made me want to grab that bottle and lope into the night.

She said, "Do you know what I do for a living?"

I nodded.

"Use your words, girl."

"I guess—you're a lawyer?"

She cast herself onto her chair, then sipped her drink. "It's a good guess, seeing as we've been next-door neighbors for years. I'd've been worried if you'd thought I sold coffee at the Starbucks in Whitefish."

I swallowed. A framed watercolor of a mountain peony rattled from Trent's sex music next door. That brought an image of him facedown on Sherry. The wind swelled through the curtains, causing a pine knot to explode in the fireplace.

Frieda said, "What's going to happen, is you are going to do a small job for me."

CHAPTER

6

The Work

SHE COULD HAVE introduced me to a talking bear. It would have surprised me less. I waited, tense, a lightbulb flickering on the brink of flare-out.

I said, "I don't get it."

"That's because you are an imbecile, young lady, in addition to being a bad person. But listen and learn. You are about to be given *parameters* of *functionality*. That's what's happening, right here, right now, tonight. It will not make you a good person. It will not stop you from being an imbecile. But it might get you through a footnote of little Emmie's childhood. Do you understand?"

It sounded horrible. Lucky for me, Frieda did not require a reply.

She said, "You are going to have the opportunity to make a little money. More than you make working for him."

She shot her chin at Harvey. He baby-sipped his scotch and soda, thumbing the snub nose's trigger guard.

Frieda's voice turned to silk. "You could use the money to get the heat turned on. Would you like that?"

"Yes?" I replied, processing that she knew my apartment had no heat. What else did she know? I looked from Harvey to Frieda.

Frieda said, "Right. First thing, you're going to get back on your medication."

"I can't afford it."

"No insurance?"

"Even with, the meds're too expensive."

"Then your pay goes to your medication. It's that important. This is what's called kindness. I am being kind to you. Do you understand me?"

I nodded—jerkily.

"Use your words!"

"Yeah! I-I get it!"

My mouth throbbed from her kind beating. I clamped my hands to stop them from shaking.

Frieda said, "It's just a one-off. You keep your job at the Hideout. You do not call me, I get in touch with you. You do not come around, not here to the house and certainly not to my office. Not unless I summon you. Do you understand?"

"Yeah, I get it."

I got it, all right. The base of my skull formed an oil slick.

Frieda said, "You do not talk about this to anyone. Not to your cousin, not to your priest. If you violate my rules I will have you arrested and you will lose custody of your child. Are we clear?"

Through an ever-constricting throat: "Yes, Frieda, we're clear."

"Good. Harvey is taking you into Kalispell now."

Harvey sprang to life. "I'm what?"

Frieda shot him a glance. "You'll find that the Tundra is nice and warm so your tender backside won't have to endure the cold."

Harvey said, "That's good news. Cuz anymore of your horseshit and I'll have to sit down to pee."

In that moment, I realized Frieda had been giving me the okiedoke. She'd never had any intention of calling 911. She'd dispatched Harvey to warm up the Tundra, knowing she was going to send us to Kalispell before she even made a show of calling the cops. I didn't know what to do about this. She faked her threats but they were also real. If I walked away, she would nail me. She marched three steps into the future because she *created* the future. She'd outfitted me in a cow halter before I ever saw it.

Frieda continued to address me. "I'm going to write down the name of a doctor who will give you a urine test. We'll see if you're telling the truth about being drug-free. If you're on something, now's the time to tell me and save us all a whole lot of trouble."

I wrung my hands, looked from Frieda to Harvey. "I'll drive myself. I've never done street drugs. My problem was with alcohol."

"Harvey will drive you."

Harvey said, "Darlin', I'll take her in the morning. I been drinking and I've had a long day."

"You haven't had that much to drink."

Frieda picked up his glass and drained it. "There. Go on, go."

"Godsake, woman."

He stashed the Saturday night special and made helpless hands at me. "You heard her."

CHAPTER

7

Dirty Doc

THE DOCTOR WAS the only soul at the clinic. The lights were off and I expected dripping water, maybe a three-wheeled gurney with a rusty saw. But it was just a regular medical facility that looked foreboding in the afterhours.

Before we left Suspicion, Harvey and I had swung by my place to drop off my station wagon and pick up my old medical printouts. Then we drove all the way into Kalispell with only one stop for coffee, two and a half hours in a blizzard. Lucky the roads weren't blocked. Kalispell had twenty-four-hour urgent cares but we came to this place, which looked closed except for the one physician who wore his street clothes and needed a shave.

He, that is, the *male* doctor, escorted me into the bathroom to watch me pee. "The sooner you fill that cup, the sooner we both get out of here."

I said, "I can't pee with you watching."

"I have to. That's the point."

I tried. Nothing happened, even though Harvey and I stopped for large coffees from the McDonald's in Whitefish.

The doctor switched on the faucet and let the water run. That got my water running, and I worked through it.

The tests would come back clean, of course.

* * *

Harvey walked me back through the slushy parking lot to the Tundra, still warm. While I'd been performance peeing for Frieda's dirty doctor, Harvey had gone to the twenty-four-hour Walmart for munchies. He'd gotten me peanut-butter-filled pretzels, my favorite, and Diet Coke. He knew what I liked because aside from being my boss, he was my friend.

"Here's your pills," Harvey said, handing me a bag full of bottles—lots of them.

Frieda's dirty doc must have phoned them in to the all-night pharmacy before he ever laid eyes on me. As in, while we were still driving out from Suspicion. He'd taken the prescriptions from my printouts and added his own flair.

I glared at Harvey. "I'll take them later. They make me sleepy."

"Now Janey, don't give me any shit. You can sleep on the way back."

Harvey turning on me felt worse than getting knocked senseless by Frieda. I probed the missing molar. Life in foster care wasn't just tough because some homes were abusive. It was tough because some families were loving. The nice families rejected me, and the system passed me from foster to foster because I was never quite right in the head. Swings from long sleeping jags to wall-climbing, bark-at-the-moon episodes.

I had vowed that Em would never live in fear of violence, and never know what it felt like to be sent away by a good family because she just didn't fit. *I* was Em's mother, and *I* would take care of her.

While Harvey drove, I washed down each pill with Diet Coke. I ignored my favorite pretzels. Let someone else choke on them.

Harvey said, "Don't look so sour. Things aren't that bad."

"Maybe for you. You've gone so low you're incapable of falling down."

He shrugged, like all was cool at school and we were just sharing beer nuts at the Hideout. "Tell me what's on your mind. Maybe I can walk you through it."

"Just trying to consider my options."

"Okay. Far as options go, you have none."

"Bullshit, Harvey. There's always options. Fortunately for me, I was born without balls, so I don't have to worry about someone else carrying them around in her cow-print purse."

"Let me tell you something. You think you can get all cute now that Frieda's not sitting here with us? Your situation hasn't changed. I'm a veteran of trying to outrun Frieda's buckshot, and trust me, you can't. Once she picks you, she's got you. She knows how to turn the screws, and for you, that's Em. Frieda caught you sneaking up on Trent with that damn gun—"

"But she had me all wrong."

"No, Janey, *you* had it wrong. *You* had it wrong. Never before have I seen anyone fuck up so spectacularly and with such precision, and perfect timing."

He exploded a breath.

The snow descended in relentless rhythm, hitting the Tundra's windshield one flake at a time, one second at a time, in no rush but with horrifying persistence.

"I'll go to the police myself," I said.

Harvey chuckled. "You sure could do that. Call who, straight to the police chief? Quincy Tigner?"

Driving one-handed, Harvey grabbed his phone and tapped the screen. "Go on, call him."

He handed me his cell. Quincy Tigner's phone number displayed, but with the label "Quince," because apparently, they were tight like that.

I said, "You're bluffing."

"You sure? It's just a phone call. I guess it *is* after three in the morning. You'd damn straight get his attention."

Harvey set down the phone, leaving Chief Tigner's name displayed. "What would you tell him? You can do a dry run on me. I'll be Quincy."

I squeezed my eyes shut. Frieda had the video. I had . . . nothing. Only the idea of something. Something I didn't want to get involved in. I knew Quincy, too. Everyone grew up together in this tiny town. Before my mother died, when I was a little girl, I used to stay over with Quincy's sister at the Tigner house. But I fell out of touch, when all the while, Harvey kept him close.

Harvey said, "What about the FBI?"

He pulled up another number and this time, placed the call, putting it on speaker. I could see the name displayed—Kenny Dunkins.

It answered on the second ring, a voice on high alert. "What's goin' on?"

Harvey said, "Rawhide, how you doing?"

Long sigh. "Sleepy. What time is it?"

"It's late. We're actually in your neck of the woods. Got someone here wants to say hi to you. Say hi, Janey."

I watched each snowflake pat the windshield. I kept silent.

Harvey said, "She's shy."

That guarded tone returned to the FBI agent's voice. "I'm startin' to feel shy, too."

Harvey chuckled. "Aw, it's all right. Go on back to sleep, my man."

Harvey ended the call, then glanced at me, thumbs hooked over the steering wheel. "You get knee-deep with Frieda before you even figure out whose shit you're standin' in."

With each pat of snowflake, the medications slid into my bloodstream. I recalled that they used to pack a wallop. And those were the meds I was used to. I'd taken each according to their respective labels but now I remembered that last time, my doctor moved up the dosage gradually. Frieda's dirty doc threw me the maximum dose.

I'd have thought the FBI agent, Rawhide, would send a WTF text after our strained phone call. But he didn't. Maybe he'd grown accustomed to mysterious three AM check-ins.

CHAPTER

8

Spectacular

THE MEDS LEFT me woozy and I drained my Diet Coke, hoping the caffeine would help.

After an hour driving in silence, Harvey said, "She hates you."

That much seemed clear. "What did I ever do to Frieda?"

"She thinks you and I had an affair. We didn't, though."

"Thanks for telling me. I'd have been embarrassed if I missed it."

He looked at me, looked back at the highway.

He said, "I'm supposed to wait for the labs to come back, but I know you're not on any drugs and you haven't been drinkin'. She's gonna need you tomorrow."

"Tomorrow, as in Wednesday? Because today's already tomorrow, which is Tuesday."

"Tuesday. She needs you Tuesday."

This sounded bad. Wolf's lair bad. Mean streets bad. I'd returned to Suspicion years ago, after that awful stretch of uncertainty in the foster system, and I'd gotten my life together. I thought those shadows would never fall on me again.

The Tundra exited to the feeder road.

Harvey said, "It's real simple. Seven o'clock, you know where the Big Bald Luck games are going down?"

"Of course I do. I'm the card dealer."

"I mean, 'ya know,' not, '*do you* know.'"

I pressed my forehead. The card games migrated on a regular basis. Originally, Harvey and I held them in a cabin at Big Bald Rock. But then the buzz traveled too far—and the sheriff told Harvey to keep his illegal gambling situation low-key or shut it down. So we moved to a trailer in Little Bald Rock. Then we moved to the back room of Maya's Salon. Currently, we were meeting at the Sure Shot Shooting Range off Cinnamon Falls Road. Since email, text, social media, or any other digital footprint triggered Harvey's paranoia, my players came to the Hideout to get the location of upcoming games.

Harvey said, "You get to the shooting range at seven thirty, wait in the parking lot for five minutes. Y'know the Cinnamon Falls Bridge?"

"Yeah, jeez, I know."

"Someone'll meet you there under that bridge. Bring'm an empty backpack. It's a particular kind. I'll get it to you. Then they'll give you a full backpack. Don't go makin' conversation. You take the backpack, bring it to the Hideout, put it in the safe."

"I can't. I have Em."

"You're gonna need a sitter, Janey."

"Harvey, come on. I have to work at the Hideout, *and* raise my kid . . ."

He slammed on the brakes and the Tundra went skidding. I gasped. Something pelted my neck and papers slid off the dashboard. His energy drink sloshed.

Harvey said, "I don't think you realize what's happening. Something bigger than you or me or Frieda or the entire town of Suspicion. A very important part is missing that usually keeps this machine in motion. You are that replacement part. You, because of your spectacularly timed, PRECISION FUCK-UP!"

My pulse pumped so hard it hurt my hands.

Eighteen wheelers made rise-and-falls as they passed on the nearby interstate. This part of Montana never slept.

I said, "Harvey? What are you talking about, important part? I am nobody."

I picked a coin out of my lap, the thing that had pelted my neck when Harvey slammed the brakes. Reflexively, I started to check for heads or tails, but placed my thumb over it instead. I'd left a decision to chance when I could have made an active choice. And yet. The superstitious kernel within my psyche believed that regardless of whether the road started with chance or choice, it would have led to the same fate.

"This is the way things turned out, Janey. I wish to God you didn't go creep-stalking Trent like that. Now Frieda's got you."

He wiped his hand over his mouth, blinked at the distant traffic. We'd stopped in the middle of the feeder road, but the Tundra was the only vehicle on it. In the side mirror, our taillights painted the snow red.

I placed the coin back on the dashboard. Harvey's brand-new Toyota Tundra cost ten times the price of my rusted-out Subaru station wagon, but his could use a cleaning.

He reached into the console and handed me spare keys to the Hideout. "When you're done, just leave the keys and the bag in the safe and go out through the kitchen. Lay low, one and done. It's important that these people accept you. But try to get in and out without saying much."

He put the Tundra in gear, and we resumed the drive. Snow laced the windshield and disappeared with the wipers. My pulse continued to flutter.

Harvey said, "You could always bring Em over to our place. Frieda'll watch her. Believe it or not, she loves kids. She's a different person around kids. Won't drink a drop."

I visualized Frieda, her face pinched in hatred, watching Em. Not in this lifetime.

CHAPTER

9

Logan

THE SUBARU'S HEADLIGHTS glistened on the road. The shooting range had a false-front Western facade and sat nestled in a snowy grove of firs. I pulled into the empty parking lot and killed the lights, the tail pipe sending puffs in my rearview mirror. No one around.

Harvey said to sit here for five minutes. What the hell for?

Because somewhere out there, someone had eyes on me.

I murmured, "Be cool, Kitty Cat," and stretched my fingers on the steering wheel so anyone watching could see I was harmless.

I'd filled up too much of my life playing stupid. It had gotten me by in foster care and group homes, and as a nonthreatening wife for Trent. When you played stupid, people didn't take you seriously, and—you believed—you were less likely to offend or get hurt. The problem was, if you turned off your intelligence too long, you forgot where the On switch was.

I'm in trouble, Janey. I need your help. I promise I'll explain.

Logan damn sure would explain, because now *I* was in a jam. His phone was still out of range on the guide trip. Phone service ran spotty in the best parts of Greater Suspicion, let alone up in the lost Kootenai wilderness where Logan took fly-fishing clients.

Five minutes passed.

"One and done, one and done," I said.

I put the Subaru in motion again, crawling the curves of Cinnamon Falls Road to the bridge. The station wagon managed well in melted snow, although two decades of salted roads had bitten rust into the undercarriage.

Beneath the bridge, I rolled down the windows as if that could help me see. The falls gushed somewhere beyond. Snow dripped and refroze from the girders, and it smelled like rain.

The cherry end of a cigarette caught my eye. Behind it, a large vehicle came into view. I parked and let myself out of my station wagon. A man leaned against an SUV, smoking, a backpack resting on the hood next to him.

He sized me up from boots to hairline. "Where's Logan?"

My mind encased the name in ice. Surely I'd misheard. I'd been thinking about my cousin as I drove over here, so maybe I was projecting.

The man fell silent. Harvey had warned that they must accept me.

Suspicion was a small town and I knew of only one Logan, and that was my cousin—the one out in the wilderness right now cooking trout over a campfire. Beneath my leather jacket, Logan's revolver, still empty, sat at an awkward angle down the back of my pants. I'd stolen it back from Harvey on the return drive from Kalispell. Not a violation of the circle of salt when you were stealing back something that had been taken from you in the first place.

In the glow of parking lights, the guy wore his jacket open, a thermal shirt tucked into his jeans. He had dark hair, though his face fell in shadow beyond his cigarette.

He arched his neck to scrutinize my Subaru. I leaned over to steal his field of vision and bring him back.

He said, over-annunciating the hard *o*, "*Loh-gun*. I asked you, 'Where is *Logan*?'"

Moving with exaggerated ease, I reached for his hand, then removed the cigarette from between his fingers. He went rigid but relinquished it and refrained from any cataclysmic reactions—such as reaching for a weapon.

I took a slow drag, and his eyes held mine. The smoke drifted from me to him. Then I dropped his cigarette to the sand, crushing it beneath my boot.

"*I'm* Logan," I said.

The man swept me with his eyes again, this time with an altered demeanor. He handed over the bag.

CHAPTER

10

The Bad Pitch

At the Big Bald Luck games, I'd have to act like all was cool. I arrived at the Sure Shot Shooting Range early and chose the merch area. There were holsters, ear protection, clothing emblazoned with the "Sure Shot" logo. I pushed aside the displays to make room.

My card table weighed 145 pounds. I used a dolly to transport it from my station wagon to the building. From there it rolled on its own wheels and unfolded in seconds. It had a dramatic red felt top with black tufted leather rails and a drink holder for each seat.

I allowed my players a pour if they used a short glass, be it water, soda, or hard stuff, but if they wanted snacks or to drink from a bottle, they had to remove themselves. That usually meant sitting out a hand.

I used a level and kept my table clean. I bought my own brush but I'd made Harvey get me a cordless tabletop crumb vacuum. He'd balked at the expense, but I'd pointed out that it worked on the psyche. The cleaner the felt, the more compelling the game.

The more compelling, the higher the bets. The higher the bets, the steeper the rake—and Harvey raked on points.

He bought the damned crumb vacuum.

I swigged my bottle of water and set it in my cup holder at the dealer's chair, my thoughts returning to the strange little backpack the man under the bridge had handed off to me. It'd had one strap and tough mesh fabric, and the zipper closed to a lock. Like a bank bag, only large and over-the-shoulder. The contents had felt brick-like. Bundled drugs, maybe, or stacked money. Perhaps something stolen. Frieda's "job" for me felt worse than barehand picking hair from the Hideout's washroom drain.

Never.

Again.

I wondered if it might boomerang back to me. How bad a thing had I "one-and-done"?

My elbow swung wide and knocked my bottle, sending water diamonds in an arc. I flung out my arm and caught them before they hit the red felt. They landed cold on my skin.

The door flew open, and the first of my players arrived—Guy Hamm. He brought in a blast of frigid air.

He stamped his feet in the entry instead of on the porch, leaving salty slush for me to clean up, and he failed to close the door.

I said, "Hey, Guy, you wanna clear your boots outside? This isn't the roadhouse."

"Christ, you look like hell. You drinking?"

* * *

I cleared Guy's slush as the others arrived. I held seats for only four players tonight: Guy Hamm, the jerk; Maycie Gaynor, the coroner; Wes Cooney, a retired politician; and Cam Scarver, a cattleman. Usually, Harvey played. He had to drive to Great Falls for a cardiac appointment. Fine. My boss and ex-friend had burned his name onto my shit list.

The other thing that bothered me was Logan. Harvey and Frieda had dragged me into something dirty, but the guy with the cigarette under the bridge had dropped my cousin's name.

Focus on the cards.

I used a timer because it curtailed the motormouths and helped me steer toward the ideal—forty minutes dragged too long; ten minutes was too short. Twenty minutes landed on target and gave the players enough rounds for real competition.

I set my timer. The players chatted. I dealt.

I'd perfected my glide on the pitch—little hummingbirds to each player. I hated when cards spun out in perfect flow and then snagged, like on a cracker crumb.

But tonight I screwed up. I forgot to deal Wes Cooney his hole cards. *Both* hole cards. Something about the way he sat in my small blind, maybe.

He let the first pitch go without a word, and then I came around and pitched the second, missing him again. The pre-flop began with Guy Hamm. He bet $1,000—with a grin at Wes.

Maycie Gaynor's turn came next, but she paused beneath her Stetson, eyeing the exchange between Guy and Wes. "What?"

Maycie checked her cards and looked at the table. "Why do you two look like you're colluding on a heist?"

I felt it then, heat blooming to my face.

Wes said with a lilt, "Is this some kind of ghosting?"

I scowled. How long would they have let it go if Maycie hadn't stopped before her pre-flop bet? I should make him sit out the entire round, since he never raised the flag.

Guy Hamm said, "Too late. I've already placed my bet."

I said, "His position doesn't impact you."

I dealt two cards to Wes—one off the top, and the second after a cut.

Guy said, "It's not right. The deal was screwed up. We should start over."

I eyed him. "My call, Guy. The show goes on."

He glared back.

Cam Scarver chuckled. "Got an ugly hand, there, Guy?"

I nodded at Maycie, and she placed her pre-flop bet. Guy Hamm continued to gripe. He clearly held a pukey hand and wanted a reset.

We continued. The meds seeped fog to my eyes. I should have asked Logan when he was coming back from his guide trip. He'd have gotten my messages by now—even when you're out of range up mountain, it catches the signal every now and then.

I wouldn't have come tonight except I really needed the money and once scheduled, Big Bald Luck games were set in stone.

Cam Scarver looked at me. "You did it again."

They stared, but Guy Hamm was grinning. I froze in my pitch to Maycie. I had skipped Wes Cooney *again*.

He raised his hands in surrender. "Was it something I said?"

Guy pointed in my face. "She's back on the drugs. Look at the eyes."

"I am not on drugs!"

Maycie gave me a somber look. "Janey, what's going on?"

I snorted, but I owed them an explanation. "Fine. I'm on new medication that's hit me hard. It takes time to adjust."

I scowled at Guy. "And for your information, I've never had a drug problem. It was alcohol. If you're gonna gossip about my addiction, at least get your story straight."

His grin never slipped.

I scooped the cards, including the ones I'd already dealt, plus the muck. "I need a breather."

Guy looked at the felt. "You can't just take ten in the middle of—"

But I stashed the cards and pushed away from the table.

Cam Scarver said, "Janey is the dealer and referee. It's her call."

Then he shouted after me, "Where you going?"

"Walk!"

"You need company?"

I slammed the door.

Never in the history of the games had I called a break in the middle of a round. If the players needed a break, they sat out a hand. Not me.

I stormed up Cinnamon Falls Road, annoyed that it led to where I met with the creep. This time I headed uphill, toward the cascades, avoiding the bridge.

For a normal person, an on-the-up-and-up person like Maycie Gaynor back there, the Frieda job might not feel terrible. But *I* came from a hard start—a wolf ready to slink back to the shadows. People like Maycie, Guy, Cam, and Wes, they came from solid families. They went to college. They had impressive careers. Their biggest dare was a raked card game. The kind of thing that got me, the game runner, in trouble with the law, while the players remained spotless.

My Aunt Sylvie, Uncle Reg, and Logan always believed in a brisk walk. They hiked in their emerald haven over in Coeur d'Alene. I discovered it made me feel better, too.

I ran my arm across my forehead, sweating in the cold, and checked my phone. I always switched it to Silent while dealing cards. Now I saw I'd missed two calls:

Logan!

I called back. Straight to voice mail. *Damn it.*

I walked faster. Cinnamon Falls Road stretched beneath the stars, and I continued until the cascades opened in a roar. Moonlight illuminated the spill, and a burst escaped, a ghost blooming into the night. I closed my eyes, listening. It sounded clean. The mountain air washed my lungs.

Maybe tomorrow Logan would return and we could talk this through. My involvement was "one and done" but it sounded like my cousin was deeply ensnared.

I listened to the falls. The whispering boughs. The snaps and rustles of the forest. I allowed myself one more breath of cold sweet air, then turned back to the games.

CHAPTER

11

Harvey's Hideout

FROM THE ROAD, Harvey's Hideout looked like a place for humans, but it originally stored rail cargo. The design was simple: a small rectangle atop a big one. No slope to the roof. The Kootenai Valley Railroad had made Suspicion a town. They constructed Harvey's Hideout in the early 1900s from local pines.

You wouldn't call the Hideout welcoming, but those logs drew you in. Suspicioners gathered on the porch to sip through the summer, Gabe serving wood-smoked barbeque for up to fifty lucky souls. Beyond that, he banished folks to the biker bar in Troy.

Harvey always gave me keys from Thursdays to Sundays. I closed for him, made deposits, cleaned, and even did his books, but I always had to pass the keys back or drop them in the safe on Sundays. Now I knew why—he kept a shady side hustle.

On a snowy weeknight when the Hideout was closed, breaking in was a cinch. I knew which window I could jimmy without leaving a mark. I helped Em first and then climbed in myself.

Em looked up at the vaulted ceiling, her face shining. "If it's okay, why did we have to come in through the window?"

I said, "It's okay but I don't have permission."

And before she had a chance to dissect that, I added, "You don't like coming in through the window, Emmie-nem?"

"No, it's all good."

We did our secret handshake. At nine years old, she was cooler than I could ever hope to be.

Em took off her knit hat and panned the dining area. "It's a hiding place. I love it."

Harvey's Hideout was family-friendly so long as Em and I were the only ones here. On the walls hung pictures of turn-of-the-century rail cars, Old West frontier folk, and a snapshot of "a real and actual Sasquatch" (as scrawled at the bottom of the photo) that Tag Benson had taken back in 1981. At the north wall stood a walk-in fireplace. Best of all, Harvey's Hideout had working heat and a functioning kitchen.

Tonight, we came for the heat.

From the ceiling in the dining area hung a rustic chandelier. Over the bar, also suspended from the ceiling, dangled so many antlers no one could tell one from the next. They scrolled like hoop wire.

We had the place to ourselves.

Em said, "Where're we gonna sleep?"

"In the office upstairs. It has a carpet floor for our sleeping bags and it's warm. It's got a separate thermostat. We can't turn on the heat down here, but we can light a fire. Would you like that?"

"Yeah."

"Cool. You can do homework while I gather firewood."

"I'll help."

I shook my head. "No, sweetie, I need to get it from the woods and it's dark."

Em said, "But there's a wood pile."

"That wood's for pay. If I took some, it would be stealing."

Em nodded. "Circle of salt."

I flipped on the lights to the kitchen, Gabe's domain—anyone who messed it up caught hell—and opened the side door, securing it with Gabe's wooden wedge.

From the Subaru, I retrieved sleeping bags and Em's prized possession: a 1960s Samsonite train case with white vinyl covering. Midcentury women packed these things with cosmetics and fit them into overhead train compartments. I had told Em it belonged to my great-grandmother. Really, I'd found it in a thrift store. Em had scribbled on it when she was a toddler, but now, at age nine, she regretted the actions of her former self. (I knew the feeling.) The train case had a handle but no rolling wheels, which made it awkward to carry, but she loved it.

I stepped out to gather wood. My phone rang. Harvey. I looked behind me at the moonlit forest, paranoid like he was watching, then answered the call.

"Yeah?"

"Tuesday night, same thing."

"Harvey, no!"

"I'll get the empty backpack to you. Exchange it for a new one."

"You said it was one time only!"

"Can't be helped."

The ground tilted. I squatted, elbows to knees, pressing the phone to my ear.

I said, "I cannot. Listen to me. I cannot."

"You can. Frieda's still got that video. It's just one more time."

* * *

I had forgotten my gloves and tugged my sleeves to cover my frozen fingers. A cold balsam scent filled the night as the wind stirred the pine needles.

It sounds like stars, Em had once said.

She'd been four years old, and she'd thought the stars blew the wind.

When I was a teenager, long after my mother died, I had run away from foster care to steal back to Suspicion. That instinct had gotten me into trouble. Running away landed me in juvenile detention. I wondered what my life would be like if I'd toughed it out—stayed in the nasty foster home in Ronan where they'd hit and starved me. Or a nice one, like in Coeur d'Alene, the loving river home with Uncle Reggie and Logan. Or even in Missoula, the weird but organized group home: a little sweet, a little flakey—but mostly nice—and brimming with therapy and freakishly self-aware vocabulary.

Where would I be now, if my younger self had toughed it out, and hadn't run away from those places? Would I still have my Emmie?

Yes. This was one of those paths that either began with the choice or the flip of a coin, it didn't matter, because either way it ended on the same main road. Em felt like a predetermined part of my main road, and I was part of hers.

As I gathered wood, I scanned the snow for prints—a habit Logan taught me. How to tell cat tracks (tiny pawprints) from a raccoon (tiny handprints); a coyote (oval) from a dog (round).

There. A fox. Like moose, fox left single-line tracks.

Earlier today, Harvey had stopped by to "check on" me. Acting sorry for all the silliness. But he'd also checked my pill bottles. Said I'd missed some doses. He told me Frieda wanted me to take another pee test, see if I was taking the pills correctly. Now I understood why. Frieda wasn't done with me.

I had told Harvey to get me a pill dispenser. No need for pee tests.

I gathered wood. Then I noticed a different set of tracks. Large shoe prints. They looked fresh.

I panned the woods. The Hideout did a fair business. That could explain footprints. But this far from the building, up the hill, in the woods, footprints made less sense.

Something snapped behind me.

The woods were full of sounds—that fox, a deer, a falling branch—and yet my pulse quickened. Suddenly I was keyed up. The medication evaporated from my blood.

"Who's there?" I called.

This was *my* forest. God save anyone who tried to come after me in my own territory.

"Hey!" I shouted.

Nothing. Wind. I replayed the sound, tried to call it paranoia. But growing up around dangerous people had taught me better.

I backed up in a half circle, scanning the pines—white and gray in the moonlight. "Come get me, pickle dick!"

I had a taste for it. I had been smacked around enough as a youth that my pulse couldn't tell the difference between fear and battle therapy.

And yet there was Em. She was alone inside the Hideout, door wedged open.

I hugged the firewood and strode back. The wind lashed my hair, blinding me. I looked over my shoulder and caught movement but when I paused, it vanished. I pushed the kitchen door off its wedge with my knee.

"Emmie?"

I dumped the wood on Gabe's impeccable bleached concrete as the door slammed shut, locking automatically.

"Em!"

"Yeah?"

My pulse returned to normal. Deep breath. Then another. I found her at the hearth, where she'd spread her workbooks. Her face looked serene and content.

Through the windows, all appeared calm. My aging, primer-brushed station wagon sat in the gravel parking area under a clear night sky. Snow drifts kicked crystal into the wind. The woods loomed black.

CHAPTER

12

The Wolf and the Train

I told Em to build the fire while I put on makeup.

Em frowned. "Makeup? You don't wear makeup."

"I'm putting it on tonight," I said, digging through the shipping box.

"I'll come with."

"It's not like that. I'm not getting ready like normal."

I could come up with no explanation that made any sense, so we went to the washroom together and unpacked. Tom Ford, Louboutin, Charlotte Tilbury. Em lit right up.

The ladies' washroom was clean but rust-stained with a leaky faucet, and we fretted over getting damp on the expensive cosmetics.

She said, "Do we have eye shadow?"

"Yeah, I—"

No, apparently not. It appeared I'd bought only contouring products, over and over, in multiple brands. And a set of brushes. Nothing else.

I pressed my brain and squeezed. I must have either bought all this when keyed up, or while going brain dead from the meds.

"How much did this cost?" Emmie asked.

"Don't remember."

Although $472 came to mind, as did the fact that the accumulated heating bill had also climbed to the four hundreds.

"Can I try some?" Em said.

I looked at my daughter, then crouched and took her gently by the arms. "Yes. But here's the thing, Emmie-nem. I gotta make money. A lot of money. I mean a crap ton of money."

Em's forehead wrinkled.

I said, "You're smart, scary smart. I have no idea where you got it from, because it ain't me or your father. It's good you're smart, baby, because—"

I looked at the ceiling, trying to cobble this into words. "In life, you'll make mistakes. A lot of times people will forgive you. But people don't forgive stupid."

I said, "So you *got* to be smart. It's real important that you go to college."

"I get straight A's, Mom. I'll get a scholarship."

I closed my eyes. It was a lot to lay on a nine-year-old.

I looked at my daughter, gave her a tiny shake. "Scholarships only go so far. I need to know you're gonna be okay. No matter what happens."

Em looked at me intently. "I'm okay, Mom. This is great."

"No, it's not. We're having fun but there's a lotta people who'd say this isn't okay, even if it's fun. *Especially* since it's fun."

I scraped my lip. "I really don't know what the heck I'm doing. The proper way to raise a child. See, I'm screwing you up. You have a good head on your shoulders, but one day you're gonna wake up and say, 'Oh God, I'm screwed up! Mom screwed me up!' and all the college in the world won't fix that."

Em listened.

I said, "I don't know how to plan for if something were to happen to me, how to take care of you, but I'm pretty sure it involves a crap ton of money."

Em knew nothing about the Hendee curse–the horrific fate that befell the women in our family. How could I tell her about such a thing? I wasn't sure I believed it myself. I couldn't see myself getting struck dead before age thirty, and I damn sure couldn't believe Em would die young. I had to end the pattern of Hendee orphans.

Em nodded. "Okay, Mom. Okay."

"You understand?"

"Yeah, I think so. We're going shoplifting?"

I exhaled the length of a twelve-car freight train, looked at my little girl. "I'm putting on this makeup."

"Why? Where're we going?"

"Nowhere. The point is to put on makeup for the sake of putting on makeup. It's called GRWM, like 'get ready with me.' I'm gonna be an influencer."

Em said, "You never actually wear makeup."

"That's why I had to buy new stuff. Expensive stuff. You gotta have money to make money."

I handed her the phone. "Hold the camera for me?"

* * *

It was hard. Influencers had patter, but I couldn't patter on my winningest day. Roxie chatted up the customers at the Hideout, and I bounced them. It helped that I had bikers to back me up. I could reward Cast Iron in chicken potpies, and every once in a while he tried to bounce someone who wasn't even stirring shit up, just because he was hungry. Rox and I called it his "potpie hustle."

These stupid antipsychotics made me too rummy and instead of pattering for my followers, I just scowled through the application.

I finally set down my brush and asked Em, "How do I look?"

"Hmm," she said, then, "like a flaming skull."

Shit.

She added, "Like the one on Ponce's motorcycle. The Harley."

I leaned toward the mirror. Em was right. Maybe I'd overdone the contours.

I pointed at the phone. "Let me see that."

She handed it over and I played it back. The washroom lighting seemed normal, but on camera it looked like something out of a Scandinavian horror flick, and my fingernails had *actually* transmogrified to black birch from gathering firewood.

"This isn't going to work."

I cast around, wide-eyed and over-tranq'ed, feeling like my feral had shed fur all over the floor. "Being a beauty influencer takes practice. I don't have time for that."

I had to get my baby out of this situation. I threw the stuff back into the box.

Em wasted no breath. "Then can I have the makeup and brushes?"

"No. You're only nine."

"Mom! I won't wear it outside the house. Just for fun. *Please?*"

I regarded my daughter's earnest little face, her long lashes and pointed chin. Em resembled my mother so much, it grabbed me by the throat. The horrifically expensive makeup would freeze and crack in my heatless garage apartment.

I said, "All right. But you are *not* to wear it outside the house."

* * *

As we tucked in for bed, we read. I had struggled with reading from a young age even with my mother's help. Not Em. She prowled Suspicion Library with a vulpine quality—stalking, selecting, then tearing through several books at once. I had to learn to read later in life, in a nonconventional way, separating the skill of reading from intelligence.

After lights-out, we ended with our ritual: what we were most thankful for today. I expected Em to say scoring the makeup.

Instead she said, "Coming to the Hideout through the window."

My eyes snapped in the darkness. "You mean spending the night here?"

"Sure. But mostly coming in through the window."

Because I am teaching my nine-year-old the art of breaking and entering.

Em said, "What are *you* most grateful for today?"

"I'm grateful for you, kiddo."

"You promised not to keep saying that."

I paused. A broken promise, but if I said anything else, it would be a lie. Once again, impossible to figure out parenting.

I said, "I'm grateful we sat by the fire. I love when there's a big fire in the fireplace."

"Me too."

I pulled my daughter in through our sleeping bags and listened to the night. Over the next half hour, Em's breathing became rhythmic. I beckoned sleep but my mind kicked and scratched.

Another backpack—it thundered over me. I pressed my cheek against my daughter's hair.

Still no word from Logan. I ought to call my Uncle Reggie and Margot in Idaho. Especially now that I knew what my cousin had been up to, it felt important to grasp fingers with this thin web of family.

I *did* need a crap ton of money, and not just to fix Em before I screwed her up. I needed a wall of cash to barricade off this mess I'd created, and I needed it fast.

The voice of the mountain seeped through the walls. Boughs ladened with snow gave way. The wind came to a crescendo in the evergreens, then quieted.

Far off toward the valley, a train.

And then another sound, an enchanted sound: a wolf. It drifted from the direction of Cinnamon Falls. The wolf answered back to the train.

Train whistle, wolf, silence.

Howl, whistle, silence.

Again and again. A rising-and-falling duet, interweaving across the distance.

The two conversed into the night to a theater of wind, and then all went still.

CHAPTER

13

The Void

THE NEXT HANDOFF occurred outside Suspicion in a mining community, more settlement than town. This corridor brimmed with miners, mines, minerals, and quarries. Black Diamond, Big Copper Ridge, Yaak Mine, Idamont, and countless others—some had been abandoned as gaping horrors in the ground. Invisible traps that lay in wait for a misplaced foot or a whole-ass person.

Our meeting spot lay down a side road along chain link. I never would have found it but for the miracle of map sharing. We met in daylight and sleeting weather.

The same guy waited for me, the one from under Cinnamon Falls Bridge. This time, he couldn't be bothered to speak to me. He talked on his phone—something about truck routes—and gestured at me to come.

I didn't want to stray from my Subaru.

I offered the empty backpack. He took it and again, waved for me to come, all the while speaking into his phone.

Frieda's threats about Em mobilized me. I exited my safe, warm station wagon and followed the stranger into the dark woods.

We passed through a rift in the chain link and entered a complex, keeping to the forest. Good. Woods gave me comfort, even though these grew on someone else's mountain.

Beyond the trees, men with hard hats milled around a large mine entrance, with trucks hauling material. I wasn't dressed for this. My shoes got wet. I folded my arms over my leather jacket.

The bridge guy took me to a second mine, an isolated one. No one in hard hats, no survey markers, undisturbed terrain. Just a tiny eyebrow in the hillside.

He crouched through the opening—still on his phone—and picked his way down as though into a tomb. He disappeared.

I did not follow. The exterior looked carved from chalk though three feet in, it turned black. I shivered, and not from sleet. I didn't do darkness. Darkness and I never got along. An earthen, choking wind emerged from that black hole.

The guy popped back out and waved me in, but I planted my feet.

Sleet and dust creased my eyes. So black, so dark was that thing, that cave or mine or whatever the fuck it was, that I could only see the man's face. The maw swallowed the rest of him.

His hand emerged, reaching for me like to drag me inside.

I turned and strode, then barreled for my car. He made a *ssst* sound after me. I accelerated. Now an all-out sprint.

I'd seen these things, mines in the wilderness. Some sank no more than ten feet deep, some meandered far enough to get lost and never emerge. They were the blackest voids. They held bones. They filled with water. They were death traps.

* * *

I shivered inside my Subaru for ten minutes, wet, wondering if I should leave, when the man knocked on my window.

I slammed my eyes shut. The knock sounded like metal on glass, not knuckles—a gun, a knife. He tapped again.

I steeled myself and opened the door. He had no gun. He'd tapped with his ring.

He said, "You'll get used to it. You got nothing to be afraid of."

He handed me a fresh backpack.

Through the material, I felt certain, were bundles of cash. I looked up, but he was gone.

CHAPTER

14

Hello Again

I LOCKED THE BACKPACK in the Hideout safe and pushed it from my mind.

Then I showered and ran errands, brainstorming money-making schemes to flip Em and me off this red-hot skillet.

On the way back from grocery shopping, I took Cloudberry Creek Road—not the quickest route, but a distraction. The creek wound from the falls and pooled in a swimming hole where Em, Trent, and I used to have summer picnics. Also in the summer, the cloudberries shone with white flowers, the fruit ripe for picking.

Now, in our extended winter, the cloudberries were dormant. The creek frothed in indigo and white with spring melt as we entered March. It would gather strength until it found the Kootenay, which in turn fed distant lakes, rivers, and forks.

I rounded the bend to flashing lights. Three police vehicles parked alongside the road—which was saying something, as Suspicioners hated paying for police vehicles. An ambulance waited nearby. Another rare sight since we had to borrow those.

This was a dangerous curve and notorious for wrecks.

Gary, the very same policeman I'd bounced from Harvey's Hideout last Saturday, waved me along, his face tight. He checked back at the creek as I rolled past, and I followed his gaze.

Police Chief Quincy Tigner stood hip-deep in the water, waders on. Opposite him stood two other officers. I couldn't see what they were doing, but EMTs were expanding a stretcher.

Tigner called, "One, two, three," and the officers gave a hoist. On Tigner's end, I caught a glimpse: a limp figure, with a wet flannel-clad arm and a torn gray glove.

But then I realized it was not a glove. It was a hand.

A horn sounded.

I gasped. Even though I'd only barely rolled along, I'd drifted toward the center line.

I recognized the other driver. Dannie Tigner, the police chief's sister. Dannie raised her hand to wave. I waved back and reclaimed my heartbeat. We each continued in opposite directions.

* * *

On my way to the Hideout for my shift, the Subaru died.

And that.

Was just.

Dandy.

The damn meds. They kept me from doing stupid crap like breaking into Trent's house, but they left me too bleary to notice when the check engine light came on.

My mind fired off the essentials: a cigarette, a scotch and soda. I didn't like scotch, but watching Frieda go at it gave me an itch. The urge to drink and smoke bubbled up, crested, and passed. My mind reset to the task at hand: The Subaru leaked oil.

My wheels and I had a long history. I had to give the car a minute, let it get over its tantrum, then add oil, which I kept in the back. My station wagon had two decades and 160,000 miles on it, and fixing it would cost as much as buying a completely different junker.

I yanked the release and scrabbled out, propped the hood. It stank like something burning. The Subaru's buzzy factory stereo played

Lizzo, and I leaned through my driver-side window and cranked the volume—a great big party for one. Me on this vacant snowy road while the wagon wheezed itself out and my ex combed the Sherry out of his beard and my little girl got farther and farther away because I was unfit, unfit, unfit, and getting evermore unfit by the day.

The stereo gave everything it had. I grabbed a quart of Valvoline and left the liftgate open, then walked around to stare at the black, snaking engine.

"We need out," I said aloud.

I needed a plan. I had to get my life on track for Em's sake. The meds cramped my brain. All ideas ended with Frieda seeing me locked up, Trent blowing it, and Emmie in foster care.

"Car troubles?"

I jumped.

Before me stood a man. He lit a cigarette, taking his time, then held it out to me. It clicked: the man from under Cinnamon Falls Bridge.

The volume on my stereo had diminished. He must have turned it down while I'd stood gazing into the engine. I longed for the snub nose. The cigarette burned, waiting.

I said, "I don't smoke."

He spread his arms and crooked his brow, because we both knew I'd shared his cigarette under that bridge. Smoke rose between us. I accepted the cigarette.

He said, "I'll give you a ride."

"It just needs oil."

He shrugged, leaned against the bumper.

Harvey's Hideout was a true hideout, tucked between outcroppings. It used to sit on a thoroughfare but the Montana Department of Highways condemned it after the avalanche of '83. Now Harvey's Hideout was a roadhouse with no road. People traveled this way solely to get to Harvey's. Locals, bikers, and in the summer, hard core YouTubers who hoped for a find. We clocked their kind the moment their shadows darkened the batwing doors, so Gabe always served them burnt offerings.

No traffic filtered up this way while the Hideout was closed, and right now I felt that fact in my facial nerves. I was alone with this guy.

I asked, "This my last cigarette before you kill me?"

He tapped out a Marlboro for himself. "We've barely met. Why would I kill you?"

"You've been following me."

He lit his smoke with a match, not a lighter, then waved it out elaborately. "I just happened to pull up."

He gestured his eyes at the Subaru. "That's good luck, since your car broke down."

His brows were expressive. A tattoo crept above his linen shirt collar. He wore nice shoes that seemed expensive though I lacked savvy in men's couture. His gray slacks hung snug enough to bow at the pockets with a glimpse of car keys. Back as a teen on the run, I'd have palmed his wallet by now.

I said, "If you're not here to kill me, tell me what you want."

He smiled. A beautiful smile that made my skin crawl.

"Do I have to want something?"

"Yes. Otherwise, leave."

He smiled again but this time for himself. Silence lengthened the reach of road. It occurred to me that quite a lot could happen in that reach—just a visual distance, but amenable to any number of dangers.

The wind abandoned the trees and their boughs fell still. No cardinals flitting. Now the only sound came from the creek rushing under the culvert.

He said, "It's not much of a car for someone who does what you do."

"Roadhouse waitress?"

"The other thing you do."

"Look, just tell me—"

He cut me off but spoke even-toned. "I *am* telling you what I want"—he gave a nod—"to *tell* you."

He tapped the ashes from his Marlboro. "I been working for my boss as long as your beater here has been in existence. Since I was a kid. His people are loyal and have a sense of self-respect."

He shrugged. "Obviously, it's not a good idea to cross him."

He pointed his cigarette at me. "You're a card dealer."

I nodded.

He said, "Where'd you learn that?"

"Finishing school."

A smile played at his eyes, and he scanned the trees. "I was a street kid with no parents. My boss took me in because I ran a clean card game. He liked that. Everyone in my neighborhood knew you could come to me for a simple night of cards."

If he thought we'd bond by swapping sob stories, he had it backward. It creeped me out that he knew my background.

He said, "Do you trust her? You trust Frieda Kanjo?"

I rose from the bumper. "Time for you to go."

He remained in place, rolling the muscles of his upper body. "Still smoking my cigarette."

He fit the Marlboro between his lips, then reached down and picked up the Valvoline from where I'd set it in the snowbank. I looked up the road to his high-dollar SUV. Harvey could drive up at any moment. What would he do if he saw me with the guy from under Cinnamon Falls Bridge?

The man unscrewed the cap and poured the synthetic blend into the Subaru, now cool and ready to drink.

He turned to me and smiled. The liquid glugged into the engine.

He said, "Do you even know who my boss is?"

I swallowed.

I thought of the backpacks, hefty with money. "A gambler?"

Maybe some high roller interested in buying into a casino. Harvey sometimes talked about taking the Big Bald Luck games to the next level. Unlikely. I didn't think I was running backpacks for gamblers. But I wasn't about to throw around words like "drug trafficker" or "money launderer" out here before God and the silver sun.

The man finished the first quart and added the second.

He said, "Oh, my boss is not a gambler, no. He takes calculated risks. But he is no gambler."

I watched him, my cigarette poised away from my thigh.

He said, "His name's Baltazar Valencia. And *your* boss, Frieda Kanjo, is his lawyer. It's no secret. You can read about it in the news."

Frost crept from my fingers, to my hands, to my middle. I knew exactly who Baltazar Valencia was. They called him the Red King, the head of a Seattle drug cartel with ties to Colombia. The Red King was known for his coke and heroin, premium grade.

Someone from my old Missoula group home had wrecked herself with alligator heroin, which left necrotic scales up her arms. Alligator heroin was a bottom-dollar synthetic for true junkies. The product brought in by the Red King was nothing like that. His was top quality. Pure snowflakes from ten thousand feet. Valencia was the one who'd elevated Frieda Kanjo from local yokel to a bigtime attorney, a face people recognized.

The Red King was also known for ruthlessness—wiping out rivals; brazen assassinations. Torture.

The man said, "And I am Roman. That's how it is when people are trustworthy. I straight-up tell you my name."

The second quart of oil emptied. Roman made a sound of contentment.

He glanced at me, screwed the cap back on the bottle. "You? You're just another Logan."

When had my breathing stopped? I dared not show fear. I knew that from growing up in the system. I forced my diaphragm to move and raised the Marlboro to my lips, but found my fingers empty. The cigarette had dropped to the snow. The creek rushed through the culvert.

He was taking my picture. He held my phone—I'd left it in the Subaru—and was unlocking it with facial recognition.

He typed something, then handed my phone back. "You might want to talk to me sometime. Now you have my number."

I shoved my phone in my pocket and forced my feet to move. Guys like this Roman always lurked in the shadows of my life. No matter where I ran. I knew his type. Dangerous people.

I yanked the prop stick and slammed the hood closed.

He said, "I'll wait here with you. See that the engine starts."

I slipped behind the wheel and got my voice working. "You do that, Roman."

The station wagon roared to life. The liftgate still gaped. I mashed the gas pedal, throwing gravel and accelerating down the road, only to hit the brakes twenty feet beyond him. The liftgate spanked shut.

I stepped out, threw his car keys into the creek, and sped off.

CHAPTER

15

Thursdays Are for Gossip

THURSDAYS AT THE Hideout were for gossip. Love triangles, gripes, and the old standby: whether Jemma slipped Visine into Conrad's coffee back in 2024. I tended not to dish. I more often gave them something to talk about. Now, as I served up hot plates, people buzzed about the fatal accident on Cloudberry Creek Road. I recalled that torn gray glove that was not a glove.

Tonight I was the only server. I had to function as though I hadn't stepped in an acid hot spring.

I served food to my customer without a word, scanning the other tables.

"What is this?"

I looked down to see Dannie Tigner, with her tiger-striped hair brushed to the side. The former friend I'd seen on Cloudberry Creek Road.

She waved at the plate. "I ordered a cheeseburger and sweet potato fries."

I had served her the meatloaf. That was supposed to go to Ponce, the biker. My meds were getting cute with me again.

I brought Ponce the meatloaf. He sat with my buddy Cast Iron of the potpie hustle. Cast Iron occupied a perpetually good mood. It balanced Ponce's perpetually bad one. Cast Iron had a full pint and needed nothing from me.

Bikers around here were mostly just people who enjoyed motorcycles—like Logan—not members of any particular gang. But Ponce and Cast Iron were *biker* bikers. They belonged to the RSOMC. The Rank Strangers Outlaw Motorcycle Club. The "Rank Stranger" name came from a high lonesome bluegrass song, a mountain song. "Rank" in context means *absolute*, though it could also mean *foul-smelling*. I'd advise against saying so to their faces. The RSOMC operated on both sides of the law, but I'd never had problems with them, and they always tipped.

I threaded toward the kitchen to check on Dannie's cheeseburger.

"I'll take some coffee," someone called as I passed. Guy Fucking Hamm.

"I have to make a fresh pot."

"All right then. Make me a pot. We still on for next week?"

As much as it pained me, I had to get along with Guy Hamm. Not just because he was one of my card players, but because he'd given me a small side job. He had a property that had been trashed by renters. I'd told him I'd clean it for a hundred bucks.

He sat at a big table by himself, and he'd angled his seat to overlook the bar. Specifically, so he could watch Dr. Jude Summers nurse his drink.

Jude stared into his glass, and then lifted his gaze to the well drinks. He'd keep that up another hour or two. His wife Kierra had died two years ago under mysterious circumstances that remained fodder for Suspicion gossip. Jude had been hitting the bar like that ever since.

I said, "Guy, are you sitting that way so you can ogle a man in his grief?"

Guy laughed, and I had to hand it to him, he had an earth-shaking laugh. I couldn't help but tilt my head.

He placed a five on the table and stood. "Go on, give him my coffee. He needs it more."

I'd known Guy Hamm since I was a kid. He'd been famous for his feud with Jude Summers—the dentist who warmed the seat at my bar every night.

The bad blood started around the time my mother died. Both Guy and Jude were several grades ahead of me, and they'd been best friends. They used to trek through the woods, play basketball, or ride bikes down Farm to Market Road. They were both really smart kids.

Then Guy sold Jude his ten-speed.

They'd agreed to the deal at school, but by the time Jude took the bike home, Guy had traded out the gear shift with an old rusted one he'd lubed to death. It fell apart in a day. Some people found it funny. Guy had wanted to get one over on Jude since Jude was breaking out as the smarter friend. Guy wanted everyone to see Jude wasn't the big genius we believed him to be.

Jude simply went to the junkyard and picked up a replacement gear shift.

As they grew older, Jude earned a reputation for his unusual intelligence at school. When SATs rolled around, he scored the highest in the district. Guy accused him of cheating. The administrator made Jude sit the test again, and he scored even higher.

Guy Hamm grew to truly hate Jude Summers. And why? Sometimes people are prone to hatred out of sheer embarrassment for their own bad behavior.

The whole thing made no sense. Guy was smart, too. Since his school days, he'd steadily acquired property across northwestern Montana. I'd love to be that clever. Jude followed in his father's footsteps and became a dentist—a brainy but servile job. You'd think Guy would get over it.

I made the coffee.

Usually Jude was quiet. But he once shot an antler off the ceiling so it fell on Guy's head. I'd had to kick them both out. Guy Hamm was the one *actually* being a turd that night, but I couldn't abide shooting antlers.

On another night, about a year ago, I came onto shift to find Jude and Gabe happily cooking together. Right there on Gabe's hallowed rubber mats. No one else had ever graced that sacred kitchen during working hours except for me, and that took years of trust-building, and then only when we were slammed. But there they were, Jude and Gabe laughing in the kitchen. Jude had sizzled me up a chicken-fried steak.

After that Jude went back to his routine of sitting on his barstool, barely speaking, staring at the well drinks and thinking about God knew what: Root canals. Cavities. Kierra, however she died—Suspicion may never know.

The coffee purred.

I said to Jude, "You doin' all right?"

Half a nod.

In my heart, I thought, *Your secret's safe with me.*

I didn't mean that night with Gabe, or sharpshooting antlers.

CHAPTER

16

Logan and the Other Logan

A HUNDRED-DOLLAR WINDFALL FROM Guy Hamm would not scrape me out of my mess. And if "one and done" wasn't really done, I had doubts about "two and through."

A dozen tables sat occupied and through my medicated fog I couldn't remember whether I'd served them or they needed anything, so I grabbed a tray to clear empty tables.

Amid the mess, a bottle of Pabst stood half-full. I held it with two fingers so it wouldn't spill when I carried the tray. Then I paused and rocked the lukewarm half-empty beer, raised it toward my lips—

Out of nowhere, Dannie Tigner snatched it from my hand. "Janey? What in the *hell* are you doing?"

Dannie stood shorter than me by a good four inches, her nose turned up as she scowled. I chuckled like I'd taken a lungful of Jude's nitrous oxide.

She flung her hand at the corner booth where she'd been sitting. "Give me your apron, and go watch my purse."

Now more than ever, I needed to function, but I was doing the opposite.

So I did as told.

* * *

Dannie parked a hot coffee in front of me. She brought cream and sugar and a spoon. I added enough cream to turn it the color of snow and half as cool, and watched Dannie move through the Hideout. The customers, cranky a minute ago, turned pliable under Dannie.

Something tasted off about the coffee. I'd forgotten to add sugar. Three packets, and life improved. Over at the pass-through, Dannie talked to Gabe, then they shouted. Gabe shot me a filthy look. Gabe could be a royal pain in the ass. I loved Gabe.

Dannie came back and refilled my coffee without a word, then left.

The single-strap backpack. Ice dripping from the bridge. Roman smoking as he poured Valvoline into my Subaru. Something tilted, and I realized it was my head shifting on my neck. I lifted it back in place.

If Baltazar Valencia was one of Frieda's clients, why did Frieda need me to mule money between them? Did it matter? All that mattered was Em. Knowing Frieda's shit business may not get me out of the Business of Shit.

Dannie returned with her cheeseburger plate and a bottle of Stella. "You never even put my order in."

I felt bad.

Dannie said, "I figure we got ten minutes before I need to check those tables again."

"Thanks for your help."

"How long you been back to drinking?"

"I'm not."

Dannie shrugged. "Okay."

She patted Heinz 57 at her sweet potato fries. Nothing came out. I gulped sweet coffee.

Dannie smacked her ketchup harder and with repetition. "I just watched you drink someone's nasty leftover COVID-syphilis-spit beer off an empty table, but okay."

I opened my hands. "As you saw, I did not *actually* drink that—"

"I stopped you."

"I work in a roadhouse. When I want to start drinking, there's enough around here to swim in it. You saw what's called, 'having a moment.'"

Dannie shook and smacked the Heinz 57. "Quite a moment."

I rubbed my eye with the heel of my hand.

Dannie finally lured the ketchup to her fries, then glanced at me. "So why are you so . . . ?"

"It's my pills."

"Ohhhhh."

"Don't say it like that."

Dannie snorted. "Please. Like people in this town don't know you got stability issues."

She disassembled her cheeseburger and worked on making it the way she liked it, starting with ketchup on the bun, then downsizing the lettuce. "I'm a gambling addict. Had to take out a second mortgage to give to the Indian casino. Police Chief gotta live in a cheap hovel cuz he loaned money to his sister who can't stay away from the poker tables. Go on, act like you don't know."

She aggressively shoved a double-sized fry in her mouth. "So let's cut the crap. You and I can go four years without a conversation, but to me you're still family."

Hearing her call me "family" caused a sting of gratitude. Since our school friend days, I had, after getting my act together, turned micro focused on my micro life. Juggling the Hideout and the card games. Raising a child in an un-wolf-like way. I had lost touch with people.

At seventeen, I used to see time as a tender green shoot. Now, at twenty-seven, I realized my life had seasons. Time wasn't tender green, it was brittle. It kept coming, but you couldn't renew it.

Dannie wiped her mouth. "What kinda meds you on?"

I could lie. The smart thing would be to tell her the meds I used to take, or evade the question. I didn't have the energy for that. I waved at the apron around her waist so she could see the meds herself. Dannie reached in, froze, then pulled out the Röhm.

Oops.

* * *

Dannie set the gun on the seat next to her and spread her napkin over it. "I *thought* your apron was heavy."

She looked around the dining area, her words snappish. "Figured you had a wallet in there, not a damned gun."

But she dug back into the apron and extracted my pill bottles, reading labels as she went. "Are you kidding me?"

"What?"

Dannie looked like she might throw them across the dining hall. "Where'd you find this doctor?"

It would have made for a tasty tidbit on gossip night to tell her where I'd gotten them, but I kept my mouth shut.

Dannie said, "When is your next dose?"

I squeezed my eyes. Had I taken the last one at lunch or before my shift? Or doubled up to be safe? The pill dispenser would say but I'd forgotten it. Maybe I ought to take one now. If I missed, Frieda would find out.

Dannie pointed to the Saturday night special beneath the napkin. "And what's *this* about?"

"For protection."

"From Trent?"

"No, 'course not."

"You using it to go after Trent?"

I shut my trap.

Dannie said, "Where'd you get this thing?"

"It's Logan's. It's not loaded."

"Come again?"

"I said I'm holding the gun for Logan. There's no bullets."

Dannie stared at me for a piercing moment. Long enough that I had to reach for another packet of sugar and flick it three times.

Dannie said, "You didn't hear? About Logan?"

These damned pills. I should have kept still about Logan, about all this sketchy stuff. Dannie had called me "friend," but she was the police chief's sister.

I said, "Sure. Logan is . . . He's guiding a fly-fishing trip. I'm expecting a call."

"He gave you this gun?"

I stared at her. *Did* manage to keep my mouth shut this time. The last thing I wanted was to cause problems for my cousin.

Dannie said, "Janey, Logan's dead. He's been killed."

I blinked. Blinked again. The sugar packet burst to sand in my fingers.

Dannie said, "Janey, did you hear me? It's important you understand this."

I said, "I just talked to him a few days ago. I mean . . . It's been—"

Longer than that. I tried to think when I last spoke with my cousin. The night I bounced Gary. How long ago? It didn't matter against the weight of what Dannie told me and yet I clung to it as proof her words were untrue.

I said, "I know for a fact he's guiding a flyfishing trip up the mountain."

But, he'd tried to call me the night of the card games. That would suggest he'd returned.

Dannie pressed her hand over mine. "Tag Benson found him in Cloudberry Creek today. Logan is . . . Honey, he is no longer with us."

CHAPTER

17

Girl, Friend

I THREW UP IN the ladies' room. It was stupid to believe I could do Frieda's nasty deeds and have everything work out.

The washroom door opened and Dannie entered. I ran the sink. Dannie pulled a lip color from her purse and applied it, top first and then back and forth over the lower, while I splashed my face with cold water.

She said, "Your tables are handled for another fifteen minutes. I left a message for Roxie to come take over."

Our eyes met in the mirror. I shook my head. I needed the shift.

She said, "You sure?"

"Yeah. I'm just stunned."

"Shocked, babe. You are in shock."

I dried my face with a scratchy brown paper towel. I wanted to go home, crawl under a blanket, cry until morning. Then load up Em and take her to Coeur d'Alene to see Uncle Reggie. But I'd finish this shift and keep the balance with Frieda, because I needed the waitressing money and couldn't risk Frieda's wrath.

Dannie said, “You wanna tell me why you’re carrying around the little revolver?”

I shrugged. “It’s Logan’s.”

I thought a moment. “Was.”

“Doesn’t explain why you keep it on you at all times.”

Dannie tapped the lipstick on the sink. “Yes, my brother’s the chief of police, but it’s not like we tell each other everything. I wouldn’t tell him your business. Even if it’s illegal. Anything you say stays between you and me. I can help you figure out Frieda Kanjo.”

I went rigid. “What makes you think this has anything to do with Frieda?”

She reached into the apron and pulled out one of my pill bottles, shook it. “Anyone in this town’d recognize Frieda’s dirty doc. His name’s right there on the label.”

I closed my eyes, opened them.

She said, “Go on, tell me what Frieda’s gotten you into.”

The pressure to talk about it nearly undid me, but I said, “Nothing to tell.”

“Really?”

“Really.”

Dannie crossed her arms.

I said, “I appreciate your help tonight. Do me a favor and forget all this. Especially the part about the gun.”

She breathed with effort. “Fine.”

She tapped the lipstick, peered at me. I pointed at my apron. Dannie hesitated, then untied it from her waist and handed it over, gun and all.

She said, “I’m going to give you the name of a good doctor. Not some creep from Frieda’s bone sack. This guy’ll fix your meds and straighten out your thinking.”

“How would I know if my thinking’s straightened out?”

“When you no longer feel like you want to shoot, smash, or jab. Let me see your phone.”

I handed it over and cinched the apron around my waist, and as Dannie added the doctor's name to my contacts, it gave me a shiver, thinking of how Roman had done something similar a few hours ago.

But then Dannie said, "Tell you what, Janey, before you head back in there. If you do me a favor, I could be a good friend to you."

I regarded Dannie from the side of my eye.

She said, "It's simple. Get me into the Big Bald Luck games."

* * *

I snorted. No way could I bring Dannie Tigner, sister of the chief of police, into my illegal card games.

I said, "Thanks for your help tonight, Dannie. Your dinner's on me."

I made for the door, but she stopped me. "Get me in. I could be of help to you. Connections. Babysitting. At the very least, I could watch Em for you."

I paused, glaring. "I cannot get you into the games. Seats are limited. And what kind of person would I be if I did? You're a gambling addict. It'd be like you buying me shots of tequila."

Dannie said, "Oh, pardon me, you think I don't gamble? That just shows how well I hide it. I'm not a recovering gambler. I *am* a *gam-buh-ler*. Yeah it got out of hand there for a while, but I won that money back. That's the gossip nobody hears about. I paid back my brother's second mortgage but he stays where he is because he's cheap."

She lowered her voice. "That last part's between you and me. His wife doesn't know they're flush. She'd kill him."

Dannie leaned against the sink, flipping her lipstick. "Quincy doesn't know I still gamble. He thought I earned it back in commercial real estate banking. *In this economy.* I keep it quiet, drive across the state to the casinos—*and wear a wig*. Because everyone knows our little police chief's sister's a gambling addict, even out there. Then I have to drive all the way back home again."

She waved her lipstick. "Still got to get up and go to work the next day. It's a lot. It is a *lot*."

I said, "As you stated, I'm in a situation with Frieda. Which means I can't mess around with Harvey. If I parade the police chief's sister around his *raked* games, Harvey would have kittens."

But in my mind, I saw Harvey pulling up Quincy's number on his phone.

Dannie looked at her ankle boots, then up at me with a smile that probably kept her clients wrapped around her little arrow-tipped tail. "If it were the police chief himself, yeah, Harvey might flip. But it's just little ole me. You been running the games for him a long time. Really, aren't they *your* games?"

I paused.

She said, "I heard that shitheel Guy Hamm's one of your players. Kick his ass out and bring me in."

Harvey and I kept the games locked up. Everyone wanted in. Few could afford it.

Dannie said, "I'm sick of slots. I'm sick of driving all that way just to put on the wig of shame. The nearest card game is full of the same beer bellies."

She flung her hand at the stalls. "*And* they post *porn* in the bathrooms."

I snorted.

She looked me over. "What an ass. I'm whining about gambling sorrows and you just lost your cousin."

Roxie burst into the washroom. "Hey, what's going on? You sick, Janey?"

I looked at Roxie, didn't have the heart to tell her about Logan.

Instead I said to Dannie, "What's it called?"

I pointed to her lipstick, curious after my failed attempt as a beauty influencer, but mostly I wanted to change the subject. "The color. What is it?"

Dannie read the label. "It's by NARS. It's called, 'Somebody to Love.'"

Even that felt like a stab through the ribs. I gripped the sink.

From beyond the walls, we heard Gabe roar: "Everyone out! Pay up and get . . . *out*!"

"Oh, God." I stormed out to the dining hall and found Gabe swinging a damp bar towel and shouting at my tables.

Dannie said over my shoulder, "I told him about Logan. He said if we don't get another server in he'd close up early for you."

Roxie said, "Guess he didn't see me come in."

Gabe strode over to me and gripped my shoulder. "Janey, I don't know what to say. This is bad shit."

I nodded.

"How you doin'?"

"I'll have to get through it."

He blinked, turned, and shouted again. "I said, OUT! All you people! Out!"

"Here we go," Roxie said, and went to ring up the stragglers.

On his way out, Dr. Jude Summers paused at a table that seemed oblivious to Gabe's shouting, and encouraged them to vamoose before Gabe cracked the towel in their faces.

Dannie said, "It's just as well. I texted my brother. He's on his way."

"*Here?* Police chief's coming *now*?"

"Sure. Something wrong?"

I sagged.

Dannie's concern shifted gear. "Whatever you're into, Janey, I will tell you this. I bet you have more power than you think. Even bluffing is power, if you're good."

She leaned in, her eyes on the dining hall. "You don't wanna talk about what's going on, but clearly you're over your head. If I can get you something, just give me a shout. You could use a friend."

I scoffed, thinking how she called me "friend" and then tried to wheedle into the games. "*Are* we friends, though, Dannie? Let's get real."

Dannie turned to look me full in the eyes. "You didn't know that? We're friends. Even if you turn me down for the Big Bald Luck games, that won't change. Hit me up for babysitting. Em's a kick."

She gave a chuckle. "We may have grown apart, but girl, you and I have always been friends."

Girl. So different from how Frieda had used that word. I could choke.

Dannie tossed the lipstick into her bag and zipped it. "You get me into Big Bald Luck, though, we become *real* good friends."

CHAPTER

18

Suspicion

Suspicion sits in northwest Montana, the greener corridor, with mountain peaks and turquoise falls. Heartache gorgeous. Suspicion had instilled in me a homing device. I'd run away from foster care and always slink back here where I was born. Where my mother had died.

Suspicion isn't as weird a name as Scapegoat, over in the Lolo Forest, which is what we always told outsiders who comment about Suspicion being a weird name. Same with Good Grief, Idaho.

Suspicion tucked itself into the Kootenai National Forest with a lone highway and no freeways. The main street here was just called Farm to Market Road.

Since we were not as dramatic a landscape as Glacier, we didn't get the tourists. Suspicioners heard tales of the Kalispell sewage system that couldn't keep up with its population boom. *But damn, the money!* Some developer always wanted to scrape trees and replace them with concrete. Long lines at the McDonald's. A surge in crime. Flathead County could keep their troubles. We were happy to stay anonymous over here.

Suspicion had crime, of course. We just did it our way. Any crimes perpetrated by outsiders were unacceptable, period. However, our own townsfolk might commit the same forgivable crimes we'd always enjoyed.

For example.

Tax fraud could mean not filing taxes. Well, sometimes a Suspicioner just couldn't get it together. Or up on Cable Hill it could mean bending the numbers; also understandable so long as they didn't get greedy.

Fleeing a peace officer was just common sense, and it created spectator sport.

Barroom brawls? Come on.

Even petty larceny slid by around here if property didn't get damaged. Small-time drugs if they kept it on the DL. And yes, please: illegal card games.

Every now and then, a body went down the mountain. Sometimes by accident, sometimes not. It could cause a grumble. It really could.

In short, we liked things to stay the way they were.

And we preferred a police chief who moved drag ass to a crime scene.

CHAPTER

19

Police Chief Quincy Tigner

WITH GABE ALL bug-eyed and protective, I couldn't talk to Chief Tigner at the Hideout. Nor did I want him at my apartment over Mr. Traverse's detached garage—especially with Mr. Traverse fifty feet away. That left the damned police station.

Quincy Tigner's desk was made of fake wood with black trim that peeled on the end near the window. It hunkered beneath spiral-bound manuals and notepads and sticky wrappers and mail and crumpled paper. No way could he find anything. He did have an enviable collection of house plants. The chair he offered squeaked when I sat.

He said, "Can I get you anything? Water? Coffee?"

"Can we just get this over with? I heard my cousin was murdered."

He reared back, aghast. Despite his leanness, his cheeks plumped like a little boy's, his lashes long.

He deflated into his chair. "I am so, so sorry, Janey. Logan's the kind of guy, you know, friend to everybody. He gave me a ride on that Victory Jackpot of his. I swear to you we will figure this out."

It put a catch in my throat, seeing his earnestness. When we were kids, I used to stay the night at Dannie's place. We'd make cupcakes and pad around in our socks. Quincy was a good kid, typical older brother, probably more fun than most. Not the brightest. The Tigner household always burst with family who shouted over one another and cracked up at the least provocation.

That was when I was young. After my mother died, I had to move. When I came back, Dannie had a whole new clique. I'd become a mismatch. I'd stolen things. I'd gone to juvie. I'd become a teenaged mother. And God, the drinking. Both Dannie and Quincy went off to college.

I said to Quincy, "What happened?"

"Well, yeah. What can you tell me?"

I frowned. "Tell *you*? You're the police."

He blinked as though he were just now learning of this. His eye synchronized the blinks with a tick of his mouth. My fists tightened. It was no accident that Suspicion appointed a chief of police smart enough to count all his fingers and toes, but only just barely. Suspicion wasn't hell-bent to fight crime.

I took a breath and asked the horrible question, "Do you know who did it?"

And then because I felt I had to be absolutely clear with Quincy: "Who killed Logan?"

Quincy's eyes widened, and he unearthed a pad of paper, then dug out a pen. Whatever he thought he might write down would surely never be seen again once this conversation ended, as it would fall lost to the wilderness of his desk.

He said, "I thought you could tell *me* who killed him."

I said, "Why would I know?" though I was thinking it had to be Roman, or someone else in the Red King's army.

Or, it struck me, possibly even Harvey.

The thought left me volcanic. My hand slipped to my throat. If Harvey had touched one hair on my cousin's head, he would answer to me.

Quincy said, "You just told me he was murdered."

I fell still. Quincy looked at me, eyes big and sympathetic, hovering his grease-smeared pen over the notepad. I'd taken a faulty step but couldn't figure out where. My ears felt like fire.

I said, carefully, "Quincy, your sister, Danielle Tigner, came to Harvey's Hideout tonight while I was waiting tables. She told me Logan had been killed."

Quincy nodded, maintaining that slack expression—bordering fearful.

I said, "So he *was* murdered?"

He blossomed. "Oh, you mean *killed*? As in—no. We don't know. In my line of work, see, Janey,"—he straightened, hands folded over his messy desk, all official—"that could mean 'killed in a car accident,' or a freak accident, or drug overdose. See? We don't know what killed him. Dannie shouldn't have blabbed like that. I *told* her. We got a process."

He pursed his lips and exhaled through his nose. "I'm awful sorry. I wanted to tell you, but I been at the scene and she happened to drive by. She asked what was going on. I shouldn't have filled her in."

He lowered his voice. "Try holding up against Dannie sometime. She's your friend, you know how she gets."

He shook his head, regarded the window. "It's crazy around here. We got four police officers and only three vehicles. The fourth one has a bad transmission, so we constantly swap. Such a pain. You get up to go to work, and you got no car. What're you supposed to do, patrol the whole mountain on foot? But anyway. You went straight to murder? What made you think murder, as opposed to, you know, a car accident?"

My eyes dropped to the notepad beneath Quincy's hands. He'd jotted notes. I hadn't realized he'd managed to do that while we were talking.

I said, "Can I get a coffee after all?"

* * *

My thumbs eeled around one other, my brain flaming.

Quincy said, "Sure, sure, let's get you some coffee."

He rose and hooked his spiral notebook with his belt buckle but decoupled in time to avoid disaster. He had to hop on one foot. Then he shouted at Gary to bring coffee. I'd hoped Quincy would do the fetching himself so I could steal a moment to think.

"How do you like it, Janey?" Gary called.

"Sweet and light."

"Sweet and light, she says," Quincy shouted.

"I heard her."

Oh, God. Gary could hear all this?

Quincy said to me, "So why do you think Logan was murdered? Really, Janey? What made you think murder?"

I said, "Will you please just tell me what happened?"

He looked at me—no, he stared hard. I felt heat ball up from my heart and radiate to my extremities.

What the hell was going on? Harvey said Quincy was part of this. What if that was a bluff? I did not play poker, I just dealt the cards. But I'd spent years learning the skill of concealing my thoughts.

Logan's death was more important than keeping myself out of hot water.

I burst out, "What the hell, Quincy! Tell me what happened to my cousin!"

He softened. "Yeah. What's going on right now is, well, we don't know yet. We're gonna have to send Logan's remains on down to the crime lab in Missoula to figure that out."

"So he *was*—"

Quincy raised his hand. "It doesn't mean he was murdered. It means we don't *know*. The medical examiner and the coroner will help us figure out cause and manner of death."

"Maycie," I murmured.

It gave some comfort. Maycie Gaynor was the coroner, and she was one of my players at the Big Bald Luck games, but also a family friend. She'd known my mother.

Gary entered the office with my coffee.

"Thanks, Gar," I murmured.

"Sure thing, Janey. Hey, no hard feelings about Saturday."

I looked up. "What?"

"I don't hold it against you."

I stared.

He said, "For tossing me. From the Hideout."

Quincy said, "We're good here, Gary."

Gary disappeared, but Quincy called after him, "Would you mind closing the door, there, Gar?"

Gary's hand materialized and pulled the door closed. Slowly. The Hideout wasn't the only hub for gossip.

I'd sat in that Tundra down in Kalispell and watched Harvey pull up Quincy's number on speed dial. Harvey had made like the two of them were tight. I felt sick. And furious. And I didn't know where that put Dannie in all this.

I said, "What *can* you tell me?"

"We are investigating. There may be nothing *to* investigate. Maycie Gaynor will let us know. But until then, we follow procedure. Which means I'm unable to tell you much other than we found him off Cloudberry Creek. That mean anything to you?"

"No. So what the hell am I *here* for?"

"In case there's something you know that would help—"

I hopped out of my chair. "I gotta tell Uncle Reggie."

Quincy said, "Janey. Your uncle has been informed. Idaho sent a unit to him over in Coeur d'Alene."

"Like *I'm* being informed? You've told me nothing." I pinched the space between my brows and grabbed my purse.

"Janey, hold on. Help me figure this out. I have questions I'd like to ask you."

"Ask me later. I'm taking my kid and we're going to Idaho."

Something I should have done the first day things toppled sideways. Idaho was safe. Uncle Reggie and Margot needed us.

I left the coffee steaming on his desk. It would grow hair and dry up before Quincy threw it out. Suspicion had been duped when they appointed Quincy Tigner chief of police. He might take it easy on "acceptable" crime, but that big dumb puppy dog act of his was just that—an act.

The question was, where did the police chief stand with Harvey and Frieda?

CHAPTER 20

Family

I PULLED UP AND cut the engine. Trent's living room window glowed purple from the TV. No sex playlist. No snow falling, but the radio said a blizzard was bearing down over the pass. The Röhm sat tucked in the back of my Subaru beneath the box of Valvoline.

The dashboard clock read 10:23 PM—Em was inside that house, in bed by now. Probably reading under the covers with a flashlight.

On the porch railing stood two forgotten beer bottles, like flipping the bird twice. Oh, how the Cable Hill pretties must love it. In the morning when Em awoke, she'd throw them away before heading to school because Em took after me. She kept it together by putting things in order, regardless of whether it worked.

Em had given me Sherry's number. I initiated a message to both Trent and Sherry. With Sherry in copy, Trent couldn't ignore me. I typed:

I'm outside. Logan's dead. Need to talk about Em.

I clicked Send. We'll see what old crunchy curls is made of. I climbed out of the car and advanced toward the house. That bottom step gaped its maw.

Ding. An immediate text back from Sherry:

omg i'm so sorry

The door opened and Trent slipped through sideways, then slammed it shut. He wore a white tank top and sweatpants with socks, and he shook his hands against the cold—or me.

He'd grown that beard. Trent had a way with the ladies, and many thought he was hot. But wow. Now more than ever I noticed his hairiness; how his arms hung low, his eyes too tiny beneath a heavy brow. And why did he always stand with his knees akimbo? The poor man really was a troll.

I said, "Beer bottles on the railing. Nice."

"You come here to file a complaint with the HOA?"

He glanced back at the door and added, "You're not supposed to be here. Should've called."

"I did. You didn't answer. Did you get my text about Logan?"

He looked guarded. "Yeah."

"I'm going to Coeur d'Alene to be with Uncle Reggie and Margot. I want to take Em."

"How long?"

"Couple of days. She wouldn't miss much school."

He frowned. "You can't take her tonight."

Before I could speak, he said, "Not tomorrow, either. She needs to keep to the schedule."

"Trent!"

"People been talking, Janey. They say you're acting weird. Like, like you're probably in a bad way. It's not good to yank Em around. I'll finish out my weekend with her, same as always."

A vise squeezed my heart. I tried to think, get my mind rational so I could navigate a calm conversation. But the only thing inside me were accusations and insults, so I wobbled at a parboil, mute.

He leaned into the column and pushed off. "Is it true? About Logan?"

My tongue swelled at the back of my teeth, and my eyes swelled, and my throat.

I got out, "Yes. He's dead."

"How?"

"They won't tell me."

"Damn. It's a damn shame. I liked him."

"Everyone did. He was good." My voice creaked on the word "good."

Then Trent said, "But you know, you hear shit," and suppressed a tiny, wavering smile.

I whipped my eyes back to him, stepping forward from the darkness. "What's that supposed to mean?"

"I don't know. He was pretty secretive and all." He let the grin harden off.

I could scream in his face for being so smug. But I also wanted to hear what under God's glory rays he was talking about.

Trent leaned into the column, pushed off. Leaned in, pushed off.

"What are people saying?"

He hawked and spat into the snow. I shuddered.

He said, "Something about a trail Logan's been blazing all the way to Canada."

I had a front-row seat for gossip at the Hideout but I'd never heard such a thing. Then again, people turn down the volume when the buzz is about one of your own.

Trent pushed off from the column one last time and stretched. "Tomorrow I'll go ahead and tell Em about Logan. Next time, don't come here, okay? You know better. Not supposed to come to the house with the order of protection and all. See you Sunday."

He smiled and pointed a finger pistol at me, eyebrow cocked. "At the *library.*"

He disappeared inside—into *my* house that I paid for. It belonged to Em and me.

I forced down an inhuman growl, turned, and ran. My foot slipped. I back-bicycled on the steps and almost put my foot through the dread hole at the bottom. I grabbed the rail and wrenched my wrist in the process.

Up above, one of the beer bottles rocked but did not fall.

The lights of Cable Hill twinkled. Springtime coming. Nearly St. Patrick's Day, a lucky time of year.

I dashed back up and snatched the bottles from the railing, then descended again. I smashed first one, then the other into the jagged black hole in the bottom step.

* * *

With a heart crushed to pea gravel, I called Uncle Reg. He was bereft. I felt almost grateful for the brain putty the pills created. It kept me from falling apart.

Uncle Reggie said, "You remember back when Logan taught you to paddleboard?"

"I'll never forget."

An indigo sky, the sun warming my face, and the cool, dark blue of Lake Coeur d'Alene washing my feet as Logan helped me find balance on the spongey board. I'd been fifteen years old. My mother had been dead eight years at that time, and Logan's mother, my Aunt Sylvie, was dying of the same cancer. Logan had taken me to a secluded area off the lake, a sunny canyon cove, because he knew I preferred listening to birdsong over powerboats. Songbirds had reminded me of Suspicion. That day on the paddleboards was one of my best memories growing up.

Years after Aunt Sylvie died, Uncle Reg found love again with Margot. They rented out kayaks, paddleboards, and paddleboats on the lake during the summer, and they rented modest cabins year-round.

I clutched the phone and listened to my uncle sort through his shock.

Uncle Reggie said, "The business could have been his. He's so good at it. Good with people. Patient. He loved it out on the lake."

I said, "I think he meant to come back and do just that. He was working with the fly-fishing outfitter over here but he told me he saw himself going back to Coeur d'Alene someday."

"He told you that?"

"Yes."

Like me, Logan had been born with a homing device.

I paused. I didn't know whether telling Uncle Reg about Logan's plans gave him comfort, or if it was cruel.

But then I said, "Uncle Reg, I'm coming out. To Idaho. To be there with you and Margot for a day or two."

I wished I could bring Em. I wanted to show Em what to do. In a time of grief, you come together with friends and family. I was bad at knowing what to do as a mother, but I knew grief.

Uncle Reggie said, "You're coming *now*?"

Then, in the background, Margot's voice: "Janey can't come *here*."

My fingers tightened over the phone. They didn't want me.

I said, "I saw Logan two weeks ago. He was leaving for a guide trip up the mountain."

Uncle Reg puffed, agitated. "Police told me. I never understood why he went all the way out there and took up with strangers."

It came as a gut punch. Me, a stranger. I'd lived with Uncle Reg, Aunt Sylvie, and Logan for over a year. They were one of the good foster families—my mother's sister. Although, I ran away when Aunt Sylvie died. It had felt too raw. First my mother, then my aunt. I was part of the reason for Aunt Sylvie's decline, with all the stress of taking in an unhinged niece. I ran back to Suspicion. Scared, teenaged, clueless. Maybe running away had caused more damage to that family than I'd realized. Maybe Uncle Reg had only been tolerating me, the head case, the screw-up, for Aunt Sylvie's sake.

Margot's voice came on the line. "Janey, you are not to come out here."

"No?"

"Now is not the time."

I blinked. "Of course. I get it."

The head case. The screw-up. The *stranger.*

Margot said, "Check the weather, hon. There's a big storm on the pass. Wait until the blizzard's gone. Then, it would be a comfort to see you."

I released my breath in a hard stream. I'd misinterpreted them. They *did* want me.

The mind plays its most sinister tricks when steeped in grief. I, if anyone, should have known this by now.

CHAPTER

21

The Dentist's Secret

It was Friday night, and Harvey took the stage. The Hideout always got rowdy when he performed. He sat at his piano—not a keyboard, but a piano for Harvey—and instead of launching into his usual rock-and-roll, burn-it-down set, he placed a bottle of Dewar's on the housing and waited for quiet.

Then he angled the microphone and said, "This is for Logan."

It was called "I Will Not Say Goodbye." Harvey didn't perform it like the popular version. He sang in a well-worn voice. He delivered that ballad the hard way. I wanted to slam the piano lid over his fingers. Smash the whisky bottle. He had no right to sing for Logan.

When he finished, silence hung in the air, and then the Hideout erupted in applause. He took a belt from the scotch and walked off the stage. The crowd kept up but Harvey was gone. The band looked puzzled. They'd have to play without him or defer to the piped-in music.

I folded my arms tight and looked over to see Dr. Jude Summers, the "Sunshine Dentist," wiping his boots at the double doors.

* * *

I caught up with Jude at the bar. "I need to talk to you."

He was surprised. He looked like a man who preferred to be left alone.

I said, "Last month, when my cousin got his wisdom teeth taken out, did he say anything? You know, did he say anything under anesthesia?"

Jude smiled, a patient—no, an *impatient* smile, bar lights reflecting off his wire-rimmed glasses. He was older than me by about six years.

He said, "Like what . . . ?"

I lifted a shoulder. "Anything unusual."

"Like how people give up state secrets under sedation?"

He grimaced, rearranged himself on the stool. "Carrie Grosvenor came to see me for an impaction once and blurted out her blue-ribbon chili recipe."

Then he seemed to register my vitriol.

He said, "Forgive me."

Because I was three seconds away from tearing off those glasses and stomping them.

Cast Iron appeared from nowhere, leaning into the bar behind my shoulder. "Janey. Is this jackass bothering you?"

He breathed twice the oxygen of anyone else in the Hideout.

Jude checked my face, confused. "Am I?"

I dusted Cast Iron away. "We're good. Give us privacy."

Cast Iron kept heating the space behind me, and I swiveled with a frown. He finally disengaged and walked off.

I returned to Jude. "You don't know about Logan?"

"What about him?"

I glanced at the now-empty stage. Jude had walked in as Harvey finished his dedication, so he hadn't heard it. But the Suspicion grapevine moved fast. Darcy Halfthunder worked Jude's reception desk and she was sister-in-law to Millie, the dispatcher at the police station.

I said, "Weren't you seeing patients today?"

"I've been in Great Falls for a CE. Tell me what happened to your cousin."

I couldn't. I blinked and pressed my lips together.

He said, "Oh," more like an exhalation than a word.

Roxie passed by with a low-five to me. Her way of telling me she was covering my tables, but I knew she could only keep it up for so long.

Jude's tone softened. "I wouldn't have joked if I'd known. You want an answer to your question. It's this: Logan never said anything out of school while under sedation. Patients don't do that. They get emotional, or even funny, but it's a myth that people blurt out their secrets. I don't know if that helps you."

I nodded. Customers were waiting, and I turned to go.

He said, "Although."

I looked back.

He said, "It's not entirely ethical for me to tell you this, but once a patient is deceased, their medical records are no longer confidential."

He gestured with his hand. "If you put in a request."

"Can I make a verbal request?"

"I suppose."

"I'm requesting them now."

Jude said, "A few days ago, your cousin came in with an abscess. You should never let the sun go down on an abscess. His had gotten bad. He said he'd been stuck on a guide trip, or he'd have come in sooner."

I stiffened. Logan had seen the dentist upon return, though he hadn't connected with me. I remembered those missed calls. He must have phoned around the same time he saw Jude. I had failed him.

Jude said, "The abscess was the result of an insult to the jaw."

"What, now?"

"He said someone hit him. He told me he didn't know who'd done it. It'd been dark. A blind attack."

I tried to process this. "Like a burglary?"

"Maybe. It's possible he surprised a burglar. That's all I know."

He'd been attacked. Some creep lying in wait? In the time he needed me most, I'd disconnected. I may never forgive myself. I felt sick, drugged, and aggressive.

Jude said, "Look, I know what it's like to lose someone. I know it hurts."

"Yeah? In that case how about I fix you a double?"

A snide comment in hopes that a taste of meanness would ease my pain.

Put that down in the No column. Nothing worked. Pain was pain.

I flipped the gate and entered the bar.

But Jude said, "In that case, how about I spot *you* one?"

That surprised me. I looked at him, and we both almost smiled.

In this suffocating hour, the secret I kept for the dentist felt quietly—

nice.

CHAPTER

22

Plain Manila Folder

I'd named Em in honor of my mother Emily, though Em was not Emily, just Em. Also, Em's last name is Hendee (same as mine) because Trent didn't want to give her his. He'd said he'd get in trouble. I had been underage. He was four years older, and the age difference stopped mattering over time, but when Em was born it posed a problem. I'd given birth in juvie. If Trent had gotten locked up for getting me, a minor, pregnant, what would have happened to Em?

Anyway, it didn't stop him from putting his name on the house deed my money paid for. He wouldn't put his name on his daughter, but he'd put it on real estate.

See? Thoughts spin vile when you break a relationship. Things that don't bother you when you're in love turn bitter when you separate. I don't like the bitterness but I don't know how to spit it out.

There were two weird things about Em taking my name.

One: "Em Hendee" sounded strange on the ear. Like I was clearing my throat every time I said it. A car trying to start.

Two: Hendee women never lived into their thirties. That's the Hendee curse.

* * *

I made it through my Friday and Saturday shifts. Today, Sunday, I'd pick Em up after close.

The entire town knew about Logan and could talk of little else. As the chief of police, Quincy Tigner released a statement. He told reporters it was an unexplained death, and that they were investing all resources looking into it.

I wanted to know, Did Logan look his killer in the eye? What if he'd had the little Saturday night special? What if I'd stood by his side?

Did he suffer?

Every Suspicioner sought the latest bulletin on Logan's death. Murder, suicide, accident. These woods were no place for outsiders like Logan, they said.

Fifteen minutes before Harvey's Hideout opened for Sunday brunch, Roxie and I gathered in the ladies' room. I had to squat over the toilet with a lab cup, the bathroom stall open. Roxie leaned against the sink with her arms folded and eyes fixed on her blinding white Sketchers. I wondered how she kept them so bright. She must clean them after every shift.

Roxie said, "I don't know why Harvey's picking on you. No one else has to take drug tests."

I said, "It's not for street drugs, it's meds. He wants to make sure I'm taking them."

Roxie's gaze flew up. "How is that any of his business?"

"It's not. I could refuse."

I peed into the cup with precision (thank God) and screwed on the lid, then finished into the toilet bowl while Roxie went back to fixating on her Sketchers. Roxie clearly assumed that my job hung in the balance, and a honkytonk waitress wasn't going to raise the matter with the Montana Department of Labor & Industry. Roxie didn't know the real reason behind the enforced urine tests.

I left the specimen cup and washed my hands. Roxie, already wearing blue nitrile gloves, screwed on the lid and inserted it into the plastic zip-top bag.

She said, "Did you at least have fun?"

"Fun?"

"With whatever batshit crazy thing you did to have to go on meds."

I reflected on breaking into Trent's with the snub nose while Sherry screamed with joy. "Nope. Wish I'd planned better and had myself a hootenanny."

"Bummer. Well. Are the meds any good?"

A nutty question in the context of my personal earthquake zone. The meds felt like death, but I knew what she meant. I pulled my apron off the counter and plucked out the pill bottles, lining them up for Roxie. Her perfume smelled like light, crisp spice. She could actually pull it off in a public washroom or a Saturday night dance floor atomized with beer and sweat—she knew just which scent to wear.

She leaned over and squinted, moving her lips as she read, then popped back up with wide eyes. "Girl, that's black market gold."

She threw her arms in the air and gave me a hip-bump. And *that* was why Roxie got all the tips.

* * *

After two PM, close of Sunday brunch, Harvey pulled in even though he hadn't worked today. He did a double take when he saw me camped out in my station wagon. I pretended to fiddle with the stereo.

He pulled up next to me. I cursed blue streamers and rolled down my window.

He said, "Everything all right?"

"Oh, sure, Harvey. Life's a song. Don't worry, keys are in the safe, same as always."

He gazed across the sunlit forest surrounding the Hideout, then down at me from the tower that was his Toyota Tundra.

"You're clearly having a hard time. I didn't want things to go this way. I'd do something if I could."

"Right."

He fell silent, a half-smile plastered on his face.

I pulled his gaze in, held it, then broke. "This whole act of yours, Harvey? 'I raise hell, but only a few inches.' You think it's cute, like we're still pals? I wouldn't let you walk me safely to my station wagon at night, lest you put a bullet in my brain yourself."

His smile dropped. "What *are* you doing out here? Sittin' by yourself in the parking lot."

"Making a phone call. Not that it's any of your business. Or do I need to clear my calls with you now?"

He laughed—through his teeth. "It'd be better if we got along on friendlier terms."

I climbed out of the Subaru and slammed the door, peering up at him where he sat on high. "What happened to my cousin?"

"Keep your voice down!"

"Answer me!"

"How should I know?"

"Because you or one of your buddies had him kil—"

I couldn't finish the statement. My throat seized up. I clutched my neck and gagged.

He growled, "Watch yourself."

I bared my teeth and rolled my eyes to the sky, clean blue with clouds pooling down the mountain. Crisp air. My breath hitched. Harvey wasn't at the games that night at the Sure Shot Shooting Range, and that might have been the last time anyone heard from Logan.

Carefully, he said, "I did not kill Logan. Don't know how to kill a man."

He cut his eyes to the Hideout, then back at me. "And I don't think our associates did. Wouldn't be in their best interest."

"Except you'd already found Logan's replacement. Me."

"We'd all have preferred to keep Logan." He wrinkled his mouth. "You know? I don't like doing this—"

He swung open the door and lurched out of the Tundra. I flung myself back against my Subaru, bracing for whatever he was about to let fly.

He reached past me and dropped something onto my passenger seat. "Frieda wants you to stop by the office next week with Em."

"Why?"

"Has to do with power of attorney."

I scowled at the thing on my seat—a folder.

He said, "She's good with children, and she'll make the right decision if anything should happen to you."

"What's going to 'happen to me'?"

"Just a precaution, that's all. Call it free legal help, a benefit of the arrangement. You know good and well that Trent's a worthless piece of shit."

He climbed back into his Tundra. "But what you're going to do, is sign those papers, and bring Em by Frieda's office. Take your medication. Do as you're told."

"Harvey? What's going to happen to me?"

He slammed the door. "Nothing, I hope. But knowing you? Bad decision-making."

He threw the truck in gear. "Better get a move on. Once your shift's over, you hang around here, it's trespassing."

He drove toward his hallowed Harvey-only parking space.

The thing he'd deposited on my passenger's seat was a manila folder with legal documents. Yellow tabs indicated where I should sign. Terms like "power of attorney" and "court appointed guardian." I skimmed the legalese until something caught my eye. It said Frieda and Harvey often picked Em up from school and took care of her on overnight stays. Days or weeks at a time. That they provided non-reimbursed food and other supplies.

Not true.

The papers trembled in my hands. What made Frieda think I would sign these?

Because Frieda threatened me with jail. My juvenile record was sealed but Frieda said she could break that, which created a "history." If I went to jail now, I'd stay there for a long time. She might be bluffing but I couldn't take that chance.

I didn't have anything to bargain with. I had no idea what Frieda was up to. I'd played stupid so long I forgot how to work my mind.

I could run. Take Em and run.

But with what? No money. And if my 2002 Subaru station wagon could creep across the state line I'd consider it uncommon luck.

I looked at my phone, open to Trent's number.

I scrolled through the call history, found Roman. Steeled myself. Placed the call.

CHAPTER

23

Better Behavior

ROMAN'S VOICE CAME through the phone in a whisper. "Do you have any idea how long I had to stand out there, freezing my ass off after you threw my keys in that river?"

I said, "It was a creek. Not my fault you come dressed like the Burberry catalog. Next time, behave better."

"You're lucky you weren't the one they found in that fucking creek."

"Thank you for finally talking straight. Last time, you rolled up like some serial killer who hands out oil changes."

Murmurs swelled in the background, then a door shut and the sounds dropped as though he'd stepped away for privacy.

He said, "How. May I *help* you?"

I scanned the snowy sunlit pine grove. The Hideout was closed and Harvey was still parked in his Tundra.

I said, "I need to know what happened to Logan."

I could hear Roman breathing. Tried to picture him.

I said, "Was it you?"

"You know better than to ask that sort of thing over the phone. Talk to your boss."

"I can't."

The station wagon had warmed—too warm, in fact, and I rolled down the window and bathed my sweaty palm in the breeze.

He said, "You'll have to meet me."

My pulse quickened. Harvey now strode across the lot with his hitching step, his expression dark. Until this point, I had observed the rules Frieda had laid down. Meeting with Roman would breach them.

I said, "Where?"

CHAPTER

24

Ponderosa Lodge

We met at a crumbling lodge that half of Suspicion wanted to tear down and the other half wanted to save. The sign read Ponderosa Lodge, but all along the drive stood lodgepole pines, not ponderosas. Maybe Lodgepole Lodge sounded phallic, or just plain dumb, so they swerved to a different pine.

The place went sleepy when I was a kid, and closed down except for special events. Then the storm of 2016 put a full stop to practical use.

Everyone my age who grew up in Suspicion, including me, had snuck in and declared it haunted. It had even hosted the occasional loss of virginity.

I pulled around the blockade, which had been pushed aside. I spotted Roman's high-dollar SUV, a black Cadillac Escalade. Part moon buggy, part hearse. Between the shoes, the clothes, and the vehicle, Roman could fit in on Cable Hill with those neighbors who wished to God Trent would up and move so they could scrape the house and put up something more attractive. Like a boulder.

I mounted the steps, thinking of the night I'd mounted the back steps to Trent's place—my once-was home—on the flip of a coin.

I tried the door. It opened. Not easily. Six inches and then it scrubbed the floor and stopped. Roman snatched my wrist and pulled me through the gap.

* * *

Roman said, "Did anyone follow you?"

"No."

"Remove your clothes."

"What? Forget it!" I wrenched away, hackles at a sawtooth.

Timbers crisscrossed the vaulted ceiling and despite the boarded-up windows, shafts of light seeped in, sparkling with dust motes.

He said, "I need to know if you're wearing a wire."

A full-grown taxidermy grizzly stood at reception. Years of dust frosted every surface, and I could only imagine the mold and rodent droppings amid the trash. It wasn't that I enjoyed cleaning, just that it hurt to endure a mess. On occasion I'd snuck into the Hideout on days off to deep clean the women's washroom even though Harvey used a service. Once I'd nearly broken my back falling off the ladder when I tried to wipe down the chandelier.

Laying my clothing on all that dust made me equally as anxious as disrobing in front of a stranger with a known criminal background.

I said, "You first."

Roman looked at me like I'd pitched his keys into the creek again.

I said, "For all I know, you're the one who's wired."

He sighed. Then to my horror, he began to strip. I averted my gaze.

The walls bore shadows where once had been mounted taxidermy fish, heads of elk, landscape paintings. All that remained was a standing grizzly bear, hide ripped and ear torn, in the center of the vast hall.

Now in his underwear, Roman turned in a circle for me. I couldn't lift my eyes beyond his feet. He might have been wired like C-3PO, and I wouldn't have seen it.

He spread his arms. "Good?"

Then he reached for his clothes, but I stopped him. "Wait."

I disrobed and folded my things on top of his, since his clothing seemed cleaner than any surface around the great hall. With no heat, it was freezing, our breath swirling white. But my self-consciousness kept me steamed up despite the cold. I wanted to crawl inside the fireplace.

Now in my bra and granny panties, I turned slowly, arms up, glaring at the ceiling timbers. Because if I saw his face and he showed the slightest hint of judgment over my body, be it dismay, shock, or joy, I'd issue donkey kicks.

After a full turn in silence, I dared to look at him. He didn't even have eyes on me. He was fixated on my neatly folded leather jacket—or rather, on an inch of faux-mahogany exposed from its pocket.

He extracted the snub nose. "Was this for me?"

I shriveled into my nudity. He held the Röhm by the mahogany grip and pointed it at the rafters. The short barrel gleamed under portals of daylight, the metal spreading a fairy dance across the hall.

He said, "I'm insulted and flattered. It's so cute."

He hefted it, spun it on his trigger finger. It got stuck. "Wow. Mountain people. Even you."

He gestured with it as he spoke. "I knew a guy who kept a tiny thing like this in his boot. It always jammed. Used to find them everywhere. They called them Suicide Specials."

He gave me that winning smile, and it reminded me that he was handsome, that he kept in shape. Tattoos in scrolling cursive. I felt ridiculous standing in my underwear making conversation. I'd gone too long without a certain kind of human touch.

He said, "My advice, put ammo in the chamber. Everyone can see it ain't loaded."

He smiled at the empty cylinder. "You won't fool anybody with an unloaded revolver."

He tucked it back in my jacket. We got dressed. A rare occasion that I strip with a man and pray gratitude for having worn sexless underwear.

He gave a tiny hop as he hoisted his jeans, then snatched my phone and powered it down. "All right. Now what was it you wanted to talk about?"

* * *

I folded my arms over my leather jacket. "Logan. Was it your people who killed him? Or Frieda?"

Roman shook his head. "I don't know anything about that."

I scowled. I didn't trust Roman. It's easier to identify the liar than the lie itself.

He said, "If we iced him, I'd just say so. 'We bumped him off cuz he stole from us.' Or, 'Because he talked.' Or, 'He spat on Baltazar's mother.' I got no reason to lie. You told me you're Logan now. That's enough for me."

I searched his face. He showed no desire to win me over, was just stating facts.

I said, "You and the Red King had absolutely nothing to do with Logan's death?"

"Far as I know. I'm the only one from the Seattle set who's been posted in this godforsaken town. If Baltazar wanted Logan unalived, he would have come to me."

"That's a weak denial."

He shrugged.

I said, "What's the money for? The cash in the backpack?"

Roman narrowed his eyes. "You really don't know a *thing*, do you?"

I frowned.

He said, "How did you get pulled in?"

"If I tell you, will you answer my question?"

He set his hands to his hips and looked up to the cross timbers. I twisted a hangnail. He was taking too long to think it over. I'd been on a roll, but now the dealer of information had me hooked on free product and it was time to pay. I felt like a turtle on its back with a bear sniffing the retractable parts.

Roman held up a finger. "See, that's exactly the sort of thing that makes Baltazar nervous."

He crossed to the bar and dusted off a stool, then sat. "Frieda Kanjo keeps her hands so damn clean. Zero risk. Her own people don't have a clue. Logan works for her, he makes her angry, and now he's dead."

"What did he do to make her angry?"

Roman shrugged. "Don't know. We didn't call the hit, so I assume it was her."

He folded his hands and nodded at me. "Look at you. You do stuff for her that could put you in prison. Knowing your predecessor was probably assassinated. Frieda doesn't seem to pay you much. So why—"

He gave a sharp intake of breath. "Ah."

His face registered surprise like I'd answered his question. "Blackmail."

He gave a micro-shake of the head. "It's bad? You want to tell me?"

I said nothing, my fists tight.

He said, "Doesn't matter."

He stopped, analyzed the situation. "People see inside one another faster than they realize. They determine trust almost immediately. Love at first sight, and *bam*. They visualize marriage, children, grandchildren, till death do us part. Know what I'm saying? It's an unconscious decision within five minutes of meeting someone: Can I trust this person?"

I stood before him. I didn't remember having crossed over to the bar to where he sat on the stool.

Roman waved between us. "What's happening now, you and me, we're speaking with honesty. We're showing respect. You want to know about the money in the backpack? I'll tell you."

He swiped the dirt from the barstool next to him and gestured to me. "Please."

CHAPTER

25

The Backpack Pact

I ACTUALLY SAT ON the filthy barstool, now less dusty with the deep swipe of Roman's hand.

He said, "You got a guess as to what the backpack funds are about?"

"She's laundering money for you?"

"No, but good guess. Know where Baltazar is right now?"

If I hadn't been so brain fizzed, I'd have read up. "Last I saw he was behind bars."

Roman nodded. "He's awaiting trial for murder at Lincoln County Jail. He continues to head the organization, but it ain't easy. Those of us working for him have to make some decisions on his behalf."

He waved in the general direction of Cable Hill. "With Frieda's connections, she's kept Baltazar out of trouble. Understand me?"

My medically basted mind extruded the realization. "It's bribe money."

He smiled, nodded. "A chief of police—"

I blanched. Quincy Tigner. So it was true.

"A prosecutor, and two judges. It's expensive, but worthwhile."

I glanced at the motheaten grizzly bear, then back up into Roman's eyes. "Expensive?"

"Very."

I thought of Dannie and her gambling. She'd lost her home, then sprung back from debt by "winning it back." The quintessential gambler's fantasy. What a bunch of BS.

Roman said, "But since Baltazar got arrested, facing trial, the accumulated total has gone from hundreds of thousands to millions."

Millions. Millions of U.S. dollars. His revelation spun at me in cutting slow motion. People like me didn't survive that sort of thing. Million-dollar bribes.

Reason number four why Frieda picked me. She'd wanted the disposable razor.

* * *

I said, "Why is Baltazar Valencia in jail? If all that money's being spread around, couldn't he have avoided arrest?"

Roman gave a pinched smile. "It's complicated."

I figured otherwise. Probably it was simple. From the way Roman watched me, he thought so, too.

I said, my voice scratchy, "You want something from me. Specifically."

"Mm."

Roman looked at me, then up at the timbers. "Baltazar should have been released by now. My team has serious concerns. It doesn't help that we have a trust problem with Frieda Kanjo. She refuses to allow contact with the key people we've been paying, including the prosecutor. Says that would be in violation of our deal. But then again, Baltazar was supposed to stay out of jail. I would say *that* is in violation of our deal."

"These things take time?"

"Maybe."

He folded his hands. "Maybe."

"You think Frieda's keeping the money."

"I hope not. For everyone's sake."

I thought it through. A prosecutor and a judge keeping Baltazar in jail well beyond his sell-by date. That was either one hell of a bluff, or—

He said, "But now we have a new Logan."

"Janey."

He smiled. "Nice to meet you, Janey."

As if he didn't already know my name. The grit of the place had found its way to my teeth, a taste of smoky, rotted wood. I wet my lips, but that made it worse.

He said, "I think you can help."

"I'm nobody. I can do nothing."

"You strike me as a somebody." Roman gestured. "You got access. You are an attractive woman with connections. You can find out if our funds hit their targets."

This man was woofing. None of that was true. Not even the part about being attractive.

I raised my voice. "There's no connections. I wait tables at a nowhere roadhouse, not some pumpkin spice bistro. We haven't replaced the felt on the pool tables since Kid Rock numbered his album covers by how many times he's flipping the bird."

Roman patted the air in a placating gesture, but I rushed on. "If I had connections, I wouldn't be working there, Mister, I promise you that."

"I'm Roman, not Mister."

I sat poised to spring.

He said, "How many people in this town do you know?"

"Here? I know everyone in Suspicion. You want to sell them beer, I can manage that. I can bounce the rowdies. But I'm not the type you pour your heart out to. Roxie's the one everybody loves."

He said nothing. He took his time. I glanced at the door, tempted to make an exit.

He said, "Still, you know them. They come to Harvey's Hideout. And you run a card game. High rollers, am I right? Influential people."

"Listen, you are overestimating—"

"Do you like working for Frieda Kanjo?"

"No."

"What exactly do you want? Tell me what we can give you."

I covered my face, then opened my hands in pleading, but failed to speak.

He said, "Let's just say we could help. What would it take?"

This felt insane. The grizzly bear stood with a frozen roar and a paw raking a ghost. In the massive fireplace, vandals had tossed paint cans and Chumpus Burger wrappers. How much money to betray Frieda, the woman who held my daughter's fate—and mine—and take a chance on these crooks?

* * *

I stammered, "A hun—a hundred thousand."

He arched his neck. "That's a lot of money."

"It's what I'd need to disappear. If I find something out for you, and it's all bad news, I can't continue a life here in Suspicion. Look what happened to Logan."

"You might uncover good news."

"Frieda's still gonna know I stepped out of line. Either way, I'll have to grab my kid and go."

"You're that afraid of her?"

Roman touched a match to the end of his cigarette, then shook it out in that same elaborate flourish.

He said, "Ten grand."

"Not worth it."

"I don't believe that. Frieda has something on you. I'm guessing it's got something to do with your daughter. In a best-case scenario, you stand to lose your little girl, and in the worst, you fear for your life. How'm I doing?"

A swallow lodged in my throat. He'd nailed it, but he just revealed he knew I had a daughter. I'd been careful to refer to Em as "my kid."

Roman nodded as he pulled in a drag. "Don't worry. We'll relocate you. Give you a new name. People always focus on money, money, money. Think in terms of what you want. We can provide what you want without stacks of cash."

The smoke curled toward the ceiling.

He said, "Along with your ten grand, we can get you a place to live. Maybe not something out of *House Beautiful*, but nice enough. Decent school."

I drew myself up. "All that, plus an upgrade to what I'm driving. And fifty thousand."

He shook his head. "Ten thousand."

"You don't understand. I'm screwing up my kid. This is only gonna make things worse."

"She needs a psychiatrist? We can provide—"

"No! I get the whole trust thing, but no dirty docs for my kid. Not even a shrink."

He squinted as the smoke burned his eyes. "I can add the car and go up to fifteen grand."

My head hurt. "Twenty."

"Fifteen. That's final."

I thought about it. "All right, fifteen thousand with all the other stuff."

Roman shrugged. "You did the right thing by coming to me. Now. I'll be gone for a week or two and as you know, Baltazar's in the clink. There's a chance some of my people will act against Baltazar's wishes."

He said, "Because I'll be traveling, you might do some handoffs with someone other than me. You talk about our agreement to no one."

"Why? You said you all trust each other."

He grimaced. "We trust *each other*, not the *situation*. With Baltazar incarcerated, it's interesting what it does to loyalties. Do your handoffs, but don't engage."

It sounded shady in a land already filled with shadows.

He said, "We should avoid public interactions. Check in every few days. Don't lose my number."

He slid off the barstool. He took a slow pull from his Marlboro, then ground out the butt on the scuffed floor.

I said, "What are the names I'm supposed to look into? The judges and all that?"

He took an envelope from his jacket, removed the contents, then jotted on the back. He paused once to blink at the timbers. Then, he handed his list to me. The handwriting ran blocky and slanted:

- chief police
- prosecutor—Barkling?
- two judges

I said, "That's *it*? Who are the judges?"

"We don't know. Frieda Kanjo says it's confidential. Even from us."

"Are these people even from around here? The county, or . . . ?"

He answered with a tight smile. "You leave first. I'll block the entrance after."

Roman headed for the door.

I jumped to my feet and followed. "Wait, just so we're clear, I haven't accepted this deal. I don't think I can get this information for you."

He paused in the doorway, his figure silhouetted by the cold sparkling sun of early spring. "We just agreed on a deal."

"No, I said I wasn't *sure*, and I probably couldn't do it. What happens if I can't get the information?"

He smiled, eyes flat, lips together and the corners pressed wide. "We have a deal. Let's keep things friendly. I like when things are friendly."

CHAPTER

26

Crunchy

THEY NAMED CABLE Hill after Cable Gross, a prospector who'd struck vermiculite along one of Suspicion's prettiest overlooks. Ordinarily you'd use the person's last name, like Lincoln Harbor or Washington Heights, but understandably, they didn't name it Gross Hill.

Cable Hill was bad enough. It sounded like a utility easement.

Lately, the highly groomed, leather-and-wool residents of Cable Hill had become restless. They wanted to rename it. I no longer had a vote but I'd have dug in for Cable Gross, just to be a jerk. I didn't believe Mr. Gross cared after his bones had stopped pumping marrow, but all these names the glossy-haired people came up with made my butt ache.

That part of Suspicion was called Cable Hill, and the rest was just Greater Suspicion, which seemed plain but when you thought about it, was kind of cool: *Greater* Suspicion.

Trent and I would not meet at my former home, my little tear-down on Cable Hill. I had to pick up my kid at the library due to the stupid restraining order—because of that one little time I'd jabbed his tire. That was my mistake and I owned it.

Fresh from Roman, I pulled up in the Subaru and spotted Trent and Sherry. Sherry's curls crunched from too much product. Em stood at the top of the library steps, hand-in-hand with the two of them, and how stupid because they could have waited in Trent's nice warm (not rusty) F-150. Em was nine, too old to hold hands with a couple of grown-ups. Like they were taking some toddler trick-or-treating at the Bates Motel.

And that Sherry. Wouldn't those crunchy curls shatter in this freezing weather?

Flash! An image of Trent facedown on her.

Spying was also my mistake, and I owned that, too.

Trent wore slacks and a tidy beard, hair combed, and Sherry had on flats and a modest dress—slim fitting but not tight. The three descended the steps with no hint this was a custody handoff with protective order restrictions. Sherry's knees had to be freezing. Any second, she'd go ass over teakettle. Em looked perfect.

My eyes zeroed in on Sherry's left hand. She was swinging Em's prized treasure, her dingy antique train case. Except it didn't look dingy. It glowed like the snow over the library lawn, gilded in the afternoon sun. Someone had cleaned sixty years of grime and Em's Magic Marker graffiti from its sweet cream vinyl.

Sherry. She could have ruined it. She had no right.

I remained seated while Trent opened my liftgate and loaded Em's things. Sherry gave Emmie a hug then paused, offered me a tentative wave. I stuck my hand in the air but failed to move it around. Sherry climbed into Trent's F-150.

Trent stepped over to my window. "Was that you who covered the hole in my bottom step?"

His bottom step.

After I'd smashed his beer bottles into the hole the other night, I was haunted by visions of Em slipping and putting her foot through that step—like I'd nearly done—only to land in broken glass. So I'd snuck back and tacked a board over it. Doing so violated the protective order. But I couldn't just leave it. Nor could I call Trent and tell him what I'd done.

Yet again, yet again, yetafucking-gain. Confused as to how to be a good mother.

Trent whispered, "I didn't tell Em about Logan. Didn't have the heart."

I stabbed my eyes into him.

He said, "I know, my bad. Better coming from you anyhow."

He rapped twice on the roof and waved to Em, who'd already buckled in.

Em said, "Mom! Did you see? Sherry cleaned my train case. It looks exactly like when Great-Grandma bought it. Let's get out and look!"

It wasn't your great-grandmother's train case! That was a big lie! It's just a thrift store find and Sherry probably ruined it!

But I made big, wide hands. "I . . . saw it!"

* * *

"Are we spending the night here?" Em asked as we slipped through the Hideout window.

Outside, the sun illumined the late winter snowfall, a refusal of spring's gentle prod.

I said, "Not tonight. We have heat at home now. We're here to try a different kind of influencer thing. Cooking."

"Yes!" Em slung her stuff onto the stage and made for the kitchen.

I'd tried and failed to get a good recording angle over my stove. The Hideout kitchen had racks everywhere—perfect for mounting my phone camera.

Em said, "What are we going to make?"

"What does Sherry make for you?"

"Lots of stuff. She says I always have to have at least a protein and a vegetable. Last night, we had spinach chicken enchilada casserole with salad and tortilla soup."

"Ew. That sounds—"

"It was good."

Em clued in on my expression and added, "I didn't eat all my salad."

My phone rang. Suspicion PD. I cursed under my breath and signaled Em that I'd need a minute. She nodded.

Police Chief Tigner greeted me. "Hi, Janey, just checking in. I'm here at the Traverse place but you're not home."

That rattled me. Like every other red-blooded Suspicioner, unannounced guests freaked me out.

Quincy said, "I could drive on over to where you are now."

"Actually, Quince, I'm not available. Is it something quick?"

"The whole thing's quick. You hopped out of my office before we could finish our talk."

"I got my kid."

His hearty tone returned. "Em's a sweetheart. Heather really loves her."

"Em's a big fan of your daughter, too. Look. I promise to stop by—"

"If you could just paint a picture of what Logan was up to in the weeks before his death."

I said, "You know he's a guide, hiking and fly-fishing. He'd gone up the mountain."

My mind's eye stared at the snub-nose .22 with the faux-mahogany grip, and its journey from the Hideout toilet to now, beneath a box of Valvoline in my station wagon.

Quincy was supposed to be on the take but Roman had doubts about that. Where did that leave me? If I confronted Quincy and he turned out to be clean, I'd be in trouble with the law, lose my daughter, and become a target with Frieda and the Seattle set.

I swam through these awful meds and tried to focus.

"Logan was in high demand as a guide," I said.

"I guess you know my Uncle Reggie rents kayaks and cabins out in Coeur d'Alene. Logan was planning to go back." My voice went raspy.

It hurt to think about this. I massaged the hinge of my jaw to remove the rust.

Quincy said, "Go on."

"He wanted to expand his father's business to include fly-fishing."

I took a deep breath. "Who else have you interviewed?"

"I'm interviewing you."

"Just me?"

"And your uncle. Family's the closest to him. Work with me, here. Tell me who I should talk to if you know something."

"That's the stupidest!—"

I glanced over and caught Em watching, and lowered my voice. "Seriously, Quince?"

I steeled myself. "All right, lately he's been coming to the Hide-out with the bikers."

"The Rank Strangers."

"Yeah. He bought that Victory Jackpot. You said he took you for a ride."

"You know he was being made."

I paused, my left hand crossing to the opposite shoulder. "What did you just say?"

"With the bikers. Logan wasn't just hanging out. Your uncle said he was a prospect."

I frowned. Something itched the back of my brain. Logan's fraternizing with the local MC had become more than casual. I knew the Strangers had rules—club business stays inside the club, including when someone becomes a prospect. But I should have seen the signs. Ponce came in all the time. Cast Iron, too. Most other Strangers disappeared during the winter, but the clubhouse would fill up again in a few weeks, like a bird migration.

My phone conversation with Uncle Reg echoed back: *I never understood why he went all the way out there and took up with Strangers.*

Uncle Reg meant *the Strangers.* The bikers. The RSOMC, one-percenters.

I said, "How long had he been a prospect?"

"Not long, I don't think."

"I really do have to go. Get with that client Logan took up the mountain. And talk to Dr. Jude Summers. He treated Logan for a tooth abscess right before he died. Tell me as soon as there's news."

"You have my word. Call if you think of anything that can help. And, listen. Stay close."

I slipped back to the window and checked the road. "What's that supposed to mean, 'stay close'?"

"I mean, don't go for walks in the woods. Stay in your apartment. Don't leave town."

"What's in the woods?"

"Nothing more than the usual, as far as I know. Just a precaution." This in his unassuming Quincy voice.

I said, "Precautions for *me*? Or to protect the case?"

"Both."

CHAPTER

27

Crispy

WE CHOSE THE deep fryer. I'd assisted Gabe many times over the years, and I liked deep frying. The trick was crispy outside and plush inside: golden, brown, delicious.

I said, "I could make fried . . . fried . . ."

Em said, "Let's make fries. Everyone loves french fries."

Fries it was.

I positioned the phone camera on the rack above the deep fryer and set recording while the oil heated up. I sliced potatoes. This did not violate the circle of salt. I could buy potatoes to replace what I took from the Hideout.

I walked on sea legs. Keeping up a patter felt impossible with my tongue glued to the roof of my mouth. Fortunately, Em chattered for us both, though she stayed off camera because of internet weirdos.

The police chief's call left me unnerved. Was he a dirty cop? Was he clean, and on my trail? I wasn't sure which upset me more.

The fry oil reached temperature.

Em said, "I don't know if all the followers would have a big deep fryer like this."

Right. Rookie mistake.

I said, "You can make french fries on the stovetop, too. You just need a great big pan."

I took one of Gabe's heavies and twirled it. It landed on the stove with a *clank*. Something plopped behind me. We turned. The deep fryer belched a micro explosion. A honey-colored spring bubbled from the oil.

"Mom. Was that your phone?"

We scanned the upper rack. Empty. My cell phone was gone.

I lifted the deep fryer basket and found my cell phone—melted and warped. Golden, brown, delicious.

I went numb. All my contacts were in there. My mode of communication with Trent for custody handoff, given the restraining order, was my phone. Dannie's new doctor was in there.

Roman was in there.

Roman was in there.

Roman was in there.

I had no backup. No synced computer. There was no cloud.

Em said, "What'll we do with no phone?"

I had no money. Zilcho. It had all gone to getting the heat turned on and the madness that was premium contouring makeup.

I waited for panic. It breathed at my ear. My brain pushed against the inside of my skull. Roman would return fourteen days from now. I was supposed to keep checking in.

A single, clear thought emerged. I floated to my purse and retrieved one pill bottle after another. There were so many. I added each to my crispy phone and lowered them back into the deep fryer.

Em said, "Good. Those pills never stopped you from doing crazy stuff."

We watched the golden purr. The hypnotic fountain. It popped and we jumped back. I lifted the basket and found cylinders that once were pill bottles, but now bowed around the phone like curled cheese puffs.

Em said, "What now?"

"Tell you what, Emmie-nem. We're going."

"Sounds cool, Kitty Cat. Shoplifting?"

"Let's hit it."

* * *

Attack.

We sang at the top of our lungs and headed west under a rippling pastel sky. Emmie pumped the stereo until the speakers buzzed. When South Fork became Pipe Creek Road, the old Subaru Legacy crossed the circle of salt, and mother and daughter whooped our war cry.

I glanced to my right at a snowy meadow. "Hey, look!"

I slowed and pulled over, staring hard into wilderness.

"What?" Em said.

She turned off the stereo and followed my eyes. "What is it? What do you see?"

"Come on, slow and quiet."

We let ourselves out and picked our way over a drainage ditch and up to the meadow, then I sat down beneath a fir, snow brickle giving way beneath me. I pulled my daughter into my lap. Her parka swished against my leather jacket. I hooked my chin over Em's shoulder and pointed at a spruce, my arm forming a plane to align my field of vision with Em's.

When the creature moved, Em gasped. A snowshoe hare in winter whites.

"I see it!" Emmie whispered.

I squeezed her. The hare raised to hindquarters to gnaw the spruce bark. The coat change, the Spartan diet, the long feet that glided atop the snow's surface—an animal built to survive.

A lump formed in my throat when I remembered how I'd learned about snowshoe hare tracks. Like all of them, Logan had taught me. Snowshoe hare had huge hind feet and small forefeet, but their tracks made it look backward. It had to do with the way they threw their snowshoes forward when they ran.

My heart beat against my daughter's back, a blanket of warmth between us.

A woodpecker hammered, and the hare bolted. It zipped a snowy wake around to the back of the grove.

I gave Em a squeeze. "Let's go look."

We trekked to the hare's banquet area, the setting sun antiquing the clouds and stretching our shadows. Just ahead, blue asymmetrical horseshoe hare tracks embroidered the pink snow. Em would keep this memory forever.

I said, "We're not going shoplifting."

Em went still, then, "Okay."

I said, "The truth is, I think someone moved the circle of salt. I think it's wider now. Maybe wider than the whole state of Montana."

My teeth scraped my lip. "Maybe even the whole world."

"I think so, too, Mom. I think they moved it a long time ago. I just didn't want to say."

Beneath her knit cap, Em's hair tousled with the breeze. The line of tracks disappeared behind the grove, where diamonds shimmered from the fir boughs in the last catch of sunset, and the woodpecker sounded off again.

How do you undo stupid things? Like taking a two-year-old shoplifting, not knowing she'd remember all these years later? And even if she didn't, there was a whole town to remind her. I'd been caught when I was nineteen. They hadn't pressed charges—I'd been lucky. That stupid decision had been a holdover from my desperate days. Now, I felt desperate again.

Emmie whispered, "There's no place like our mountain. We live in the best place on earth."

Chance leads to luck leads to fate . . .

I said, "We're leaving, baby."

CHAPTER

28

Escape

DARKNESS FELL.

Em wanted to know:

But where are we going? How long is "for a while"? What about Dad? We can't tell him because your phone is golden, brown, delicious. Did you make us a crap ton of money? What about school? I'm hungry.

I started with, "We're going to see Uncle Reggie and Aunt Margot first. Would you like that?"

"Yes! Is Logan there? Me and Logan are making you a surprise."

I'd tell her about Logan after dinner.

Back in the car, I checked my wallet. Thirty-two dollars. Plenty. No oil light. Gas: half a tank. I even had an emergency apple for my daughter.

Though it pained me, I'd ask Uncle Reg and Margot for help. Maybe I'd admit a little about the situation. Not about Logan's part—that would upset them. They might loan me a little money for a fresh start.

Then . . . what?

Las Vegas. Em and I could abscond to Vegas. A card dealer could make a living there in cognito.

The Subaru's headlights shone along the road. The odometer counted a mile of asphalt. First one, then another. Taking us farther away from our home.

* * *

Sixteen miles in, the Subaru died.

It was not the usual oil leak. We still had gas. I had no phone. We hadn't seen a passing car since . . .

Since the hare.

Em and I stewed for forty-five minutes. Then a middle-aged couple finally drove by and promised to call someone they knew. I didn't catch the name.

When he showed up with a wrecker truck, I asked twice and still didn't catch his name, but he wore an Earthquake heavy equipment hat. He let me borrow his phone.

I had far more troubles than getting stranded forty-some miles west of Suspicion. I couldn't think of a soul I could call.

This stretch of road lay three hours from Coeur d'Alene. With Logan not even buried yet, it felt like we were trying to barge in on Uncle Reggie's grief. But I had a child, and we were desperate.

So I called. Voice mail. I didn't leave a message.

I stood half-blind in the glare of Earthquake's headlamps. The moonless night had grown particularly dark, and Em huddled against me for warmth. She didn't complain, but I knew the apple didn't cut it.

I looked down at Earthquake's phone.

Trent? No.

Harvey? Hell, no.

Dannie? With her dirty police chief brother? Nope.

Roxie? Yes.

I opened a browser to a hidden page on the Hideout's web site, where we kept contact info for employees and suppliers. I found Roxie, but it went to voice mail, too. This time, I left a message.

Gabe. Ask Gabe the Broncos score, and he'd see it as a passive-aggressive pugnacity because the Grizzlies never won a national championship. Ask Gabe for ketchup, and he'd think you're denouncing his food. But ask Gabe for a forty-mile lift back to Suspicion, and he'd cheerfully drive us that and beyond, all the way to Coeur d'Alene, then ask to use the washroom and drive straight home again.

On the same hidden web page, I found Gabe. But the call not only went to voice mail, it went *straight* to voice mail, because he kept his phone turned off. Phones annoyed him. To Gabe, phones were for outgoing calls, only.

Earthquake took off his cap and rubbed his hair. "Look, no offense, but I can't just—"

I said, "Can you just take us home? Do you take checks?"

He kicked dirty snow along the side of the road. "All the way to, where did you say you live?"

"Suspicion."

"God. That's like, forty, forty-five miles, and—"

He shook his head. "I prefer cash."

I looked at the Subaru, threw my hands in the air. "I got thirty-two dollars. Wasn't planning on breaking down tonight."

The Earthquake cap took another trip up and back down on his head. "I guess I'll have to. My credit card attachment's on the blink."

I gave him sympathetic eyes, though it meant good news for us. However much he'd charge, I wasn't going to have that amount in my bank account or room on my credit card. I'd have to float poor Earthquake. I felt bad about that.

Also, I felt so grateful to get my daughter off the road that my mind arrowed past the reality of the situation: My escape attempt had failed.

* * *

Later, in my garage apartment, which never felt so cozy as it did in that moment, I made Em semi-homemade egg noodle soup with crusty bread. It was one of the few things I remembered my mother cooking that I could re-create when I grew up. It tasted sumptuous.

Homemade broth, which I kept in the freezer.

Store-bought extra-wide egg noodles.

My mother liked to slice fresh scallions on the top, and so did I, but I didn't like the garnish as a child and neither did Emmie. The flourish that made it strange and wonderfully rich and Hendee-only: a pat of butter that melted across the top. The scent of broth filled the kitchen, and we warmed our bellies. The bread had a crusty surface but a soft center.

Afterward, I told my daughter about Logan. I held her while she wept.

She confessed they'd had a surprise planned for me. Logan was going to show Emmie how to make me a birdfeeder out of pine cones and peanut butter and seeds they'd gathered last fall. Once he showed her, he'd said, she could make them herself, and she could give one to her mother every year.

It hurt to lose someone, and there was no way around it.

C H A P T E R

29

Resale

"CAN'T USE IT." Jemma's braid ran down her back, her chin lifted.

"Come on, Jemma!" I polished the ring on my shirt and tried to coax the silver plating to a dance under her halogens.

Jemma's Finds differed from the thrift stores I could afford. I had to work my shopping into visits to Libby or Whitefish. Here, secondhand merinos and name-brand accessories stood on display. Even in the back room, where Jemma stocked flannels and denims, she maintained upscale selections.

She pointed to a basket at the bottom of her glass case. "You can toss it in there if you want."

It overflowed with rings like my nickel-core, silver-plated one. The sign read, "Toss One, Take One, or $10 Each."

I had to cover a hot check with Earthquake, plus get the Subaru fixed. I could walk to my job at the Hideout but getting Em to school was a nightmare. Mr. Traverse let me borrow his phone for fifty cents a call. It took seven tries to find someone to play chauffer—Sherry, of all people. Sherry was delighted.

Metallic squeaks erupted from the flannel-and-denim room as someone sorted impatiently through the racks.

I glanced over, my gaze landing on a tangerine-colored Montana wool quarter-zip pullover. I recognized it for having once belonged to Em's teacher, Mykayla Jansen. Not even a sweater—a pullover. For jogging. Spun from the Treasure State's own alpacas, the long-necked darlings with yoga smiles. I could imagine how I might look in such a thing. I would alchemize into a different human.

My daughter's grade school teacher sent cast-offs here, and I couldn't even hawk my wedding ring to the owner, a woman who probably slipped eye drops into her husband's coffee.

From the back room, someone groaned.

Then Danielle Tigner with her tiger-striped hair strode to the front of the store. "Jemma, do you have one single size six back here?"

Jemma said, "Be with you in a minute, Dannie."

Dannie said, "Oh, hey, there, Janey."

Rigid, I turned my back to Dannie and leaned over the case, lowering my voice. "This is worth more than those cheap rings in that basket."

I felt eyes. If Dannie possessed any tact, she'd discreetly move along and wait her turn. Instead, she draped herself over the counter, hands folded, as though we'd planned this outing since our morning jog. Jemma glanced at Dannie, accepting our togetherness.

Jemma said, "Give me that little Samsonite case I always see Em carrying around. Let me put a tag on it and do up a nice display."

I swallowed hard.

"Samsonite?" Dannie said, frowning at me. "Is she talking about Em's little train case?"

Jemma said, "Come on. That's why you're really here, isn't it, Janey? We've been through this with the ring. You're finally ready to put that Samsonite on consignment."

Dannie clapped a hand over mine. "Oh no, she is not."

I couldn't meet either woman's eyes. Jemma's long braid reminded me of a noose.

She said, "Your daughter is enterprising. Bring her in here, she can help create the display. We'll fill it with eighteen-inch necklaces and take photos for the online listing. It'll be good learning."

Dannie pulled my wrist and looked up into my eyes, then without turning, said, "Jemma? Business seems slow. I'll watch the shop while you take a break."

Jemma lit at the opportunity. She grabbed a giant coffee mug that said "Jemma" from the back shelf.

She said, "Back in five. Don't leave till I return."

As if anyone would dare steal from her. Jemma flipped the sign on her way out the door.

I'd had it with Tigners. Before Dannie could utter one single word, I pushed away from her. *I* was going to drive this conversation—and no more bullshit.

* * *

I said, "Your brother's on the take."

Dannie's mouth dropped open.

I said, "Harvey told me."

"Told you what?"

"Quit pretending. It's just the two of us here, *girlfriend*. I know everything, including the real reason you paid your gambling debts."

I jabbed my finger on the counter. "Quincy's putting on some sham investigation. Why? Because Logan's from Idaho? An *outsider*?"

Dannie's expression reset. I could see the calculations.

She said, "Listen."

Then she said, "So you think—"

She put a hand to her hip and looked down, breathed through her nose. Whatever she intended to say ended there. Instead, she pulled out her phone and slammed it on the display case, and dialed her brother on speaker.

He answered, "Hey, sis."

Country music thumped in the background.

Dannie kept her eyes on me as she spoke. "Quincy. You alone?"

"Yep, just on my way to—"

"Are you on the take?"

"What!"

The country music ended. Buffeting air through a window ceased, like he had pulled over.

Dannie said, "No judge, big brother. Just tell me. *Are-you-on-the-take?*"

"No! Where in the *hell* did you get an idea like that?"

"I mean it. You can tell me."

"The answer is no. Dannie, where is this coming from?"

"Favor exchange?"

"Favor—what kind of favors do I need? Elk? Got a deep freezer full of that."

"Serious now."

"Dannie, there is no freakin' favor exchange. Now I think I deserve an explanation."

Dannie shook her head as she raised her eyes to the drop ceiling. "There's been a rumor after what happened to Logan."

"Well, God. You know people talk. Wouldn't have expected *you* to pay any attention."

"Just crossing my t's. Catch ya later."

"Hey, am I on speaker—?"

Dannie ended the call and folded her arms.

I said, "That proves nothing."

"Best I can do."

I thought, *Fuck Harvey*, and said, "Want a seat at the games?"

"Bet your ass I do."

CHAPTER 30

Black Clouds

Suspicious Perks was known for cloud coffee: two parts whipping cream to one part sour cream, sweetened, over dark roast. Grace and Abby, the owners, made the sour cream themselves. Cloud coffee was an acquired taste, and another way to scare off tourists. We locals gulped it like it reversed aging.

Jemma returned with her now-steaming double-sized "Jemma" mug. She flipped the sign to Open and Dannie and I took off.

Jemma called after me, "Talk to Em about that train case. She might surprise you."

The med bombs were on a slow leak from my system. My freshening brain told me that once I got my car fixed, I could skip town, but in the meantime, I should work on Roman's bribery problem. Either way led to danger. If I ran, the cartel would hunt me down. If I worked on the bribes and failed, they'd kill me. If I succeeded, they'd probably still kill me because I knew too much.

I had ten days left to sort it.

Dannie looked left and right. "Where're you parked?"

"Peak Auto Repair."

She halted. "Isn't that where Trent got fired a few years back?"

"Theoretically, it was a mutual parting."

"You walked all the way over here from your place?"

I shrugged. "Pretty day, pretty walk."

A three-mile drive, but the deer trail behind the Traverse property cut it down to one mile on foot.

Dannie looked at her shoes, which seemed expensive even to my low-couture-brow. They had a buckle with mirrored T's. If I wore them, they wouldn't survive the curb.

Dannie said, "We're taking my Jeep."

The Land Rover gave me a thrill, like riding a terrain rocket. Her briefcase sat on the back seat. I could see Dannie cruising over the passes to pick up her clients for lunch, interrogating them on their loan documents, figuring out if they were financial fakers and if not, helping them put together a plan—and then cruising back over the mountains again. All because of this SUV. And maybe because she could walk around in sharp shoes that stayed clean.

Dannie said, "By the way. Did you know Em was selling makeup to the older kids?"

I straightened in my seat. "What?"

"My niece Heather told me."

"Contours?" I said, remembering Emmie's interest when I'd gone down in flaming skulls as a beauty influencer.

Dannie shrugged. "No idea."

I'd taken Em by the shoulders and told her we needed a crap ton of money. I'd meant that *I* had needed to work that out. Not nine-year-old Em.

Dannie said, "So what do you need from me? Tell me what I can do."

I regrouped to the more pressing matter. "Right. I need you to figure out Barkling."

Dannie glanced at me, hit her turn signal at the stop sign. "Barkling? As in the county attorney?"

"You know him?"

Dannie shrugged. "I'm friends with his wife Meredith. What exactly am I figuring out?"

"See if he's on the take."

"What on earth, Janey!"

I closed my eyes. In my heart, what I wanted most had not changed: to give Em a better life. Em needed a secure place to sleep. Meals at mealtime. The certainty that someone loved her. The more I grasped at this desire, the more I clawed it to pieces.

Dannie said, "I can't just call up Douggie Barkling like I did my brother and say, 'Hey man, you on the take?'"

"So he's 'Douggie' to you?"

Dannie made a blink that synced tension between her mouth and eyes. I'd seen Quincy do that same thing.

I said, "The way I heard it, you figured I was in trouble, and you were motivated to be a friend to me—a 'real good friend' was how you put it."

"All right, don't say it like that. Who's he supposedly on the take from?"

She glanced at me. "Oh, of course. The dirty doc meds. Frieda and Harvey. God, that's some crap."

She paused. "You'd better tell Quincy."

Flat out, I said, "No."

Dannie's eyebrows knitted. She was working through a decision, and I didn't like it. She turned onto my road, once paved until the weather peeled that away. The Land Rover didn't mind.

I pressed on. "If Barkling's into something with Frieda, I need to know. And no offense to your brother, but if there's any question at all whether the prosecutor and the police chief's involved, I don't exactly trust the law."

I made sure my voice held steady: "Already, my cousin got killed."

Dannie sharpened. "Logan was caught up in this?"

I didn't answer. Dannie's attention returned to the potholes.

I said, "So of course you can't just up and ask Barkling if he's on the take."

Dannie's voice receded inside her, like what she said aloud fell as backdrop to her thoughts. "Don't worry about that. I'm smooth."

Then she cleared and blinked, cutting eyes to me. "Tell me everything. Start from the beginning."

"I can't. And Dannie, hear me when I say, you don't want to know. It's no good for you that I've told you this much."

She scowled. Along the right side of the road, the Traverse log cabin came into view. My home was the apartment over the detached log cabin garage. We turned into the long gravel drive, grass and the remnants of snow dividing the tire path into two wavy lines.

She said, "At least give me something to go on with Doug Barkling. I can't just walk in there and babble till he says something hinky."

"It has to do with Frieda's client, Baltazar Valencia. Even *that* is saying too much. Find out where Barkling really stands on Valencia—not just what he gives as a statement to *The Missoulian*."

Dannie turned to face me, eyes wide. "Did I hear you right? Baltazar Valencia? As in, the Red King?"

"Yes."

Dannie stared, her system buffering. I recalled my vertigo at hearing Roman utter that name for the first time.

I said, "You can back out. Nobody knows I've spoken to you."

Dannie kept spinning in glitch mode.

Crows cawed from the tree line to the meadow, warning each other that two women invaded their territory. Mr. Traverse's car was absent. He must have been running errands in town. Dannie gazed into the steering wheel as though it foretold her future. Storm cloud thoughts. I waited, letting her churn, trying not to stare. But even from my periphery I saw the moment she registered her decision.

Dannie set the hand brake like a proper mountain woman accustomed to steep inclines, then switched off the vehicle. "Why don't you show me that cozy little apartment of yours and we'll figure out our angle?"

My shoulders released.

I knew gamblers. I'd learned cards back when I'd lived in that Missoula group home, and I kept those skills as a teen on the run, even in juvenile detention. I wasn't a gambler, but I knew gamblers.

The thing about gamblers, they were thrill-seekers.

CHAPTER

31

Frightening

DANNIE DROVE US to Guy Hamm's rental. It was as appalling as Guy had promised. Guy told me I could take home anything the renters left behind, and said we might find clothing that'd fit Em next year, maybe some that'd fit me. I hoped for unexpired pantry food. Emmie and I armed ourselves with cleaning supplies and boxes.

Dannie video recorded the "before."

"God, the bugs," she said. "And look, brown water in the sink."

She regarded Em. "You're getting in on it, too?"

I said to Em, "You don't have to, kiddo. You can read or play with your dolls if you want."

Em said, "I ain't afraid. I like bugs."

Dannie whispered, "That kid is frightening. Call me when you're ready for me to pick you up."

Dannie headed for the door, but I said, "Hey, Dannie."

"Yeah?"

"I had to write a note for Em's teacher. Do you think you could look it over for me? My spelling's so bad. I'm dumb."

Dannie huffed, then clicked her mirrored-T heels back to me. "No, Janey, you are not dumb. You have a visual processing disorder. And you've compensated by developing an excellent memory. It's why you can take everyone's order without writing it down and you actually get it right, not like those restaurants where the staff think they can remember but they can't. And by the way, Gabe can do the same thing. The entire town watches the two of you chirping orders and it's always accurate. Except during that silliness with the meds. Of course I'll look over the teacher's note for you. I'll do it every single time."

Dannie left, and the Land Rover scraped out of the drive. I stood swallowing against a tight throat for a full minute beyond the silence.

* * *

Emmie and I donned rubber gloves and started on the trash. We filled a sack that covered the kitchen and a second one for the living room. Em thought nothing of working around insects, dead or alive. We used to throw spider eggs into the Cable Hill pond to watch fish feed. Em was a true child of nature in all its horrors and glories.

Em found a girl's sweater tucked in the sofa. I kept my eyes sharpened for anything we could take on the run, along with the $100 Guy was paying me. After I got my car fixed, we'd still have a chance to disappear. Also, messy people left money lying around. I once cleaned a house that yielded over $200 in bills and change. I handed it over to the owner in a paper lunch sack.

Not this time. Our lives were at stake.

I knelt and tossed a wad of sick-looking tissues into the trash. "So, Em. I heard you've been selling makeup."

Em kept her head bent over her work. "Where'd you hear that?"

"Wanna tell me what's going on?"

Em grimaced, looked me full in the face. "Not really."

"Why not?"

"You're mad."

I considered this. Was I? Not yet.

I said, "Explain it to me, and I'll try to keep cool."

Em could see she had little choice. "I sold the contour makeup. You said I could have them. So . . . I figured it wasn't a big deal."

"You were secretive. When you're unsure whether something's wrong or right, check your actions. If you feel the need to be sneaky, that tells you something."

As I said it, I saw myself sneaking Em into the Hideout afterhours.

I rose, trash bag in hand. "You can tell me anything. Even if you're doing something wrong, I may be more understanding than you think."

Em nodded. "Was it wrong, then? Was it bad?"

I shrugged. "It was kind of shifty, kiddo. You made like you were playing dress-up. You could have just told me what you wanted to do. I don't have a problem with you selling it unless the school objects."

I paused. "What on earth do kids your age want with contouring, anyway?"

"Not my age," Em said quickly. "Older kids. They come pick up their younger sisters and brothers after school. They have big bucks."

I put my gloved hands to my hips and tried not to snort.

Em said, "Trish Harris in my class did try to buy one but I told her she was too young. If I had a bigger store, I would have sold her a lip gloss. That's appropriate for kids our age."

I gave my daughter the side-eye. Dannie was right. Em was frightening.

I said, "Bigger store?"

"I sold all the makeup, and now I want to open a backpack store."

"A *what*?" The word "backpack" struck lightning in my nerve complex.

"Don't freak out, Mom, it's just something I made up. I can take the money I made off makeup and buy candy, and maybe lip gloss, and sell it to kids during recess."

"Em, no."

"Why not?"

"I'm the one who needs to make money. Not you."

"But it's fun."

"It doesn't sound like a good idea."

"Why?"

"Stuff could go wrong."

Em spread her hands. "Stuff always goes wrong."

"What does the school say?"

"It would only be during recess. Recess is my time. And lunch. It's not like I'd disrupt math."

I folded my arms. Em waited, straight-faced, with the good sense not to try puppy dog eyes.

Other moms always knew what the hell to do.

I said, "You can have your store, but you alone are responsible for it. If the school shuts it down, that's their prerogative. You must accept any consequences with grace, chin high. Think about that before moving forward."

"Okay."

"And absolutely no transactions during class."

"Mom. Goes without saying. So! I kept the money in my little white train case. Once we get the Subaru back, will you take me to Rosauers for a grocery run?"

"Em! What did I just say?"

Crickets chirping. The child had no idea.

I put my hands to hips and willed it out of her.

Nothing.

I said, "I just made it clear that you are *on your own*, even if you get in trouble at school. So think it over before you decide."

"Okay. I thought it over. I want to do it."

Em looked over at the stereo. "Can we crank the music while we work?"

CHAPTER

32

Band Phone

I CONTINUED UNTIL SWEAT stung my eyes: scrubbing Guy Hamm's toilets, gathering his trash. It yielded $11.32 in sticky coins, no folding money.

I dared a fantasy of everything working out: The mess with Roman and Frieda would evaporate, and I'd get money and supplies from cleaning this place. I'd give Em a better life.

My body ached from lifting, scouring, and hauling. Like me, Em drew satisfaction from seeing a mess transformed into something inviting. Now she'd fallen asleep inside the rental.

I slipped outside with the cordless phone that either Guy or the renters had left connected. Since internet and cell service were unreliable in Suspicion, people used landlines. Beneath moonlit trees, I dialed Harvey's number, placing him on speaker so I could work hands-free.

I said, "Harv, it's Janey."

His voice rose. "Took you long enough. I've been calling and texting, the texts are bouncing. Thought you skipped town."

I groped under the crate I'd stashed earlier tonight. "I need a new phone. Mine's gone."

"You lost it?"

"Destroyed it."

I retrieved Logan's revolver, once again bound in flour sacks. I'd brought a bore brush, swatches torn from an old T-shirt, and a squirt bottle with 50/50 vinegar and peroxide.

I said, "You there?"

"Yeah. I'm thinking. Did you back up to the cloud?"

"No."

"That's good. No trail. I'll get you two phones. One to use for your day-to-day, and one for communicating with me."

"Sounds like a pain in the ass."

I checked the barrel in the spill of floodlight—its illumination weak here at the edge of the woods. Even so, a lifetime of lead build-up cast shadows from the gun's crevices.

Harvey said, "We'll call the second phone 'band business.' For the band at the Hideout. That'll be our code. You're now the band coordinator. Keep checking the band phone, okay? I'll get'm tomorrow."

I glanced at the handset where it lay in the pine needles. "Does that mean you're coming to the games?"

"No. Can't."

That was a relief. Harvey usually came to the games, but in recent months he'd gone scarce. I didn't want to tell him about Dannie's seat at the card table. He'd object. Harvey always said the Big Bald Luck games were mine. That was bull. When we'd started, I was nineteen, washing dishes and busing tables at the Hideout. Harvey facilitated the games, picking floating locations, which meant he took the rake. I worked only on tips from the players.

Taking tips was not illegal. Taking a rake was.

If the sheriff came after us, how egregious would my role be in the eyes of the law? Harvey's take was the illegal part, but nobody ever saw him do that. I, being the dealer, set aside his rake to give him later.

Casinos and card rooms dotted Montana's landscape. My players could go anywhere. But they relished a migrating, underground, high-rolling card game. Something rough. A ride they couldn't get from an ultra-regulated, high-tax tourist casino.

Harvey said, "Someone there with you?"

"I'm alone in the woods behind Guy Hamm's rental. I'm cleaning it for side money."

I looked up at the stars. "My car broke down, too. I can't afford to get it fixed."

"Christ, Janey!"

"Trust me when I say I'd rather rip out my tongue than come to you with this, but I can't be doing your dirty drops without my car."

"Where's it at?"

"It's with Roy at Peak Auto Repair, but I don't want you going over there to work something out with Roy. I need you to give me the money so I can pay him. I don't want to be oh-so-overly-associated with you."

He made a sucking sound through his teeth. I'd fed his paranoia, something with bottomless hunger.

I said, "Also, it's not just Roy. I gotta pay Earthquake."

"Who the hell is Earthquake?"

"The guy who towed me. I had to scam him just to get home and it felt awful. I'm so dirty now. All this dirt attracts more dirt. I can't stand it."

"Calm down. Tell me what you need and I'll get it to you."

"Don't make it sound like you're bailing me out!"

"All right! All right!"

I glared at the phone in the bed of pine needles. We both grabbed a moment to breathe. The forest crackled.

I resumed dissolving and scrubbing lead flakes.

He said, "Look. New location. Same time, same day of the week. Go to where I took you last summer."

I ran oiled cloth through the Röhm, then aimed it at the floodlight, peering down the spiral. Oil danced on metal as I moved it within my sightline, the barrel shimmering. A few stubborn remnants of lead remained.

He said, "Earth to Janey. You know the place I'm talking about?"

"The fireworks stand off Tatlock Road."

"Dammit, don't say it!"

He wanted me to speak in code? Like his phone was tapped.

The fireworks stand had closed for the season. Last June, Gabe, Roxie, and I had ridden out there with Harvey in his truck. To think, I counted Harvey as a close friend back then—it felt like a lifetime ago.

I said, "I know where to go. It's far. You wanna tell me how this ends?"

Click.

"Harvey?"

No sound but night rustling in the forest, the wind of the stars. Then a dial tone. He'd ended the call. Those dial tones were an unnerving holdover from days gone by. I pressed the button to quiet the handset, my fingers aching with chill.

I should have shaken him down for more money—getaway cash. Roman was due back in nine days. I packed up, wrapped up the gun, rose, and started back to the rental.

Something snapped to my left. Not a typical forest sound. It sent a jolt up my spine. I turned.

Eight feet from where I'd been sitting on the crate, a figure emerged from the trees.

CHAPTER

33

Replaceable Parts

I CRIED OUT, THEN put my hand to my heart. "God, you scared me."

The skinny legs. Guy Hamm shoved a fist into his jeans pocket and moved toward me in the clearing. His jacket opened to a shirt pressed so stiff he probably cut his fingers on the creases.

He said, "Didn't mean to give you a fright."

"How long have you been standing there?"

"Just walked up."

That wasn't true. Sometimes it was possible to spot the actual lie.

I'd been talking to Harvey on speaker phone so I could clean the gun. "Did you overhear my conversation?"

He said, "I went to the house and saw Em sleeping there, followed your voice out back."

I looked down the driveway but didn't see his truck, and wondered where he parked.

I said, "You should have told me you were coming."

"My house, last I checked."

I angled away from him. Something about the way he spoke caused the trees to loom taller and darker.

I said, "Well, I'm sure you saw inside. The place is spotless. That'll be a hundred bucks, like you said."

"No can do, Janey."

"Come again?"

"I won't be giving you a thin dime."

I put the phone to my hip. "What exactly are you getting at?"

"Secret drops. Secret cell phones. I heard all about your dirty dealings."

I took a step back. He'd heard everything. And though on a clear day, I couldn't care less what Guy Hamm thought of me, he'd used the word "dirty," and that stung.

Guy said, "There is no way in hell I'm paying you for illegal activities on my property. The deal is off. Get your things and get out."

I skewered my gaze into him, trying to keep my voice level, resisting the urge to unwrap the snub nose from its flour sacks. "No you don't, Guy. We've done a tremendous amount of work. You can't renege now."

"I can, and that's what I'm doing."

Then he said, "I never understood women like you. No makeup, never put on something pretty. You're a five but if you'd put in a little effort, you could be an eight. But this?"

He flung an arm at the phone clutched to my chest. "This makes you a four."

My throat caught.

He switched to sounding like he had to placate a child. "No need to cry or make a fuss. It's over. You're good at what you do, which is waiting tables, and you should stick to that and figure out how to keep your nose clean. Now I'm tired and I want you off my property."

I was nowhere near crying, but I was very much near what Dannie called "shoot, smash, or jab." My fists balled. I looked at the back door thirty feet away. I'd only stepped outside to make the phone call. Guy Hamm could only have rolled up without my noticing if he snuck up, deliberately.

I wanted to helicopter those sacks of trash all over the rental. If Em weren't here, I'd do just that.

Guy must have seen it in my eyes. "I *will* call the police."

I said, "You are out of the games. You're barred."

"Is that right?"

"Eighty-six'ed. And if you think you can go crying to Harvey . . ."

He stepped toward me, nose-in, disgustingly close. I refused to back away. It forced me to tilt my head up to look at him. He smelled like aftershave and sausage, causing a rise in my gorge, but I held my stance. Detoxing from the medication couldn't have come at a worse time.

He said, "From the sound of your phone call, Harvey might be in on that little deal you got going on. That right? Something shifty. You think Police Chief Tigner be interested? Or is he in on it, too?"

Guy Hamm grinned, moonlight glinting on his teeth, and he angled his head around me so I had to look at him from the side or back away. I stayed planted.

He said, "Maybe the FBI would be a better choice. Got a buddy went to school with, he's an in-resident agent at Kalispell."

The forest kept crackling, gasping, snapping. It had covered Guy Hamm's approach. I never saw his headlights as he drove up. Maybe he'd turned them off.

I dialed the phone, put it to my ear. Guy took three steps backward.

I said into the handset, "Can you come pick us up?"

Dannie replied, "Heading out now."

I hung up without another word, hoping she'd hurry. Guy smirked.

To think, I had planned to take home shelf-stable scroungings for our getaway food stash. I'd brought boxes because Guy Hamm had "generously" told me that I could keep anything the renters abandoned. Clothing, canned soup, ramen.

It took twenty minutes for Dannie to extricate herself from whatever she was doing and get to the rental.

I would have traded twenty hours, standing in my granny panties before Roman and the Red King himself, just to escape those twenty minutes with Guy Hamm.

CHAPTER

34

Baltazar

THE NEXT DAY, I had two cell phones and an envelope of cash—enough to pay Earthquake and come close with Peak Auto Repair. Roy had ordered the part and said he'd get the Subaru to me tomorrow. That fell on my next rendezvous—my first non-Roman drop. The fireworks stand.

Tonight's games would go down at, of all places, Harvey's Hideout. A last-minute cancelation meant Harvey had to scramble, and in the end he gave up and put us at his own roadhouse. Paranoia be damned.

I wouldn't have to worry about setup. Harvey said he'd get the card table (and my crumb vacuum) over there without my having to lift a finger.

From my window, I watched Dannie pull up in that terrain rocket of hers. Since the inception of the games, this would be the first time we'd ever changed the number of seats. With Dannie, we'd have six players instead of five, but Harvey wasn't coming so that brought us back to five, anyway.

It also marked the first time I made a major decision without consulting Harvey. It thrilled me. How hot would Harvey get over it? The police chief's sister, coming to his illegal games? Especially after he'd pretended Quincy was in on the dirty business, and therefore he couldn't say a damn thing? How hot would he get?

Seismic.

I bounced inside my boots as I opened the passenger-side door. The look on Dannie's face gave me pause.

I said, "You all right?"

Dannie looked off to Mr. Traverse's log cabin, gave a snort. "Peachy, Janey. Get in."

I climbed in, guarded. Dannie ought to be excited now that she finally got a chair at the Big Bald Luck games. She'd campaigned hard enough for it, and she wasn't the only one.

She said, "I spoke to the Barklings."

"Already?"

I felt a swift and massive swerve—from excitement to dread.

Dannie put the Land Rover in gear and maneuvered a three-point turn to head down the Traverse driveway. "If Douggie Barkling is putting on a front, pretending to go after Valencia just so he can take a dive in the fifth round, he's a good actor. Because when I talked to him, he was frothing. He despises Valencia. He wants to make an example of him. He's got political aspirations, and he thinks a win in this case would advance his career."

I listened. It sounded compelling—in a "guess you had to be there" kind of way.

Dannie said, "Do you even have an inkling of who you're dealing with?"

"Barkling?"

"No, dammit. Valencia. The Red King. And his army. The entire pack of lowlifes. Do you have any idea who they are, really?"

Taking a cue from Dannie's grave expression, I'd prefer to avoid finding out. A slow drip of foreboding trickled to my stomach as the last hints of light faded from the sky.

I said, "Look, I know they're bad. I'm afraid of them, of course. Baltazar Valencia is awaiting trial for murder."

"It's multiple murder, Janey, and it's not just—"

Dannie exhaled through her nose. She mashed her fingers around the steering wheel as though pressing her thoughts into place. The Land Rover turned out of the drive and onto the partially paved road, then accelerated.

She said, "What I'm about to tell you is between us. It's going to come out during the trial, but it needs to stay confidential until then."

I nodded, my pulse quickening.

Dannie said, "Morris Cooper was murdered by the Red King. Cooper lived in Montana and was the Red King's right-hand man for drug-running up here, their northern U.S. distribution. Everything they slip in here goes on to Seattle, Kalispell, Portland, and so on."

"Isn't that backward? I would think it would be easier to bring drugs in through a port city like Seattle."

Dannie said, "You'd think. But right now there are too many eyes on the ports. DEA is watching the vessels, so the Red King found alternatives. Anyway, he got wind of Cooper talking to law enforcement."

"So Valencia had Cooper murdered."

Dannie shook her head. "No, not at first. Valencia had Cooper's *bodyguard* murdered, and then his wife. And then he murdered his own bodyguard, whose only sin was he'd introduced him to Morris Cooper *twelve years ago*."

I felt sick. "Don't tell me any more."

"Oh, you are going to hear this. These are the people you're dealing with. So then Baltazar Valencia and his people severed Cooper's right hand."

I took a sharp intake of breath.

"Right-hand man," I murmured.

"You got it."

Dannie was speaking of faraway shadows, things unreal. I couldn't allow it into my head.

But I knew I had to. I'd opened the door to wolves, and I needed to keep Em safe. I had to listen to Dannie.

She said, "But that wasn't enough. They bound up his stump and took him along with them, but left his right hand there at the Coopers' house with the three bodies. They kept him alive for a couple more weeks. During that time, they took a power drill to his right eye and shoved a hot wire down his right ear. In the end, he succumbed to exposure in the wilderness. They must have abandoned him to die alone."

I clutched my gut. The others, the ones who'd simply been murdered in a quick death, they'd gotten off easy.

* * *

The Land Rover hummed across the main road to the Hideout. My mind tilted. Roman must have participated in those atrocities. With his mild, businesslike air, his talk of trust, Roman had said that he was the only one of Baltazar's associates who'd been in the area.

Dannie said, "As shocking as all that is, how does that tell us one way or the other whether Barkling's on the take, right?"

"Right," I said, my voice thick.

And then I blinked, digesting her words. "Right. Barkling never would have told you any of that unless he was genuinely outraged. If he were on the take, he'd have buried the horrible parts. He'd have found a way to get the case thrown out of court, or work out a sweetheart deal."

Dannie nodded. "Good start."

She stole a glance at me. "But there's an even more cut-and-dry answer."

"Which is . . . ?"

"The prosecutor's office is rounding out their due diligence right now. In just a couple of weeks, they're going to make the filing and hold a press conference."

I listened, waiting to breathe.

She said, "They're seeking the death penalty."

CHAPTER

35

Big Bald Luck

ORDINARILY, I ARRIVED at the games first. I gave myself an hour for setup, depending on location. Now, since we were meeting at Harvey's Hideout, I allotted only twenty minutes.

Except the entire brat of players had gotten there early, too.

Why? Did they think since the games were at the Hideout, Roxie would bring them stew and stouts?

We parked the Land Rover around back. I was still processing Dannie's tale about Baltazar Valencia and Doug Barkling. You can't get cute with the death penalty.

Dannie said, "Don't worry, the other players'll love me. I'll be sweet as pie."

I shook my head. "Don't you dare. They'll eat you alive. March up there tits out and mean mugging."

Everyone watched our approach, waiting to be let in.

"What's *she* doing here?" Wes Cooney said, making no attempt to be cool.

Our boots clunked across the wooden porch, and I fit my key into the lock.

I said, "Everyone, this is Danielle Tigner. You can call her Dannie."

Dannie snorted. "You kidding me? I know everyone here."

"But what's she *doing* here?" Wes said.

I swung the door wide and entered. "Dannie is taking the fifth chair at the games."

Guy Hamm said, "We already got a fifth chair, and that is for Harvey."

"Sixth, then."

I strode to the card table. Harvey, or Gabe, or whoever had set it up, had moved some tables and chairs out of the way and put it dead center under the chandelier to give it good lighting. Other than that, it looked disgraceful. They hadn't brought my damned level, either. I went to work with my brush and crumb vacuum.

"You two coming in?" I called without looking, because I could see in the hearth mirror that Maycie Gaynor and Cam Scarver lingered on the porch, a shooting range of meaningful looks between them.

I weighed the situation. On the one hand, I'd acquired one of my info commodities on the Janey-Seattle Exchange. On the other, a death penalty case against the Red King could only mean bad news for me. Roman wouldn't hold up his end of the bargain. He might see me as carrying Frieda's virus of sins.

Baltazar had one of his own murdered for making an unfortunate introduction twelve years ago. What would he do to me, who was supposed to work for both Frieda and him? He'd see me as loyal to no one. I was a dead woman. Worse than a dead woman. He'd torture me first.

Guy Hamm pointed at Dannie, then me. "She is the police chief's *sister*! Have you lost your *mind*?"

I said, "Do not shout at me."

If I could have checked in with Roman as promised before I deep fried my phone, I'd tell him Barkling was a False Bribe. Quincy Tigner, a Probably False Bribe. The judges—still unknown.

This wouldn't work. It didn't matter what I uncovered. I was handing raw meat to a bear.

As for the upcoming rendezvous at the fireworks stand, I dreaded meeting the new guy because Roman had hinted at some unrest. What did *that* mean?

Me, alone with a whole lot of money, meeting someone who might be mutinous.

Mutiny meant danger. The fireworks meetup felt bad, very bad.

I heard the *tick-tick-tick* of the Hendee curse counting down to zero.

"Are you sure this is a good idea?" Maycie said to me.

"Really? You too, Maycie?"

Guy kept shouting. "Janey has lost her mind! I mean it, she has *lost* her *mind*!"

Cam Scarver put his hands up and ratcheted his voice ten decibels above Guy's. "Janey runs the games. And Dannie's okay. I mean, we could give Harvey a holler."

I climbed up onto my chair.

Which increased the volume of Guy's shouting, and then Wes Cooney swarmed above them both. "You *know* she's got stability issues!"

BANG!

The recoil yanked my arm and I nearly fell off the chair. Screams burst through the dining hall. I looked down at my players, Logan's snub nose still pointed at the ceiling. Smoke rolled.

Everyone crouched with hands over ears. Their wide eyes searched each other. And then up at me, calmest soul in the room.

The flash had been too bright and the smoke too heavy. *I should give it another soak in my 50/50 vinegar-peroxide*, I thought. *It's a wonder this thing fired at all.*

Dannie said, "Hot damn. This is exactly why I came."

I said, "Anyone who'd like to opt out can leave. It'll be the last time you attend the Big Bald Luck games."

Glass shards lay on the card table I'd just cleaned. The bullet had shattered a light from the chandelier. That would throw a shadow over my games and now I'd run out of time to change the bulb.

"Damn it!" I switched my crumb vacuum back on.

Maycie cleared her throat. "Janey?"

I switched it off and threw her a glare. "What?"

"I'd like to offer my condolences over the loss of your cousin. He was a fine man. He will be dearly missed."

A murmur of agreement among the players.

"Thank you, Maycie."

I resumed vacuuming.

CHAPTER

36

Fireworks Stand

I LOVED MOSS. MANY people hated it. It ruined lawns. But I counted it among one of my favorite things about Suspicion, and in the war of winter versus springtime, the moss won. Spongey and green, proliferating in the corridors of forest. The moss and the conifers, the dwarf alpines between rocks, and the wildlife—a thousand unexpected treasures within the landscape—these things won.

The mountain had moods. Milky cascades today might turn green and purple tomorrow. An ice formation could burst into existence, surging from a feeder stream, larger than a house.

As we walked in the woods, Em asked me, "Can I take home some moss? I want to make a terrarium for Sherry."

It should have sounded nice. Instead, it hurt. And where did Em learn what a terrarium was? She had this whole life beyond my reach.

I said, "Of course. Sherry would like that."

We found perfect green pillows and carried them back to the garage apartment, our fingers wet and red. We spent the rest of the day letting the vanilla mint one-gallon jar candle run down to nothing—unheard-of decadence—so we could peel off the label and wash it out for Sherry's moss terrarium. Emmie added a tiny rubber cow to graze.

Then Dannie arrived with her nieces to take Em and the girls for hot chocolate.

Dannie pulled me aside. "Did you hear the news?"

"Old news, or new news?"

In Suspicion, we recycled news.

Dannie said, "About Wes Cooney. Slipped on the ice at his ranch."

A perilous sensation crept over me. And rage: Why would anyone, in mountain country, with means like Wes Cooney, allow any place on his property to get so slippery? We had ways of fixing that.

I asked, "Did he . . . ?"

"Yes. He's dead."

The air escaped my lungs. What a nonsense way to die. Wes could be a horse's ass, but he was a solid Suspicioner and one of my players. He'd have family to look in on. Dannie and I squeezed hands.

Dannie herded the girls to her terrain rocket. I climbed into my (now fixed) Subaru Legacy for a long secret run to a shuttered fireworks stand. Roman would return in six days.

* * *

The sun cast lilac rays across the fireworks stand. Much of the snow had melted on the gravel turn-off, with a parking area hidden from the road. The new guy drove a Nissan—not as flashy as Roman's vehicle. Good. Criminals should swim beneath notice. Especially when I swam alongside them.

Mutiny. Danger.

I murmured, "Be cool, Kitty Cat."

Then I saw: *Two* guys in the Nissan. Why two? Like Roman, they were smoking.

I wore my red plaid shirt jacket. Emmie always said she could spot it from the school steps, even when I was sitting in the car on the other end of the parking lot. It had sherpa lining and a hood, but it also had a broad front pocket with easy access to the Saturday night special.

I wiped sweaty hands on my jeans and tried not to twitch toward my gun. "Hello."

The men exited the Nissan with a "hello" back. One looked older, with thinning hair and a smile too taut for his face. The younger one had no smile.

We were far from home, even farther away than that godforsaken mine in the hillside. I handed over the empty backpack, and the younger one accepted it. The thin-haired smiling one gave me the new backpack, weighted down with cash.

All done. My feet felt lighter.

I hit the button to my liftgate and it opened with a hydraulic yawn. I could breathe again.

The fireworks stand exploded.

A sledgehammer hit my left side. I spun, my forehead colliding with the liftgate. I crashed to the ground.

The two men were already inside their Nissan. They looked at me and scanned the woods, weirdly calm.

A second explosion erupted.

My forehead stung where I'd hit the liftgate, but worse: My arm felt like fire. Blood poured through the plaid. And yet the fireworks shack stood whole.

Nothing had blown up.

Those explosions had been gunfire. I'd been shot.

Among the trees, I saw a retreating flash of denim.

I shouted, "I am going to rip out your throat!"

I pulled the tiny gun from my pocket and dashed for the fir trees. "Did you hear me? I'm coming!"

CHAPTER

37

Supersonic Mosquito

MY TWO COHORTS from the Red King's army peeled out, tires kicking gravel.

Clamor erupted from the forest, a pinball course of hunter-green firs. White-golden prairie grass rose to knee height between them, dense enough to hide anything—fallen branch, animal, or shooter.

I yelled, "You killed my cousin!"

I stumbled ahead, my foot plunging into snowy muck. Wind soughed through the conifers, stirring mist, transposing the shooter to a constantly shifting periphery. I listened. The scent of evergreen and musty earth mingled with the blood coursing from my gunshot wound. Then footfalls differentiated from the forest *whoosh*, and I pursued. He grunted.

I shouted, "I am going to hunt you DOWN!"

There. I saw his back. Blue jeans—*with NO ASS, the little weasel.* Gray sweatshirt with the hood up beneath that denim jacket.

"I see you! Turn around and face me!"

The forest swallowed him again. I swung my arm and fired.

Fir needles exploded and he cried out, more from startle than pain. Too far for accuracy. Other than popping off at the card game, I'd only ever before fired a shotgun.

He fired back. The bullet whizzed past my ear, a supersonic mosquito.

I laughed in a single convulsion. "A little more to the right, asshole!"

Another glimpse of denim. I dropped to one knee and extended my arms, my wound bursting pain. I zeroed in on the foliage where he'd just disappeared, but my damaged arm shook and zigzagged the sights.

I squeezed the trigger. Missed. Fired again. It jammed.

I growled, kicking at sticks and prairie grass, my knee wet with mud. The shooter thrashed an increasing distance ahead.

I pried at the jammed bullet.

Then reason drummed into my mind.

I was shot. I'd chased a murderer into the woods. I'd armed myself with the most unreliable of weapons. I'd be better off with a Daisy BB gun.

Had he heard my dry click? What if he turned around and came for me?

He'd disappeared. I jumped to my feet and swung the revolver to my left, then heard a wrenching sound and corrected to my right. Daylight faded.

The forest danced with the wind. He crashed ahead somewhere, the acoustics in the tree maze playing tricks. I'd roamed beyond my home territory. The conifers here grew shorter, bushier, more sparse than on my mountain.

I brimmed with rage. I wanted to look into his eyes and demand blood. Stab, shoot, tear, jab, smash. I cared little for my own welfare—

But what about Em?

This could be the day Em became an orphan. The day I fulfilled the Hendee curse.

I turned and lurched two steps in the direction of the fireworks stand, then looked back. I staggered forward a few more feet. And then I began to run.

The gunshot wound coursed afresh with blood, but I barely felt it. Instead, my sopping, muddy knee wanted attention, wet fabric slapping against cold skin. It drove me mad. I reached down to release a damp clod as I stumbled on, but found my left hand didn't function properly.

The woodland lay patchy with snow and mist. A glance over my shoulder showed movement—but the entire forest pitched. Waving branches. Remnants of light, winking and bursting. I'd lost track of where he might have headed.

By the time I reached the Subaru, blood coursed freely from my hand despite the padding of my sherpa jacket. I felt lightheaded. I threw myself at the vehicle and yanked the door handle, leaving a handprint on the frame. Then I noticed the open liftgate.

The shooter had managed to get back here and steal the money.

But, no.

I still wore the backpack slung over my shoulder, had been wearing it the whole time.

CHAPTER

38

The Uninvited Guest

I STOMPED THROUGH THE deer trail toward town, and called Harvey. He wanted to know what I was going to do about the gunshot wound.

I said, "I'm handling it. Not your business."

"Except it is my business."

"Supposedly, I'm working for Frieda, not you, and you're just the poor schmuck who—how did you put it? Who can't outrun Frieda's buckshot."

He let it hang there.

I said, "No police were involved, and no hospitals. Go get the drop bag out of my Subaru. I parked it in the garage beneath my apartment. Mr. Traverse is in bed."

"Is this a trap?"

"Seriously, Harvey? That's what you're worried about? I was shot. I could have gotten killed."

I tried to keep my teeth from shaking as I walked the deer trail.

I said, "Listen. Just get the money and put it in the safe."

"Who are you talking to? Who's tending that wound? Tell me where you are. I can bring you stuff."

I hung up.

* * *

I looked up at the lighted window and shouted, "Hey! You home? I'm coming up!"

My feet clanged the fire escape, loud as possible. No one on this mountain liked uninvited guests. Snow clung to the thin iron railing and I carrot-peeled it with my finger.

I'd already texted Dannie to see if she could keep Em overnight. Dannie had texted back a thumbs-up.

I looked over my shoulder. Down along the street, the commercial district lay dark and quiet—Jemma's Finds, Suspicious Perks. I could hear the town's heartbeat. Suspicion acted prickly, but it belonged to me.

A security light hung at eye level, but it had burned out. I pounded on the door.

My momentum finally at a halt, my body began to quake. I leaned back against the railing. My left hand turned icy and my arm vibrated. He didn't open the door but I could hear him rustling beyond the wall. I hoped to heaven he was alone.

I pounded again.

The door flew open and I gave a fun-sized scream. Dr. Summers stood in boxer briefs, an undershirt, and a shotgun. His hair gleamed like he'd recently showered after a day of fixing people's teeth in his clinic downstairs.

I gestured at the shotgun. "You better put on some pants if you're going hunting on a night like this."

He cocked his head, clearly unable to see much in the dark. "Janey? What in God's name are you doing on my fire escape?"

"I need help."

"What time is it? I was having dinner."

I didn't smell food. The kitchen lay in darkness but for a nightlight. The only other illumination came from a living room lamp by the recliner. No plates, no snacks.

I said, "You weren't having dinner. You were reading that paperback."

In addition to the book and the lamp, the end table displayed a framed photo of his late wife, and a bottle of Jack. He must sit around gazing at these things just like at the Hideout.

He waved at the recliner. "If you must know, I intended to finish a chapter and then eat."

He raised his voice. "Well, come on! I'm getting hypothermic. Get inside and tell me what you want so I can close the damn door."

I looked at my boots and the high-pile snow on the fire escape. "I'll track snow everywhere. I need you to go downstairs and let me in down there. At your clinic."

He sucked in to argue, but I raised my hands to stop him. "It's not a dental thing, it's medical, but I can't go to a doctor. Because . . . I can't."

Dr. Summers moved behind the door to block his half-naked, goose-fleshed body from the cold, his neck bulging with anger. After driving home, then walking a mile with the gunshot wound, my body shook so hard I worried my legs might buckle. My arm had softened to lava.

He slammed the door.

I didn't know what to make of it. Was he putting on some pants? Heading downstairs to let me in? Or did he return to his book and his bottle of Jack, and the framed photo of Kierra?

I raised my fist to pound again, but the heat and pain flared to unbearable. I scooped a line of snow from the railing and mashed it against the wound. It both tortured and helped.

The door flew open again.

Dr. Summers, now wearing joggers, in an angry action figure stance, said, "Meet me at street level."

I nodded. My legs crumpled.

He grabbed me just in time. "What the hell happened to you?"

I tried to answer. He scooped me up and dragged me inside, along with a whole lot of snow—*dammit, the mess*. Then he carried me down the stairs to his dental clinic.

CHAPTER

39

Mr. Action

I LAY IN HIS tilt-back dental chair, bleeding onto paper blotters that crinkled beneath me.

He held me by the chin and examined the gash. "How did this happen?"

"I ran into my liftgate."

His lips tensed into a line of disbelief.

I said, "It's true, Jude. There was an explosion, and I flew into my hatchback—"

He donned a light scope and held up his hand. "Follow my finger."

I did. The light held steady, his finger swung side-to-side, then he examined my other eye. He switched off his scope.

He said, "Nasty bump, but it doesn't look like you have a concussion."

I said, "Jude. It's not my head. It's my arm. I've been shot."

He followed my gesture and noticed the red stain I'd left on his paper blotter. My plaid shirt jacket camouflaged the blood, which had soaked to the interior of the sherpa, my hand sticky and scarlet.

He said, "Hunting accident?"

I licked my lips. Hunting could be a good cover story, but it might fall apart.

He said, "Let's get this off."

Together we tugged the plaid, section by section starting with the easy parts, until it came down to the wounded left arm. He worked at it like a person accustomed to dealing with patients in pain: gentle, quick, sure. The jacket off, I now sat in my beige long-sleeved shirt. I suppressed my tremors so he could get a good look.

But he stayed put without even leaning in. "Go to the emergency room."

"Can't. I need you to fix me. You're a surgeon."

"*Oral* surgery. Not a gunshot wound to the brachium. Your shirt fabric is embedded into the wound. You'll need a surgeon and continuing medical care. I'll call the Libby volunteer ambulance on your behalf."

"Jude, no. Hear me on this. I cannot . . . go . . . to the hospital. Please, just look at it."

He scowled, contemplated it. I held my breath.

He said, "Who shot you?"

"I don't know."

He pulled his cell phone from the pocket of his joggers.

I stilled his hand. "Whoever it was, I think it had to do with my cousin's death."

"Logan?"

"He got caught up in something bad. Now I'm caught. It's a long story, but—"

I looked at my arm, looked up at Jude. His brow remained furrowed behind that magnifier-scope.

Finally, he said, "Just an examination. Nothing more."

* * *

Jude owned the building. At over a hundred years old, it was divided into two commercial tenants: the dental clinic and the barber shop. Jude's exam room felt reassuring—I'd come here enough times.

Wood floors and a high ceiling of stamped tin, just like at the barber shop. The barber had tilt-back chairs, and Jude had a tilt-back chair, though he also had a spit sink. I suspected Jude deliberately held off prospective tenants so he could lease to a barber. He liked the barber pole, and whenever I came in for an exam, he used to say how in the good old days, the dentist and the barber were the same person.

He *used* to say that, before Kierra died. They would come into the Hideout together. They had a pretty cabin. After he lost her, he sold the cabin and moved into the living space above his dental practice, and his conversation skills took a plunge.

He returned in full scrubs and a mask, and readied a cart with implements. I hoped this meant he was willing to do more than just examine. He used his toe to swing his rolling stool in a single, swirling gesture so fluid it could only come from someone who'd done it countless times a day, for years, and with that particular stool. He was seated before it came to a stop.

He said, "Keep still."

With the scissors, he cut my shirt surrounding the wound. The fabric had gone stiff from blood, and snipping took patience.

He pointed at my top. "We're going to have to take this off. I can give you a paper covering and step out—"

I was already pulling it over my head. Pain seized my arm with the motion. He seemed to understand, and assisted. I considered throwing the shirt onto one of the chairs but cast it to the floor instead, thinking no one wanted to sit on my blood.

His gloved hand probed the area surrounding the wound, now puffed and angry. My arm looked like a gourd that had sat around too long past Halloween, then ruptured. The skin from mid-arm to collarbone had taken on an ashy appearance and a shined-leather texture. At the wound itself, even with a remnant of shirt stuck to it, I could see gaping red.

He wet a sponge and washed my arm. He grumbled: That he needed a nurse. Said he shouldn't be sitting here at all. Didn't even finish that chapter he'd been reading. And then he supposed there'd be no harm in taking an X-ray.

"I'll bet it hurts," he said.

"Damn straight."

"I can give you something."

"No."

A shrug. "I forgot, you're my 'no painkillers' patient."

Since I'd quit alcohol, I never took anything for pain, not even aspirin, and not even at the dentist. Fortunately, I'd only had the one cavity, but the drilling was hell.

On his way out, he tossed me a paper blanket. I unfolded it one-handed while he left to retrieve what he needed for the X-ray. I smoothed it to my neck, but it drifted forward. I tucked it into my bra like a sweetheart neckline to hold it in place, and that graduated from stupid to silly, so I let it fall.

Oral surgeons were doctors. Jude and I could handle a little skin between us.

Though the license on the wall called him an oral surgeon, the value of this fact had escaped me until now. In Suspicion, we thought he was our dentist. Because, well, he was. He did maxillofacial surgery on a limited schedule in Libby, but saw many of us locals for basic cleanings. It never occurred to me that most oral surgeons probably didn't do that.

A For Sale sign was posted in his window.

The blinds were closed, but I could make it out through the slats.

My God, was Jude leaving Suspicion?

He was a luxury we'd taken for granted. People came from all over the state to see him.

Once again, I'd been so absorbed with my crumbling marriage that I'd failed to pick up on things happening around me.

* * *

Jude X-rayed me, bellyaching the entire time, then disappeared again. My shirt swatch jutted from my wound like I was wild game shot with a dart. Sweat poured from my hair and neck, and my teeth chattered. The wound continued to puff.

Blood seeped afresh even though that swatch corked it in. I needed more of that damned snow from his stair railing. I found paper towels and cleaned the drips, hoping to downplay the severity for Jude. I needed his continued cooperation here.

He returned, adjusted his glasses, and angled a computer screen for me. It displayed an X-ray of my arm with scattered white foreign bodies. He told me I'd lost blood. Infection had set in. A scrap of bullet remained embedded in my arm, and it had dislodged comminuted bone fracturing.

With his gloved hands, he palpated my arm again, releasing more blood, which he dabbed with folded gauze. I breathed in measures through the pain.

He said, "It missed the radial nerve, though I don't like the proximity to the brachial artery. Leave the fabric in place. The heat is from increased blood flow so your immune system can fend off pathogens, but it's also a sign of infection. Without a blood test I can't be certain, but I'd be willing to place a wager."

He bound my arm with the shirt swatch in place. Then he rose, toed his magnificent rolling stool, and turned his back.

I said, "What next?"

When he regarded me again, his face held an expression so fierce, I recoiled.

But then he smiled—the kind that made me uneasy, like what I'd seen from Roman. He found a pad of paper in one of the drawers, scribbled on it, and tore it off for me.

Rx—
Go to a hospital.

Jude was already walking away when I looked up.

He called over his shoulder, "I'll get you a clean shirt for transport. Then my work here is done."

A bright red stain bloomed on my new binding. He thought his work here was done. That's where Dr. Jude Summers, the Sunshine Dentist, was wrong.

CHAPTER

40

Dealing

I HEARD HIM DOWN the hall, opening the door to his secret staircase, the one that led from his clinic to his apartment. The sound of his footfalls switched to stair mode. I leaped up after him, wearing my paper blanket like a shawl.

He said, "You shouldn't be walking and you have no business climbing stairs."

He continued up into his unit, through the dark kitchen to the refrigerator. It cast him in a soft glow. I paused at his small living area, next to his easy chair. Jude retrieved a carton of orange juice.

I said, "I appreciate what you've done. I'm asking for more."

He sighed, poured the juice and set it on the counter, then disappeared into the bedroom.

His reading light still shone. I picked up the photo of Kierra. Not a speck of dust on it. She had soft beauty with large, brown eyes and full lips. I remembered her love of the woods and her generosity. Also, a trickster. Kierra had christened him the "Sunshine Dentist," though Jude had about as much sunshine in him as a blind mole.

He emerged from the bedroom and took the photo from me, setting it down next to his book, then handed me a clean shirt. It should have been an old T-shirt but he'd given me a soft, warm flannel button-down.

He turned his back while I dressed, then handed me the orange juice. "Drink this. It'll help."

I sipped.

He said, "I'll call the hospital of your choice and speak to the attending physician."

"But—"

"I don't know what you think I can do. Maybe you believe I can provide ongoing medical supervision for you up here, while I hold clinic downstairs. Or do you think you can convalesce at home? With your daughter to look after? Let me disavow you of that. You require blood plasma and intravenous fluids. You need antibiotics and medical supervision. There is nothing I can do."

"Please, I can't just do that."

"Now we walk back downstairs and hope you avoid further injury since you've already fainted once. You are going to either await the volunteer ambulance, or allow me to personally drive you to Cabinet Peaks Medical Center. *Immediately.*"

The orange juice felt cold. I pressed it to my flaming shoulder, my eyes on all the melted snow we'd tracked in. It would calm my nerves to erase the mess but I said no such thing to Jude. I sipped, forging a mental pathway. If I went to the hospital, they'd treat me for a gunshot wound and call the police, and then I'd have to explain why I'd been shot. I was willing to lie but my skills at fabrication could earn me a Raspberry Award.

I guessed at what had befallen Logan. I would never know my chances of making it through this—or for how long—until I found out what happened to him. My fate seemed tied to his, and Emily's fate tied to mine.

Jude took my empty glass and placed it in the sink, his back muscles shifting beneath his shirt. How vulnerable a human body is.

Jude said, "Let's get downstairs. I'll lead in case you—"

"I can get you into the games."

* * *

With his back turned, the indirect kitchen lighting cast him in shadows. He swiveled to face me. He narrowed his eyes. I tugged the sleeve over my icy left hand, my heartbeat forceful.

Jude said, "Will you repeat that, please?"

"If you're still interested, I have a chair for you at the Big Bald Luck games."

"Walk me through it."

I stepped forward. "Buy-in is five thousand dollars. The locations migrate. Harvey sets the dates. You come to the Hideout to find out where the games are to be held. This next one goes down at the Cedar Mountain Christmas Tree Farm."

He said, "I know the general premise. I thought they were locked up. Why is there sudden availability?"

"You may have heard about Wes Cooney's accident."

"Yes. Hemorrhagic hypovolemic shock."

"Eh, what? No, he slipped on ice and hit his head."

"That's what I just said. I spoke with the coroner, Maycie Gaynor. It was an unattended death, so they ordered an autopsy from the crime lab in Missoula."

I blinked. "Well, Maycie's got a seat, too. You can sit together and have some laughs."

He said, "Are you telling me this is about Wes Cooney's membership in the games? The man hasn't even been buried yet, and now his chair is being offered around?"

"Not *around*. I'm offering it to *you*. It's got no bearing on how we mourn him."

I waved at his wall calendar. "The games happen a week from Wednesday. Once they're scheduled, they go down, blizzard, flood, or plague."

The fact that I'd just added a new seat for Dannie Tigner did not matter. We had a sixth seat now, and that meant one seat was vacated.

Jude said, "I don't like this. You're going to the hospital, and that's the only matter under discussion."

"If you dragged me to a hospital, I'd just walk off and dig this bullet out with my folding knife."

His face grew dark. "Then I am calling the police."

"Jude! Why?"

"Because I like you. I fear for your safety. Did you intend to barge into my clinic and hold me in moral hostage? 'Treat me or watch me succumb?'"

I said, "Think, Jude. You know me. It's not like I was out selling crank. I got shot because I'm in an awful situation. These people killed Logan. I will tell you everything, but only if you truly want me to. There might be police and judges involved. Lawyers . . ."

I wiped my face with my good hand. "See, it could be dangerous for both of us. You'd expressed interest in the games before, and—"

"That was before."

"Before what?"

I flung a hand at the bottle of Jack by his recliner. "Before all that took a turn?"

Jude glared at the bottle, then turned away from me.

I instantly wished I could take it back.

* * *

Jude's heavy drinking began after Kierra died. That mysterious, now-you-see-her-now-you-don't death that only Jude and Maycie Gaynor seemed to understand, but Suspicioners might forever explore on gossip night.

That's when his heavy drinking started. But as his waitress, I was the sole person who knew it had ended.

My comment had come out cheap, badly timed, and I'd had no right to say it. He leaned on the counter.

I said, "Look, Jude, I'm sor—"

"Alcohol's bad for the teeth. Bad for the gums."

That never occurred to me.

He said, "How long did it take for you? Before you felt like you were on solid footing?"

I rubbed my hands and stepped toward him, thinking back to the early days. They'd passed on gale winds.

"I guess, from the time when I decided to quit, to when I actually took my last drink, it was about six or eight months. A few false starts."

"Is that why you refuse painkillers? Is that what I'm supposed to do?"

I pulled up a barstool and sat. "It's different for everyone."

I looked at his bottle by the easy chair. "Some people get rid of all their alcohol. When my house was completely alcohol-free, I'd panic and binge drink. That's just how my personality works. For most people, keeping booze around when you're trying to quit would be a disaster."

I tilted to look up at him. "You like to sit at the Hideout and stare at the well drinks. Keep a fake Jack and Coke in front of you and let people believe you're still a drinker."

He said, "Roxie still serves me the hard stuff. You always ask what I want. She just puts it in front of me."

"We have regulars who get the same drinks, same food, for years. When she gets the order in front of them before they even place it—it's a way to show she cares."

He said, "When she puts it in front of me, I pretend to drink it and just pay for the damned thing. I try to come in during your shift."

"I think I know why you do it."

"Why?"

"So you don't get questions. If people think you quit drinking, they hand you advice, and they ask how it's going. This way, if they never know you quit, then they'd never find out if you failed. You don't get the looks. You're keeping your options open."

"That would be correct."

He actually smiled. It looked like sunshine.

I told him, "Did you know Guy Hamm's got a seat at the games?"

The sun grew teeth.

CHAPTER

41

The Other Hideout

I REFUSED ANESTHESIA. I committed to ride even the monstrous pain. But Jude would not move forward unless I accepted a local. He said he couldn't have me twitching while he worked near that artery, and so I relented.

Now, mopped in sweat, I held a vial with the three bullet fragments: two tiny copper pieces, and one large coppery tube, curled and bent, that reminded me of my deep-fried pill bottles. He'd also removed bits of bone. The bone I elected to leave out of my vial.

Jude drove me beneath a gibbous moon to the other side of Cinnamon Falls where he kept a fishing cabin. It overlooked a pond that most would call a lake. Mountain peaks and a constellation of stars spread at our feet until a fish rippled the surface.

His cabin lacked any dust accumulation. The canned goods had years of life before they'd expire. No signs of insect or mouse infestation. He told me he no longer went fishing or hunting, so what did he do here?

He switched on battery-powered LEDs and gave me the tour. In other words, "Turn around." It had one pantry with a wooden latch, a bed, a wooden chair, and a recliner—the only thing that looked out of place, but I understood Jude needed his recliners. Everything in the cabin pointed at a river-stone fireplace. An outhouse lay beyond a porch with a dry sink and outdoor spigot. No indoor plumbing.

Everything, from the log timber forming the walls, to the floor planks, to the stones at the hearth, looked like it had been constructed from materials gathered from the property a century ago.

In a parallel life, in an off-grid life, I could live here even without the plumbing. I'd bathe out at the spigot and watch eagles dive on the lake.

Once the fire got going, Jude sat in the recliner. I took the bed.

He said, "I'd like you to take a sedative."

"Out of the question."

"I thought you might say that. We'll forgo the sedative. Now, you are going to experience pain. It might get pronounced. In the same way you ask your customers what they want and you don't make assumptions, I won't make assumptions with you as my patient. Even though in the past, you've declined analgesics, that has no bearing. When I say the pain could get bad, I mean it."

"No painkillers, Jude."

"You keep an emergency stash of liquor even though you don't drink. Would you like an emergency stash of painkillers?"

That gave me pause. If I hit a pain crescendo, knowing I had a stash could stave off panic, even if I never touched it.

I said, "I'm good."

"Fine. We'll leave it at antibiotics."

He walked me through dosage and how to keep the wound dry, elevated, and untouched. He'd be the one to change the dressings.

Then he said, "Time to fill me in about all of this."

That was part of the bargain, so I told him everything. From finding Logan's gun in the Hideout ladies' washroom, to Frieda, to the dirty doc, to Roman, and on to the part where I'd landed on Jude's fire escape. It felt like an unsanctioned release—I was taking a risk in confiding in him, but at the same time, I'd already gone too far by seeking his help.

He listened, his thumb beneath his chin and a knuckle at his lips, his wire-rimmed glasses reflecting firelight. I spoke for almost two hours and gulped three glasses of water. He drank nothing and made no reaction.

When I wound myself down, he said, "Is that it? Have you left anything out?"

"You want more?" I wanted to curl up and pass out. Like a deep-fried pill bottle. Like a spent, bent, copper bullet.

He said, "You agreed to explain it all."

"I did, yes."

I smoothed back my hair where it spread over the pillows, and saw the first hint of morning wash over the mountain. The only part of the story I omitted was Dannie. I wanted to keep her safe.

I said, "It's an ongoing saga."

He got up from his recliner and stretched, stepping to the window. Fog drifted across the water's surface.

He said, "What about the FBI? If you're looking at a conspiracy involving police and the judiciary, it would make sense to seek assistance from the FBI."

"Oh, God, there's that whole thing with Rawhide. And Guy Hamm's buddy."

"Guy Hamm's buddy?"

I'd left out the sickening conversation at Guy Hamm's rental and his threat to call his FBI buddy, because it was humiliating and irrelevant. But now that I thought about it, Guy Hamm had eavesdropped on my call with Harvey. Guy knew things. Also, Harvey had that friend, Rawhide.

I said, "There *is* more to the story. Some of it involves Guy Hamm. The FBI connection is murky."

I shrugged. "That's the problem. I don't know what's safe and what's not."

He nodded. "I've got to get ready for clinic. Don't forget: Sleep all you can today. Water from the spigot is potable, but other than that and the outhouse, try to stay in bed."

He waved at the shelves. "There are books."

I nodded. "Thanks, Jude. I mean—"

I opened my hands. "I mean, thanks."

"You're welcome."

Then he smiled. "In case you were wondering, you're not my first gunshot wound."

That gave me a jump. "Really?"

"Not by a mile. Not even the worst."

I grinned. "Well, maybe you can tell *me* about that sometime."

"Maybe. And you can show me how to play poker."

My jaw dropped. "You don't know how to play?"

He shook his head.

I said, "You never wanted into the games?"

"Oh, I want in. I want to go head-to-head with Guy Hamm. I just need to figure out how to play."

"Jude. These are high-stakes games. Guy will grind your bones for biscuits."

"From what I read, poker is not a game of chance. It is a game of skill."

"Of which you have none."

"Skill can be learned."

"Sure, while you go bankrupt."

I felt ill. I thought about the FOR SALE sign in his window, the photo of Kierra in his dark apartment, and his prop bottle of Jack Daniels.

He said, "I'm used to cramming for exams. In my profession, it never ends. I've got a week to learn."

He opened the door with a wave to the surroundings and said, with a completely straight face, "Don't look so morose. Now you've got your very own hideout."

He disappeared, closing and latching the door.

I said to the space he'd vacated, "And, one could argue, my very own dirty doc."

CHAPTER

42

Cutely Courteous

When I awoke, my arm felt like some creature had nested inside and begun chewing. The more I moved, the harder it chewed. Heat flooded my shoulder. Jude had said not to touch the dressings, but I took a peek. My skin glimmered from ointment, and the crater had turned black and oily.

No signal on my phone.

My body demanded water. Urgently.

I stumbled out to the spigot, cranked it, and thrust my hands beneath the icy flow. I drank from my cupped palms. Cold water sluiced down my throat but even after several gulps, my mouth felt parched and gluey, and my hands went numb. I gave up and stuck my mouth directly beneath the flow.

Finally, I stood up. My shirt and hair were freezing wet, and it felt good.

Blue, marbled clouds haloed the peak, the sky a soft purple. Charcoal trees swept from the water's edge on up the mountain. I could hear rushing somewhere in the distance, possibly from Cinnamon Falls. Black-headed birds with round amber eyes bobbed on the lake. Coots. They took flight, their paths trailing a runway across the surface that opened, formed a wake, then disappeared. I watched them vanish over the treetops, their breasts open to the landscape as they flew. Freedom.

I used the outhouse, then came back to the spigot and washed. Jude kept treacherous soap, green and gritty, in a slotted dish. My wound dressing had gotten wet and now gaped.

A chill took hold, and I slunk back inside. My band phone rested on the chair where I'd left it. The screen showed 1:13 PM, with seven missed calls and some text messages. They'd dumped all at once when the network caught a signal.

I called Harvey.

With barely a ring, he picked up. "The money's gone."

My heart lurched. I could hear him breathing through his nose.

I said, "I put the backpack in the trunk."

"Yeah, well the hatch was open. Whoever got to it was cutely courteous enough to leave the backpack behind. Sliced open and empty."

* * *

The longer the silence mounted between us, the faster my heart-rate. Harvey's fury radiated through the connection. My thoughts scrambled atop one another.

On each of the three occasions I'd made the exchange, the weight of the backpack varied. I took this to mean the cash sum varied. Last night it had been quite laden. Heavier than the previous drops.

Harvey said, "Well? You got something to tell me?"

"How much was in the bag?"

"That's not the something I had in mind. Were you followed?"

"How the hell should I know? I'd been shot."

But then I recalled how at the fireworks stand, my rage flipped to fear. That continued on the drive back to Suspicion. I kept searching my rearview mirror for headlights, paranoid the shooter would come finish what he'd started. But there'd been no one else on that twisty road.

I said, "No one followed me. The shooter came from the woods. I drove home and left the backpack in the car for you, then went for help."

"Where'd you go?"

"As I said. To get help."

"Who helped you?"

"I'm not answering that."

"You damn well better!"

"Chill your bones, Harvey. It's irrelevant. That backpack was in the car, waiting for you."

I pulled hair from my eyes and wished for more water. For some of Jude's fake Jack.

Harvey said, "The window was broken."

"What window?"

"Garage."

I thrust my hand to my hip, forgetting the wounded arm, and regretted it. "Seriously? Someone broke into the garage? You didn't think to mention that first thing?"

"Where are you now? I'll come get you."

"In bed."

"At your place?"

"Swear to God, if you try to wheedle information one more time. It's like this. I'm recovering from a bullet wound. I'm not going anywhere unless it's a hospital, and neither of us wants that."

"Janey. You're scaring me with this. A whole lot of money's gone, and you're missing. Do you know what the Seattle set does to people who disappear with their money?"

A terrible whole-body tinnitus swept over me, ringing from marrow to hair follicles, leaving me cold. Fear, rage. My breath heaved—perhaps from the injury, but more likely because I wanted to kill him. Them. Harvey and Frieda, who had tossed me into a deadly situation. They threatened to take my daughter.

I spoke carefully. "Watch how you talk to me, Harvey."

He really must have believed I was clueless, complaining to *me* about missing money he and Frieda were stealing to begin with, from torturers and murderers.

I ended the call before I said something I'd regret.

CHAPTER

43

Miracle of Three

WHEN I CAUGHT a signal again, I Googled Harvey's FBI agent, Rawhide. He seemed real—a Kenneth Dunkins worked out of the Kalispell field office.

The gunshot wound throbbed, and I blew cool air over it. I didn't know if I was the target or the money was, I only knew that danger followed me home. I couldn't risk Em getting exposed to this. Dannie had taken her to school and said she would pick her up afterward and swing by the house to pack her a bag.

I called Trent and (quickly, before he could protest, though I knew it was underhanded) patched Sherry in for a three-way call. I told them I'd been in a bad accident and asked if they'd look after Em awhile.

Trent dithered.

Sherry cooed, "Of course. Are you all right?"

I gave her a vague reply.

Trent cut in. "Have you called the school back?"

"Called them back?"

I'd deep fried my phone. I forgot to give the new number to the school.

Trent said, "Your daughter's been fencing candy like some street dealer."

Sherry gave a nervous laugh, and I groaned. "Are they making a big deal about that? I told her she could."

"Nice."

I said, "I'll talk to her."

"She's right here."

Em got on the line. "Mom? You okay? What happened?"

"I'm fine, honey. You're gonna stay with Dad and Sherry awhile."

I could hear Trent say, "Tell her about your little street dealing," and I winced.

Why did he have to talk to her that way? I should have told him about her enterprise. Communication between Trent and me was terrible.

Em's voice sounded weighted with lead. "Mom, they stole my candy store."

"What? Who stole it? Tell me the name."

"*Their* names. Three of them."

I bunched the sheet in my fist and lay back on Jude's camp bed.

She said, "I don't want to say any more about that."

"Em . . ."

"Don't make me tattle. I won't make a stink. Mrs. Jansen's mad and I'm in trouble. I understand I was on my own with this. I'll just deal with it, okay? Like you said."

"But—"

But I wanted to know who the fuck stole my kid's candy. Em sounded miserable. How did mothers *manage* these things?

No, I wasn't going to make her tell me. I had to recognize her poise. I could hear Trent and Sherry murmuring in the background.

The stiff mattress beneath me, I grasped Jude's flannel over my heart.

Em said, "Sherry told me I could redecorate my bedroom here. She's going to take me shopping."

I tried not to choke. "How nice."

Stab. My hand clutching my heart in a different way.

Em said, "Yeah. She sells insurance and she makes good money. I like her. And Dad's working again."

"You're kidding."

"Yeah, he got his old job back at that mechanic place."

"Peak Auto? With Roy?"

Em said, "They went out for beer and darts. Now he's working there again. I'm going to decorate my room like a wilderness escape. Like a chalet. Nothing too themey."

The kid had seen her share of decorating shows.

After all these years, Trent got a job. He could pay the mortgage. Especially if Sherry had a job, too—double income.

It would mean that Em could keep the house. Just not with me.

A tear slid down my face. This was good news. So why did it hurt? And Trent—beneath everything, I knew he was capable of being an upstanding man. Maybe I'd triggered a lazy side of him. Or Sherry brought out the better man.

Em continued, "Sherry's going to turn my room into something Logan would have thought was cool. So don't worry. You just get better."

* * *

When Jude returned, he brought sacks of food and medicine. And news: They said Wes Cooney's death was a wolf attack. Jude had downloaded security footage for me.

From Jude's phone screen, both Wes and the wolf appeared on night-rendered video. Two pairs of glowing eyes—human and canine—as if they'd gone supernatural. The wolf had broken into Wes's garage. They surprised each other as Wes climbed the steps to a side door. When the wolf bolted into the open, Wes cried out and both of his feet shot up, his body falling backward, and his skull hit the concrete.

On the icy driveway, the wolf spun hind-end-down, barking, its jaws snapping at the air. Then it recovered and scrambled off.

Hardly a wolf attack. But if the Hendee curse claimed me, I'd rather my obituary showed something epic like "death by wolf," even if was a lie, rather than "slipped and fell."

My arm was puffed and oozing. I paid for my sins in pain approaching delirium when Jude debrided, cleaned, and swabbed. My eyes streamed, a brute sensory reaction.

When he finished wrapping, we each sat back and regarded one other: I, drenched in sweat, and he, a little spooked and curious.

He asked, "Is it addictive?"

"What?"

"Pain."

"Good God. Not for me." I tried to laugh but convulsed instead, the body confused by the close proximity between laughter and tears.

He chuckled. His eyes were bloodshot. He'd pulled an all-nighter to get me through the gunshot wound, and the man needed sleep.

I said, "I'll be fine now. You can go on home."

"I'm sleeping in this chair, unless you've come to your senses and decided to let me take you to the hospital."

"My senses are long gone."

"Then I'll make us some canned chili while you finish telling me about your situation."

That marked the second time he mentioned chili in the past week.

He said, "You told me it had to do with Guy Hamm."

The phantom odor hit me, aftershave and sausage. I groaned.

With the sunrays waning over the pond, a damp cool seeped into the cabin, bringing a scent of pine sap. Jude stoked the fire. I relayed the events at Guy Hamm's rental. The full humiliation. Funny how I'd wondered whether people blurt secrets under sedation—this rolling wake after acute pain felt like the actual truth serum.

When I finished the story, Jude said, "We'll kill him."

"What?"

"Guy's ego is his most prized possession. We'll murder it."

I smiled, sort of, but given my circumstances, even little jokes about murder came at me in dripping font.

Jude said, "It'd be good for him if a man who didn't know how to play poker took him for all he's worth."

I said, "Jude . . ."

"Even if I lose, he'll just gloat. Not like his ego can get any bigger. There's no risk but to my pride."

He stirred the pan. "Between patients today, I had a chance to look at Lincoln County jurisprudence. It's an odd system. The fact that we're remote means that we get floating judges from Missoula County. Obviously, I can't guess who the bribed judges might be—"

"If anyone."

"Exactly, but it's safe to say Frieda Kanjo would only work something out with a judge who sits the bench in Lincoln County. Someone accessible."

I nodded.

He said, "So I made a short list for you."

"How many names?"

"Three. Two local judges and one floater from Missoula. As far as I can tell, the floater only handles bail hearings, then the trials go on the local judges' dockets."

He handed me my chili and set down a sleeve of saltines between us. Suddenly, it felt within reach to figure out these judges. I needed two. He'd narrowed it down to two and a half.

CHAPTER

44

By Proxy

I WAS AFRAID TO go home, and I avoided Harvey's calls. That was easy since the phone network hated Jude's hideout. Jude said I could stay there as long as I needed, and he kept an eye on the wound while I taught him cards.

My point of view fell short. I provided game fundamentals. The rules, the constants and variables. In short, a card dealer's perspective. But Jude needed the heartbeat—how to *play*. For that, he went to Constant Companion Books and asked Val what she had on strategy. He also watched videos while I slept, but he had to download those before driving up to his secret hideout. Streaming was an urban luxury.

By Thursday, my arm was still too weak to haul dinner plates around, so I called Roxie to cover my shift. She didn't know I'd been shot—gossip had it I'd wrecked a snowmobile while drunk. I told her to confirm that as truth.

She said, "They're going to make you take another pee test."

"Are you kidding me?"

"I saw the lab kit."

I groaned. I'd hoped to squeak by with the "I've been shot" excuse.

Roxie said, "You're not taking them anymore, are you?"

"God, no."

"Ha! Didn't think so. You sound alert."

Frieda had arranged to put me on a high dose in order to reduce me to a zombie state. Unfortunately, my return to the living was attracting attention.

Roxie said, "I'll take them for you."

"You'll *what*?"

She snickered. "The Seroquel? I used to be on that. I won't take as much as your prescription says. That's nuts. I'll take partial doses of the rest, too."

My heart thumped. This was crazy.

She said, "They won't know how much from a pee test, just that it's in your system. I mean my system. Tell Harvey I'm picking up your pills for you. But I'll just keep them."

God save me and my heart of sin. I let her do it.

* * *

Friday, I still had a hard time moving my arm around, but by Saturday, I called Harvey and told him I was going back to work.

I said, "Did you find the money?"

"What do you think?"

"Have you told our buddies?"

"I told them, all right. They saw you get shot. Said the theft happened on our end and we're liable."

"Glad everyone's priorities are straight."

Harvey doubled down. "They're pissed. It's a security breach. You don't want those people rolling around our town, paranoid, quick on the trigger."

"Actually, when the shooting started, they peeled out in a hail of gravel."

"That was the B team."

I understood that the A team meant Roman, back in a few days.

Harvey said, "Listen. I didn't tell you this before. I'm sorry you were hurt, and I'm—I'm glad you're okay now."

I'd said I'd return to work. I hadn't told him I was okay.

He said, "I don't want something bad to happen to you. It's good we'll see you back at the Hideout tonight."

I almost ended the call there, but he said, "Frieda wants to see you. It's important, Janey. You need to bring Em down to her office. Today. It's more important than coming into work tonight."

Frieda wanted to control me by taking control of Em. No way could I allow this. I kept quiet, thinking hard.

He said, "I know you think of her as some monster. She cares about children, and this can get tricky in terms of legal stuff. Just talk to her. Bring in those papers I gave you. Come in late for your shift. It's fine."

* * *

As Jude drove me into Suspicion, my phone network blinked into service. It dropped two messages: one from Maycie Gaynor, and one from Quincy Tigner. The coroner and the chief of police.

Jude noticed my tension.

"What's going on?" he said as we pulled into my driveway.

Without hearing the messages, I knew. "They finished Logan's autopsy."

CHAPTER

45

How to Part

Morning sun gleamed over Mr. Traverse's log cabin, coaxing green shoots from the meadow. Beyond, a dense conifer forest. If any animal, or anyone, were hiding out there, I'd never see it; not even in the brightest stretch of day.

I checked the first message—from Maycie. The crime lab had completed its preliminary examination of my cousin's remains and submitted a report. She said Police Chief Tigner would be getting in touch, but that I could call her with questions.

Despite Jude's rule about taking it easy, I opened the door and lurched out of his Sequoia. Maycie's medical examiner had pulled a slug out of my cousin, I felt sure of it. A folded-over bit of copper like that thing I'd put in a vial.

Jude caught up and touched my elbow, gesturing at my door. "You think it's safe?"

I looked down at the key in my hand. "Probably. It's been days."

He took my key and unlocked the door, entering ahead of me, stepping in sideways.

He had a point. I wasn't paying attention to my surroundings. Even though whoever had come for the money was likely long gone, I still didn't know whether I was a target.

The garage had three doors: the roll-up for the car, the side entry Jude had unlocked, and the door at the top of the interior stairs that opened to my apartment. Whenever I entered or left, I always had to pass through two locked doors.

Beyond Jude's shoulder, sunlight bled through the window but the garage was otherwise cast in darkness. I could barely make out my Subaru. I flipped on the light, and realized Jude had his pistol out.

My car sat parked amid thirty years of Mr. Traverse's potterings: a vise and workbench, the peg board with each tool occupying its designated space, bins with hardware, the snowmobile he never used.

The window was broken. Mr. Traverse had sent a text about that. But no boogeyman crouched under the white-painted stairs. Jude was being paranoid.

My bloody handprint smeared the door frame and handle. I'd have to wipe it down before work. Probably a bad idea to let the entire town of Suspicion gawk at my bloody Subaru in the Harvey's Hideout parking lot. The whispers would fly tomorrow over Sunday brunch—an even bigger gossip day than Thursdays.

I nodded at Jude. "I think I'm set. See you at the Hideout later?"

"Save me a seat with a view of the well drinks."

And then an odd moment occurred. Neither of us knew how to part. Too much had passed between us to end it with a cordial wave. Do we hug? A light peck on the . . . ?

He squeezed my good arm and vanished.

Right.

My foot creaked on the inner staircase to my apartment. Jude's absence took the breath from me in more ways than one. It helped having someone to confide in. Now alone, I felt vulnerable.

I slipped my key in, and the door swung inward with barely a push.

I hesitated. The lock was scratched. I rattled it, tried to lock it. It had been forced and no longer worked. Someone had broken in.

I peered into my living room. *I shouldn't go in alone.*

I stepped inside.

* * *

I brought out the—unreliable—Röhm. The junk gun, the Saturday night special, what Roman had called the Suicide Special. They jammed in the very moment of danger, when you needed them most.

I held it in front of me, one bullet down—wait, no, two—and still jammed. I searched my kitchen, my bedroom, the closets.

After taking all that money from the Subaru, why bother with my apartment? I owned nothing of value.

I felt violated. I checked the window like I could catch someone who was only just now skulking into the woods, even though days had passed. I was going to have to strip off my clothes and take a shower. How could I possibly get through that? Someone could walk in. The garage window was broken. The door didn't lock.

I remembered the second voice mail, the one from Police Chief Tigner, and played it.

He wanted to talk to me—face-to-face.

Just like Frieda.

C H A P T E R

46

Another Kind of Pitch

FRIEDA COULD HAVE put her law offices in Suspicion but then she might as well set up a sno-cone stand on a lava field. Suspicion teemed with folks who needed lawyers, but few willing to pay. People like us held faith that if we held out long enough, legal troubles might air themselves out.

Frieda's office overlooked the courthouse. If I were a normal criminal, I might see that and think, "Oh, crap, there it is. I better shovel my money at this lawyer."

I thanked God we didn't have a view of the jail. Already my palms were sweating.

I didn't know lawyers opened their offices on weekends. She kept a snake plant made of silk. The edges had gone threadbare and it needed dusting. Other than that her office felt airy and stylish. She displayed a law library of rich, embossed-leather books in slate colors. Frieda herself seemed different. Her brows had smoothed away the bat in flight. She wore a high-dollar gray pantsuit that left me self-conscious of my dryer-shrunk sweater and jeans with the thermals peeking over the waistband.

And yet I could smell her fumes. An hour past noon and Frieda had gotten started—a little kick to her pod-machine coffee. I wondered if the news of my arrival had triggered her.

She pointed at a chair. I threw my coat over it, the inside open to me, and I sat on my warm, cozy parka like it was prophylactic to a bench covered in bird crap.

Frieda said, "I'm a busy woman, Janey. You were supposed to bring Emmie and signed paperwork. Did Harvey not deliver the message or do you just enjoy wasting my time?"

"You also told me you didn't want trash like me around your office."

"Unless summoned."

The receptionist, Tamara, appeared with my butter-toffee coffee—my second cup because I'd been parked in the waiting room.

Frieda drew her own mug closer. It had a plaid motif with teddy bears.

Frieda said to Tamara, "Print out another document for Miss Hendee. She forgot to bring hers."

"Will do," Tamara said.

She backed out of the office and closed the door. Worth noting that the receptionist was scared to give Frieda her back.

* * *

Frieda said, "Look, Janey, I don't care if you slept with my husband."

"I never—"

"He's a twat. This has nothing to do with that. The other night got out of hand."

I leaned back, crossed my legs.

Frieda said, "I apologize. What's happening now is we're helping each other, and it's a good thing. It's called symbiosis. You are here today because I am helping you."

"Frieda. You are trying to take Em away from me."

"That is *not* what it is. I'm glad you are voicing your concerns. That paperwork I sent is me backing you up, missy. It's a show of faith. Anything happens to you, your child will be taken care of. Look at you! You've been shot!"

I clutched the less painful part of my left arm. "Am I missing something? I was shot *because* of you."

"Young lady, it is possible you don't understand this situation. You do not work for me, you have been working *under* me in a much larger federated group of organizations."

"You make it sound like I get vision and dental."

She said, "I am an attorney assisting a client. I act as liaison on his behalf. But I am also acting in *your* interests. I am making sure that no matter what happens, your child is cared for, properly, and not left to the mercy of the state or unsuitable parenting. *That* is what those papers say. The kind of lifestyle you live, you should have done this the moment she was born. Do you have a lawyer?"

"No."

Frieda smiled. "You do now."

She sipped her jacked-up coffee, and in a certain universe, I'd have liked to jack up my own buttered-toffee coffee.

She said, "Things change when you have a good lawyer. You go from the puppy getting kicked around to big dog in the park."

Frieda raised her eyebrows. "Back when you gave birth to Emmie in jail?"—shaking her head—"That wouldn't have happened. Not with a good lawyer. You would have given birth in a hospital and brought her home with you, enjoyed a bonding period. Tell me about your parents."

I gritted my teeth. "I had fosters."

Frieda shook her head again, triumphant. "Not with me, you wouldn't have. You would have landed in a happy, stable home, because I would have fought to keep you in one. If it was a matter of getting you excellent psychiatric care, then I, as your attorney, would have helped you get that. Even as a helpless child."

She jammed her finger onto her desk. "Especially as a helpless child! That's what good lawyers do."

Frieda waved at the desk. "Say what you want about me in some regards, but one thing you'll find out, is I'm a good lawyer. I fight tooth and nail for my clients. And I love children. Have you ever Googled me?"

I watched her out of the side of my eye. I shook my head.

"Well, look me up."

She handed me a business card as though I'd never heard of Frieda Kanjo, the woman who'd shared my back fence for eight years and smacked the spit out of my mouth. It felt like she was pitching me.

She said, "You're gonna find that I'm extremely active in children's causes. And, you'll find that my clients win. Now I'm on your side, Miss Janey Hendee. And I'm on Emmie Hendee's side."

I sat mystified. Frieda was hyping her wares like she wanted me to host a Pampered Chef party.

She continued, "You are a very lucky young lady. You get to have an attorney at your beck and call in *addition* to what you get paid to do the drops."

She hadn't paid me anything unless you count a bunch of medication I'm not taking. That and the privilege to avoid jail.

She peered at me, her eyes drawing something out. The silence grew until it grimaced between us.

"Good," Frieda said.

Like I had uttered some statement of enthusiasm.

She dragged a half-filled pad of paper over and turned it to a clean sheet. "You want your house back. You put together the down payment. You kept up the mortgage and supported Trent. But the deed's in his name. Why?"

I coughed, stuttered. "I—When we bought the house on Cable Hill, I was in juvie. That's when Em was born. I had the money from the trust."

"What trust?"

"My mother died. Same as my aunt."

God, I couldn't just blurt it all out like this. Not to Frieda.

She waved it off and slammed her hand on the desk. "What are you talking about? What trust? Like you're some rich orphan?"

"The cancer. The mesothelioma." I swallowed, drew my lips back and held them there.

Her eyes shot up. "Here?"

"They were both from Libby."

Her eyes bulged, her brows practically itching. "Do you mean to tell me your mother died as part of the public health emergency? Your mother and your aunt both?"

I could only grit my teeth.

CHAPTER

47

Bag of Bones

In Libby and the surrounding area, for a hundred years, a mine had tapped a glimmering vein of vermiculite that provided jobs. Unfortunately, this vermiculite wound through an unstable vein of asbestos. Nobody really understood the dangers of asbestos for the first part of the twentieth century. Industry used it in concrete, fabricated goods, and insulation—until we figured out the troubles. In the case of the Libby vermiculite mine, asbestos had penetrated the air, drinking water, and soil. The EPA called it one of the worst environmental disasters in history. Just from digging in the dirt. My grandmother, my mother, and my aunt, all three worked for the mine.

Some received tens of millions from the lawsuits. I received about $28,000 in a trust before I ever understood courts existed. I would have much rather had my mother.

Frieda said, "Sssshhhhhiiit!"

Because before my eyes, she worked out that there'd already been a settlement on my behalf, and she couldn't get in on it.

Anxious to move past my mother, I told Freida, "When I got pregnant with Em, I got the trustee to put all the money into a down payment on the house, but I was seventeen and in juvenile detention."

Frieda nodded. "You came up with the down payment but couldn't qualify for the loan. So Trent got the loan on your money. And you made the payments once you got out of jail."

"Not *jail.* Juvenile detention. For running away."

"You're entitled to a portion of that house. He doesn't get to keep the whole thing just because his name's on the deed. Montana's a community property state. I have enough to go after him."

My heart soared. "Really? The house is all I really want for Em."

Hope multiplied in rainbows. Em could keep her school, her friends. She'd feel safe. She would grow from a girl to a teenager to a young lady in a stable home. She would never be a wolf.

And then I remembered my phone call with Em and how happy she'd gotten over Sherry helping her redecorate her bedroom. Trent with the new job—he could afford the mortgage now. Probably. With Sherry's help.

I understood that I was entitled to a portion of—my!—home, but I couldn't trust Frieda to get involved. It would be like trusting Guy Hamm, swindler of bikes, to pay me for cleaning his rental.

I said, "The house is off-limits."

"It's a straightforward and obvious—"

I shook my head. "Forget the house."

It hurt to say it. At least I was sitting down.

Frieda looked at me cock-eyed. "We'll set that aside for now. Let's talk about Trent. Does he drink?"

"Some? Why?"

Frieda made a note and asked, "What kind of drugs does he do?"

That antsy feeling. Trent was a shit, but he was Em's father.

"He got clean? Back then?" My voice kept sliding to the wrong end of the seesaw.

Frieda pounced. "I told you not to lie to me."

I pleaded, and hated the sound. "I'm trying to figure out if pot is considered a drug."

Frieda's eyebrows had assumed the bat in flight, but they relented. "That's understandable. It's the kind of question you can bring to your lawyer. You see?"

I gave a jerky nod.

Frieda said, "In Montana you can have up to one ounce of marijuana. It can be for medical or recreational purposes, either one. You cannot possess marijuana and a firearm at the same time. Does Trent keep a firearm?"

I shook my head. Again jerky.

Frieda rolled her eyes and raised her voice. "No you don't know, or no he doesn't?"

I spoke fast. "He doesn't have a gun. Least not when we were together."

Frieda wrote something down, underlined it. I slumped, exhausted, a full shift at the Hideout ahead of me. Frieda was looking for a way to attack Trent's custodial rights, too—get at Trent to get at Em to get at me.

I said, "I have primary custody, and that's it as far as I'm concerned. I'm not trying to go after Trent."

"Except you did."

Heat flooded my face.

Frieda said, "You went after him with your little revolver. Remember? That was attempted murder."

Frieda's circus lights cleared, made a hole, and crowded around the words "attempted murder." Flavored coffee threatened to leave my stomach. I saw no garbage can in which to puke in this carefully appointed office.

Frieda saw that her words had sunk in. "In Montana, attempted murder falls under deliberate homicide, same as murder itself. You have no witness to say it was unloaded."

I narrowed my eyes.

Frieda said, "Harvey took the revolver from you, but you stole it back. We didn't come forward about your crime because I'm your lawyer."

My head reeled. Surely everyone knew it had been unloaded. If Frieda went hard, could she pull it off? What about Harvey? He wasn't my lawyer.

Frieda leered. Bioelectric sparks popped from my extremities. I could lunge at her and sink in my teeth.

Frieda said, "The penalty for deliberate homicide in Montana is a minimum of ten to a maximum of a hundred years."

* * *

The door swung open, and Tamara walked in with the manila folder. A reprint of that same horrible document that Harvey had tossed into my Subaru, dragging Em's fate beneath Frieda and Harvey's mercy. Tamara placed it on the desk in front of Frieda and then backed out without a word, closing the door.

Frieda shook her head and laughed. "God! I've had such a morning."

She opened her desk and retrieved a pint-sized bottle of Dewar's, poured some into the plaid-with-teddy-bears coffee cup, surely ice-cold by now. Then she reached across the desk and took my butter-toffee coffee, lifted the lid, and added some Dewar's to that.

She said, "Just this once."

She pushed my cup toward me then raised her mug in salute, and took a long pull that never would have worked if the coffee had been hot. She gazed into it—swirling, making a tiny tornado—long enough to read someone's fortune.

She settled back into her chair and looked at me. "Where were we?"

Her eyes hazed. "Right. Trent. The truth is Janey, you *do* have me now. I *am* on your side. And *that* is what we both want. I help clients like you stay out of jail. I provide a comprehensive, satisfying, legal way to frustrate an adversary. Trent is your adversary"—waving a finger—"not me."

She said, "If we ignore your desire to hurt Trent, your mental illness will eventually take over and you'll try to do him bodily harm again. That will land him in the grave and you in prison."

She shook her head, reasoning with poor stupid me. "Then what happens to little Emmie?"

She made slicing motions onto her desk. "We need to think of every scenario and plan for Emmie's future, and make sure she is taken care of, and that you. Are. Satisfied. Do you understand now?"

I didn't bother with the head nods. I would have fractured my vertebra. That folder stared at me.

A ping from Frieda's computer. "My next appointment is here."

She slid the folder to me. "Go on and sign these, and we're done for now."

I said, "I need to look at them first."

Frieda's bat in flight reared. "You've had plenty of time for that."

"I only just glanced."

I picked up the folder and made for the door, braced for a spear between the shoulder blades.

"Janey!"

I stopped.

Frieda said, "You bring those papers back, signed, next week. And bring Em. Or you got legal problems you never dreamed of. I'm not talking about traffic tickets, missy. Legal problems of a criminal nature."

My hand gripped the doorknob. I could run through that door. Part of me wanted to do that. But my boots wanted to turn around and go back for Frieda.

I said, "What happened to Logan?"

"Logan?"

"Yes. I want to know why he was murdered."

Frieda's face contorted. "I don't know what happened to Logan. He's dead."

"Did you have him killed?"

"I most certainly did not."

"I will find out if you're lying."

Frieda pressed her fingers into her desk and rose. "You may go ahead and do that, but while you're at it, consider whether it's a good investment of your efforts. Because if you go around Suspicion asking questions about your own attorney, it will send the wrong signals."

She pointed at me. "I can ruin you. If you cross me, it will be your end."

My boots twitched. What were the chances that this woman had nothing to do with my cousin's fate?

I let the boots have their way, stalking toward her, feeling the drunken euphoria of shoot, smash, jab sweep over me with every step toward her desk. This woman who wanted to take my daughter, to put me in prison.

Her eyebrows melted, her lips parted. Cold fear. Delicious fear. Snow on a gunshot wound.

I stopped short as she gave a squeal.

My voice sounded unrecognizable, calm. "Here's the thing, Frieda. If you ever threaten to separate me from my child again, you can have Tamara schedule our next meeting in hell. And you better come swinging a bag of bones."

CHAPTER

48

Pushing Back

I BURST FROM FRIEDA's office to the street, shaking and gulping. Alternating warm and cold air swirled in ribbons over my skin. Winter on the verge of letting go. Soon Libby's hills would feather into green trees, trout streams reflecting blue instead of white.

Despite its charm, I thought of what this town did to my family. Death had closed in from all around. My grandmother, my aunt, and my mother never saw it. They enjoyed glad oblivion until it was too late.

Frieda wanted everything from me.

I had to keep it together through my meeting with Police Chief Tigner in a few hours. I pounded my chest as though to defibrillate. I had a secret reason for coming to see Frieda and it wasn't so she could crow in my face. Now I had to mobilize with time slipping away—only a few seconds to do what I came here to do.

I dabbed superglue to the fold of duct tape in my pocket, then opened the door and pushed the wad into the jamb, fixing it in place.

Much would depend on Tamara. When she locked up tonight, would she turn the key and give the door a firm yank? If so, this would fail.

In five days, Roman would return. The thought bloomed fresh sweat to my neck.

As I tampered with the jamb, Tamara returned. She'd walked Frieda's next client back to her office, and now she looked up and caught me at the door. She did a double take.

I threw the door wide and strode back to reception. "Me again. You got a washroom I could use before I head out?"

Tamara's puzzled stare vanished to a smile. She pointed down the hall.

* * *

I met with Quincy in the employee parking area behind the Hideout kitchen, near the dumpster, which we locked to discourage foraging bears. The Hideout had already kicked into full swing. Harvey would perform again tonight, a rare occurrence that he should take the stage two Saturdays in a row.

Quincy apologized for having taken so long. "I was delayed due to a poaching situation, but we got Fish, Wildlife & Parks on it now."

He took off his hat for me, his expression turning solemn. "I spoke with the crime lab in Missoula."

I listened, neck tensing.

Quincy said, "What happened to Logan was an accident. Just a godawful accident, Janey."

"Wait. You're joking, right?"

"We looked all up and down the area, but you know it'd snowed and it wasn't real clear when he was up there."

"Didn't you talk to the guy he was with? The fishing trip client? It's absolutely clear when he came back. Logan went to the dentist after. He had some problem with his tooth and—"

"Yes, I'm saying, we don't know what time he went for a walk."

"This is ridiculous. It was no accident."

Quincy said, "Or *why* he went walking up there, other than, you know, he's a hiker."

I wanted to shake the brass right off Quincy's uniform.

He said, "They found injuries consistent with a slip down the falls and drowning."

I backed away and dug my fingers into my hair.

Quincy raised pleading hands. "Aw, I know you're upset. This is real frustrating. I'm sorry. Like I said, everyone loved your cousin. He was a real sweet guy."

"Slipping and drowning? If that's all, then what took so long to get the autopsy back?"

He rolled his shoulders, slow and ursine. "It got complicated because he'd been in the water awhile. It obscures things. Time of death."

He paused. "And there were animals . . ."

My hand flew to my face.

"Sorry, I don't know how to make it easy for you."

"There's no way to make it easy. He didn't just fall, Quince! Can't you see that?"

He straightened. "Except he did. That's what happened. He wasn't wearing spiked shoes. You gotta wear spikes if you're going walking up there this time of year. People who aren't from around here don't realize."

"Don't you dare hand me the outsider talk. My cousin knew this mountain with his eyes closed. He was a *guide*."

Quincy lifted his hands to placate. "I'm sorry. Sorry. Just—you wouldn't believe how often this happens. A few years back, during a wedding photo shoot, the groom took a wrong step backward out by Kootenai Falls. That's not even a steep drop like Cinnamon Falls, just a rough churn."

"Steep drop?" I had to rewind, because my anger had flared too hot, and I'd missed something.

I said, "What steep drop? You pulled Logan out of Cloudberry Creek."

Gentle, spilling, pooling in the summer. Cascading torrent in the spring. But still, Cloudberry Creek ran a shallow stairstep.

Quincy said, "We *found* him in Cloudberry Creek. We believe he slipped over at Cinnamon Falls. That's more than a fifty-foot drop. And then he drifted about half a mile to where we pulled him from the creek."

It made no sense. Where was the sicko in the denim jacket and his bent copper slug? Footprints in the snow, the Seattle set, Frieda and Harvey?

A frigid night breeze swept down the hill and broadsided me. I welcomed the impact. I needed to push back against something, and something needed to cool me down.

Quincy said, "That's some gash on the head, Janey. What happened?"

Jude had patched my forehead but I'd removed the bandages.

My fingers went to where I'd hit the liftgate as I'd taken the bullet. "Drunken snowmobiling."

I said, "If Logan went for a waterfall hike, why *wouldn't* he have worn spikes? Something's off. I saw you pull him out of the water. He was just wearing a flannel shirt. Not even a coat."

Quincy shook his head, shrugged. "Look, you're out here on a cold night, you're not wearing your coat."

"Twenty feet from the Hideout!"

"We don't always do what we're supposed to. Maybe he saw a buck and pursued it up the trail. The tox screen hasn't come back yet."

My spine went rigid.

He said, "But at this point, it wouldn't change anything. We'll probably never know where his mind was."

I give a small shake of the head, then a violent one.

Quincy said, in the gentlest voice, "It's just that I'm sorry. Logan fell down a waterfall. And we lost him."

CHAPTER

49

Feeling All Right

"I HAVE QUESTIONS," I said to the voice mail beep.

Up on stage, Harvey sat at the piano. The Saturday night crowd lost their minds on the opening riff. Four notes, a pause, then eight more and a vibraslap—a sound like a rattlesnake in a culvert. Harvey bought it just for this song: "Feeling All Right." The crowd whooped. They poured from their seats onto the dance floor.

Harvey swayed into the refrain and looked directly at me. Roxie gave a shout and dragged a random couple to dance by the stage. Signature Roxie move. She would stop serving and dance her ass off for one minute, then resume taking orders.

Stetson in place, Maycie Gaynor strode up to me with a bottle of Bud and leaned on the bar. I hadn't realized she was already here among the customers.

She gestured at Harvey with the bottle. "Interesting song. The lyrics sound like he's feeling good, but really, he's singing about two people after a fight. Something between them is coming to an end. Check out how Harvey's watching you."

I looked over and listened.

The song said it all.

Suspicioners reveled. The Logan tragedy—behind them.

Maycie set her empty Bud on the counter. "If you'll find me another one of these, I'll spot whatever you're having. We can grab someplace quiet and talk."

* * *

Maycie Gaynor was Libby born, just like Mom and Aunt Sylvie. The three were grade school friends. Then Maycie's family moved here to Suspicion while she was in the sixth grade. Later, after my mom finished high school, my grandmother died. Aunt Sylvie moved to Coeur d'Alene, but my mom moved here to Suspicion. She and Maycie reunited.

But that became a long-distance friendship when Maycie went off to serve in Iraq as a corpsman, a Fleet Marine Force medic during Operation Phantom Fury—the Second Battle of Fallujah.

Then, Maycie abruptly switched to MOS 5811, the marine version of military police. Maycie confided in me about it one night at the Hideout. She'd witnessed something while trying to save a life. A soldier had been mortally wounded and died beneath her hands. But given what was going down on the battlefield, Maycie couldn't work out how he'd sustained his injuries. She believed friendly fire was to blame—not the accidental kind. Murder.

She reported it but nothing happened. It haunted her to the point she switched her MOS and extended her tour for another four years.

That happened around the time my mother died. Maycie flew home for the funeral. Seven years later, she stood by me again, arm over my shoulder, for Aunt Sylvie's funeral. I always secretly, guiltily, fearfully, wondered if their same fate might one day claim Maycie. They were all born in Libby. Why had she escaped?

But I knew why: Maycie was a Gaynor, not a Hendee. Maycie was not susceptible to the curse. It meant I could keep her.

At the end of her tour of duty, Maycie returned to Montana and entered the police academy at Bozemen and earned her degree in criminal justice at MSU. The job suited her, and she worked her way up to a detective shield, then returned to Suspicion. Now she served as our county coroner in cowboy boots, drawing from both her medical and law enforcement backgrounds as a death investigator.

I liked Quincy. I trusted Maycie.

* * *

We stood by the high-tops surrounding the scruffy pool table. Harvey and the band still rocked the stage, but Maycie and I could hear each other over here. One of my tables attempted to catch my eye and I shouldered them out of view.

I said to Maycie, "Quincy told me the whole thing was just a big misunderstanding and Logan went sliding down a waterfall by pure bad luck."

She sipped her Bud, shrugged, her gaze following to the band over in the great hall. "Probably true."

"'Probably.'"

"You are welcome to the autopsy report. I don't see you getting hysterical at the sight of a broken bones diagram, and it won't include any investigation photos of Logan's body. You could request that separately, but I recommend against it."

She looked me in the eye. "My ME found an unexplained death. Hear what I'm saying? Unexplained. An accident is a type of explanation. If Quincy calls it an accident, that's coming from *his* end of the investigation, not mine."

I explored this, divining an interpretation.

Maycie said, "It might help to know Logan didn't suffer. From what my ME told me, he was probably unconscious at the time of drowning."

"From the fall?"

"Possibly."

I was starting to understand. Maycie was relaying individual facts to me and interpreting nothing.

I said, "If Logan had been unconscious, how would we know if it happened before he'd gone over Cinnamon Falls, or after?"

"We wouldn't."

He'd been in the water for days. Animals had gotten to him.

I said, "Quincy didn't mention Logan could have been unconscious before he even entered the water."

She waved it off. "No harm to Quince. He hasn't exactly had miles of experience, and it's not like he ever wore a detective shield. Between you and me, I think the only other person who applied for police chief at the time was Gary."

"Oh, dear God."

"Yeah. Happy to have Quincy Tigner now, right? Listen, the simplest explanation is probably the best. That your cousin slipped and fell. But you can try to get the sheriff involved. I'm not saying you'll get much further. If you want, I can put in a word."

She let that hang. A "yes" flitted to the tip of my tongue and stopped. She'd warned that bringing in the sheriff may not take it any further, but Maycie would ensure a full investigation went down.

She said, "I gotta ask . . ."

My eyes lit, because her expression had changed.

She leaned closer, searching my face. "Last I saw Logan alive, it was here at the Hideout. It was a Saturday night. Something went down between you two. You looked mad. I saw him put something in your apron."

I swallowed. Maycie's eyes pinned mine. She was near retirement and had more investigative experience than the entire Suspicion police force combined, and half the sheriff's department. With that one statement, not even a question, it felt like she'd whisked me into an interrogation room with my pulse points wired to a polygraph.

I didn't dare relinquish her gaze, though my head lowered as my eyes held hers.

She said, "It might have been the last time anyone around here saw him. What was it he put in your apron?"

My gunshot wound throbbed. I licked my lips, blinked. My mind raced.

The guy at the far table who'd been trying to get my attention shouted, "Waitress!" and banged an empty bottle on the table. Someone else echoed him.

I said, "I got customers. Logan went to the dentist when he got back from his fishing trip. I wasn't the last one who saw him."

There would be no sheriff's investigation. How could I have even considered it?

That didn't mean I was done.

CHAPTER 50

Percent

PONCE WORE TWO thick salt-and-pepper braids. His vest colors displayed the Rank Strangers Outlaw Motorcycle Club, 1%, with a skeleton resting beneath a leafless tree. Other waitresses, like Yun or Roxie, always popped the cap on his Michelob Ultra when they heard his Road King pull in. We liked to get him started as soon as possible with his meatloaf, his beers, and his one whiskey.

By the time the band got to rocking, Ponce usually took inventory of the revelers and declared them all a bunch of tourists, though every soul here in springtime was a Suspicion native, born and bred—with the exception of Cast Iron, the very person who would drive Ponce's drunk ass home. Cast Iron was from California. When Ponce finished his whiskey, he'd grumble about tourists as his brother in chrome led him out the door.

To Ponce, a Stranger—a Rank Stranger OMC brother—could never be an outsider.

Tonight I needed to talk to Ponce. He rolled in late after the band had already kicked in and Gabe wanted to close the kitchen. It irked me that Ponce came in alone. I needed Cast Iron, too. I was tending bar tonight because my gunshot wound kept me from carrying food trays, but I told Yun I'd take care of Ponce.

He'd already downed his first Michelob Ultra while still removing his wallet, glasses, and phone and lighting a smoke.

He didn't even look up. "Meatloaf and mashed potatoes. I want an extra roll. Gimme real butter, not them crap squares you pawn off on everybody. That other girl tried to pull that shit last time. I'll take another Michelob, too. Get a cold one from the back."

I said, "Can I have one of those?"

He looked up at me, possibly for the first time in all the years I'd waited on him. I pointed at his American Spirits and he passed one to me. Tossed the lighter on the table.

"You wanna fuckin' sit?" He said it as though if he had to endure my company he might head-butt the table, but he was raised right, so he did make the offer.

I said, "It's against the rules."

He looked at me smoking the American Spirit while I was supposed to be waiting tables—ignoring a rule about smoking but not one for sitting.

I said, "I'm still processing what happened to Logan."

His expression changed, and he nodded. "He was a good kid."

"Is it true he was a prospect? I mean, I know he was interested in joining the Stranger brotherhood."

"Don't see you wearing a patch. RS business ain't for no one but club members." Ponce looked with pain upon the emptiness of his beer bottle.

I said, "Seems to me that if Logan was being made a prospect, what happened might rub you the wrong way."

"Can I help you? Cuz I could sure use another beer."

"Yeah, Ponce, matter of fact you can help me. Has to do with what happened to Logan. I can't manage it on my own. I'm thinking if his death didn't sit well with the club, this might be an opportunity to make things right."

Although an ashtray sat at the corner of the table, Ponce tapped his cigarette to the empty beer. The embers sizzled. His gaze had gone distant.

He brought his eyes slowly back to mine. "Tell you what. I changed my mind. I want fries instead a mashed potatoes. But I want gravy for the fries. Put that on the side. And I want ketchup, too. Gravy and ketchup, both. Don't let Gabe give you no shit. You need to write this down, Janey, cuz you been goddamned forgetful lately."

Paint the world in glitter. Ponce knew my name.

I crossed one arm and took a drag with my free hand. "The Strangers' part would be tiny. Just some inquiries. But there's money in it for you."

"Money."

"Sure."

"How much?"

I licked my lips. "Two grand."

I'd have to clear it with Roman. If Roman were leading me to my death, then I'd be no worse off. But if he was playing straight, then it was in his best interest to find out who killed my cousin, because that same creep stole Baltazar's drop money.

Except Roman's contact info had fizzed inside my golden, brown, delicious phone.

Waving cash I didn't have at a one-percenter, even without specifics or a firm deal, stepped closer toward getting myself killed than getting out of trouble.

Ponce slapped tiny little glasses on his nose and started reading on his phone. The screen showed indianz.com.

Conversation over.

If only Cast Iron had come. Cast Iron was half Ponce's age—in his twenties like Logan and me. Cast Iron acted like a translator between the Strangers and us normies, and he kept Ponce in check. Also, Cast Iron had been Logan's friend, and I hoped he'd advocate for him.

I slipped my American Spirit into Ponce's empty bottle, then turned to battle Gabe for the off-menu requests.

CHAPTER

51

The Scented Night

AROUND MIDNIGHT, I left Yun to take over, did a partial close-out, a safe drop, the books, and headed to my station wagon.

The Hideout would keep at it another hour or two, but not for me or the band. We let the customers down easy. Jude had left thirty minutes ago. Quincy's police cruiser was still parked in the lot, and my heart skipped. I still didn't know whether to trust him or keep watching my back, but I was getting used to that scent in the night: this perfume of fear.

Beneath the floodlights, a figure was leaning against my Subaru. Harvey.

His hands shot up. "Don't worry. You don't have to go getting your toy pistol out."

"What makes you think I haven't upgraded it?"

He stuck his fists in his pockets, leaned against my door. "That what you were talking to Ponce about?"

He'd been performing in another room and couldn't possibly have seen that.

I said, "Nice. Now you got spies on me."

He opened his jacket and pulled out a flask. "It ain't like that, and you know it. If I did something, they'd be tellin' *you*. Everybody tells everyone everything."

He offered me a sip. I shook my head.

He said, "Sorry, forgot you don't drink. You want breakfast? We can see if the firehouse is open."

"Hell, no, Harvey. I'm going to bed."

I was not going home to bed. I was driving to Libby to break into his wife's office.

I made for my car door, which he leaned against, and he moved to let me pass.

He said, "Look. I hate all this between us. It hurts me. You been my friend, and that's damaged, but I want you to know I'm sorry about what's happened."

"Not what's happened. What's happen-*ning*. Ongoing."

I climbed in the station wagon and slammed the door, and saw my window was down. *Shit.* After I'd gotten to the Hideout, I'd found more blood and cleaned it, then neglected to roll up the window. It must have been open my entire shift.

Harvey wiped his face and leaned his elbow on the inside of my door. "You didn't take Emmie on over to Frieda's office like I asked you to."

"Like you ordered me."

"You seem lively for someone heavily medicated."

"Harvey! Those pills are antipsychotics. They're not supposed to put me under for surgery."

Harvey saw my lucidity just like Roxie did. I needed to get out of here. I dug into my purse for keys—no joy. Not in my pockets, either. *Why didn't I have Roy fix that stupid dome light?*

Harvey said, "You're paranoid. Frieda got you scared. But she's looking out for you and Em. You're unstable, hon. And Trent is a fuck-up. Mark my words. You don't want Em getting thrown into the system if something goes wrong. Frieda has flaws but she loves children, and she adores Emmie."

The most unthinkable thing under the frozen stars happened: I made tears in front of Harvey Elliot.

Stupid, painful tears. Acid on my skin. I hoped he didn't see them, but of course he did. Even tipsy.

The more I fought them, the harder they pushed through my eyes and tumbled free. Then they sank into my throat in the corporeal mutiny that is sobbing. Loud, rolling bird cries.

He said, "Aw, it's all right, honey."

He patted me. This madness made me want to shriek. I would have bitten his hand, but I feared it would only make the horrible, wet throat *ca-caws* worse. I couldn't even pull the Röhm on him because he knew it was a junk gun.

He said, "Nobody's trying to take your kid. That is a fact before Jesus. It's just a precaution. Okay? You hear me?"

More sobs. This was unbearable.

He said, "I mean it, now."

He kept patting. God, he kept patting my shoulder like he was burping a baby. His heavy heat filled the inside of the Subaru despite the freezing temperature. Why couldn't I work my mouth to tell him to fuck off?

My keys dangled from the ignition. This whole time, with the window down, I'd left my damn keys in the ignition.

He said, "I'll tell Frieda you'll take Em to the office next week for sure."

The heat of him inside my hallowed station wagon. My safe space. The only place left I could call my own. He'd been performing, and his sweaty overworked heat orb suffocated me.

But—

He smelled like perfume. Crisp, cool spice. My shudders stopped. My breathing: restored.

I said, "How's it going with Rox?"

I looked up at Harvey, hitched a breath.

I said, "How's the thing with Roxie?"

"What thing?"

I opened the door and shoved it against him. He stumbled back against the sky. His body heat dissipated to fresh air.

I got out and glared, shaking my head in mock commiseration. "The *thing* between you two. Frieda thought you and *I* had a *thing* going. What would have given her that idea, right? Unless *you* gave it to her. Because right now you smell a whole lot like Roxie's perfume."

He glowered. His face contorted like he wanted to throw a fist through my windshield.

I heated my voice. "I don't get the *point*! Why did you tell her it was *me*? Cheating is cheating!"

Harvey shouted back, "Because you're not a *threat*!"

He spun away, then turned and got in my face. "She sees you as stupid. On paper you're still some brat out of juvenile detention, pregnant, someone who gets caught shoplifting. *You*, she can accept. She sees it as some kind of male urge because men are inferior beings."

He pointed at the building. "Freida would see *her* as a threat."

Stunned, I looked at the Hideout. Much love to Rox, but she was taking my meds for fun and probably fencing them as "black market gold." *She* was the threat?

He pushed against the hood of my station wagon, leaned in. "She almost caught me and Roxie one time. I told her it was you, and it was a one-night stand. A mistake. You're no threat to anyone."

I understood what I was. The crazy bird. The one who fixed up for nobody, wore practical clothes but showed up clean and neat. I worked too much because deep down I believed my romantic partner had no obligations to me. I wore my lack of self-worth like a sign.

Roxie and I were opposite types of roadhouse waitresses. I could drag a rowdy twice my size by the ear—as long as I had someone like Cast Iron to back me up. Roxie could earn double my tips and get through an entire weekend without hurting anyone's feelings.

With all Harvey's trips out of town, he'd never had any cardiologist appointments. The only thing wrong with his heart was that he was making time with Roxie. That's why he kept missing the Big Bald Luck games.

I folded my arms. "You're in love with her?"

Harvey breathed in, nodded.

I said, "You thinking you want to leave Frieda over this?"

He blinked like *Yes*, but he said, "Frieda's a hard woman to leave. She got her hooks in the Hideout a long time ago, and if I leave her, she'll have my butt in jail faster than the ink can dry on the divorce paperwork. I never did anything illegal until she blackmailed me."

I snorted. Frieda's calling card.

He said, "She's rotten on the inside. Didn't used to be that way. I'm here to tell you. She used to be really special."

"Spare me the 'once was a peach' tale. You already bored me with that one."

I glanced at the Subaru, put my hands on my hips. Jude was waiting at my place, believing we'd head to his fishing cabin. Except I needed to break into Frieda's office. Jude thought he might talk me out of that.

I was about to truly burn a bridge with Harvey—one more person who'd just as soon see me dead.

I looked him in the eye. "You run interference with Frieda on that Emmie paperwork. Because I won't be bringing Em down to Frieda's office. Not next week, not ever. And I damn sure won't sign those nasty documents. We both know it's not in Em's best interests. It's just Frieda's way of keeping me on her string."

I slid behind the driver's seat. "Frieda needs to forget all that stuff, and you need to help her forget."

"Frieda doesn't listen to me."

"You better *make* her listen. Or else Frieda's gonna hear about Roxie."

CHAPTER

52

The Break-in

I STOOD IN MY driveway. Jude was fast asleep in his Sequoia, seat let back.

I tapped the roof. He was not a man to startle awake, and in fact he barely stirred. He opened one eye. I waved. Then I noticed his hand on his pistol.

He eased out of his Sequoia and stretched, moving his neck from right to left.

I said, "You do know there've been a lot of break-ins lately."

"Those turned out to be a wolf looking for food."

Right. Except a wolf didn't break into my hatchback.

I said, "Glad to know you're capable of sleep. Look, I'm going to Libby. I need to do this."

I braced for his attempt to talk me out of it, but he said, "I'll drive you."

"Jude. You have clinic tomorrow. I can't involve you in this and I can't let you go without sleep."

He waved me off. "I went without sleep on the trauma unit, and I do not intend to break into anything. Just drive."

He gestured toward our vehicles. "Look at your car, and look at mine."

My poor twenty-odd-year-old Subaru Legacy station wagon wore primer splotches to keep the rust from going infectious. Jude drove a respectable black Toyota Sequoia like a lot of people in the county.

He said, "Yours would draw attention and it can easily be traced to you. With mine, it's anonymous."

"But your license plates."

"Take a look."

I did. Snow partially covered the back one—enough to obscure the numbers. I checked the front and saw the same thing. The springtime warming had begun a steady melt across the mountainside. How did he get it to stick?

He said, "I went downstairs into the clinic tonight. Darcy always works this miracle during the holidays where she flocks the windows with snow."

He pointed to a spray can in the rear passenger foot well. "I found that in the storeroom."

* * *

The door to Frieda's office building did not budge. My duct tape had failed.

I felt exposed. Anyone who passed would know I had no business loitering here.

Two more tugs, but nothing. I glanced up the road. At my insistence, Jude waited in his Sequoia well away from the building—in a lot hidden among other cars, lights off.

Perhaps Tamara had noticed my folded bit of duct tape. Or maybe I'd failed to stick it properly. Either way, someone would find the wad. If not today, then next week. They'd work out I'm the one who—

One last yank. The door opened. My heart gave a thrill.

I strode past Tamara's kidney-shaped desk and her industrial-quality sticky-note system. Down the hall, Frieda's office stood last on the right. Only now did I realize the other offices seemed vacant. They had monitors, but the cables hung free.

I snapped on the nitrile gloves Jude had brought for me and tried Frieda's door. Locked. "Damn it!"

I turned around. It never occurred to me she'd lock her door. A locked office inside a locked office building. Office people were an alien species.

I could try to pick this lock. But although I spent my teenage years on the streets, it's not like I'd become some master criminal. I'd risk damage like what had happened to my own door. Frieda would know.

I went back to Tamara's sanctuary and opened her desk drawer, found keys. Good old Tamara. Also, it looked like some of those sticky notes included passwords—she'd written "cookies" and "password," but with numbers instead of vowels.

Oh, Tamara. We should do another butter-toffee coffee and have ourselves a heart-to-heart.

I took the keys back and tried the lock, one by one. Each key failed. Every. Damn. One.

Headlights washed through the corridor. I dove.

Through the windows, a vehicle rolled along the street, washing the snowmelt red in its brake lights. It continued until it disappeared.

I took a shaky breath and climbed back to my feet. Thought. Thought harder.

I ran my hand over the top of the jamb. Found a key. It fit the lock.

I rode into Frieda's office on a wave of relief.

Probably, the key had sat on the molding ever since the subcontractor installed the doors. I knew this from Trent. Carpenters popped the spares above the jambs to keep all the lookalikes from getting mixed up.

I swept the office with my penlight and settled on the bookshelf, under which stood Frieda's lateral files. If she kept that damned thing locked, I was liable to shoot, smash, and jab.

It opened on a glide.

CHAPTER

53

Judge

I DUG THROUGH FILES until my eyes went numb, then finally spotted something: a charity dinner.

Frieda had hosted it to raise money for children with cleft palates. She'd held the dinner right there at her house on Cable Hill (probably while I sanded floors in my little tear-down next door) and in attendance were Quincy Tigner, Doug Barkling, and two judges: Abigail Brontez and Mitch Goshen. Both of those judges had featured on Jude's list.

I sat on the short-pile carpet with the file across my knees, scanning details. Each attendee's name showed a subsequent donation to the cause, from Quincy Tigner's hundred-dollar contribution to a five-thousand-dollar one from Judge Goshen. Frieda Kanjo and Harvey Elliot matched their combined donations and then rounded up, so the entire dinner raised $20,000.

That dinner had represented a lot of power under Frieda's own roof. That must have felt intoxicating.

On her desk stood a PC with a Mystify screensaver chasing in vector lines. I wondered if one of Tamara's sticky-note passwords applied to Frieda's computer.

* * *

The "cookies" password got me in. Frieda didn't strike me as a "cookies" type.

Computers and I were never besties, so it took over an hour and a check-in with Jude before I found something. Then I discovered the folder called Misc.

Under the Misc folder sat another folder called MGosh for—I assumed—Judge Mitch Goshen, and in *that* folder I found photos. They meant nothing to me. Some guy (Goshen?) talking to or walking with various people; women, to be exact. They also meant nothing. Until the hidden camera porn.

It showed Goshen with a woman, and he stood while she knelt in front of him. It caught his face, but not hers. Then in the next image, both faces displayed. Same woman, different sex act. She'd thrown back her head. Her bra spilled beneath her breasts. Her thigh looked taut as she clutched him.

His face heralded God's holy rapture. She seemed . . . theatrical. Maybe she got paid to do this sort of thing. Or she knew the camera had its eye on them and she had her own reasons for wanting to look good.

Okay, fine. Goshen had indiscreet sex. Did anyone really care?

Maybe he was married. Or these women were sex workers.

Still: Who cared? Would the goofball actually throw a case over a week in the news?

I should have slipped some high-tech drive into Frieda's computer and downloaded the photos. But I didn't have a drive or know how to use one. So, I hoisted my phone and ultra-low-tech snapped a photo of the image on her screen. Then advanced to the next image and did it again. One by one, over and over, until I had them all.

Nowhere among Frieda's electronic files—and I pored over them—could I find anything on Judge Abigail Brontez.

* * *

Dannie met with a client in Bigfork, then as the shadow of the peak spread to full dark across Suspicion, she joined us at Jude's secret hideout. She brought a deck of cards, and Jude had a jar of pennies that had accumulated long enough that several had sprouted wheat. He said whenever he had a pocket full of change, he'd throw the pennies in the jar. His father had done that, too—same jar.

The elder Doc Summers had been our dentist a few years before Jude entered practice, but was quick to retire. I don't know what that said about the dental hygiene of our Suspicion citizenry: either really good or really bad.

Tonight we'd run through Texas Hold'em and five-card draw, two staples of our Big Bald Luck games. Maybe we'd get to stud, but I preferred to put that off until after Jude had a chance to soak in what he'd learned. The man had a sharp brain, but I'd never known anyone to operate on four hours' sleep and catnaps. That was his default. Not just since I'd kicked in the door to his life.

* * *

At midnight, after Texas Hold'em, we took a break outside to stretch and gaze at the pond. I showed Dannie and Jude my photos of Judge Goshen. Jude recognized one of the women as a patient—not the one from the sex photos. So that gave me one name. Dannie confirmed the man in the photos was Goshen but didn't know any of the women.

No internet connectivity at Jude's cabin, so Dannie said, "Send me what you got. I'll figure it out."

We went back inside and Dannie showed Jude the ropes for five-card draw. Not too many ropes. She'd play against him in a few days.

After Dannie left, I settled into bed while Jude crashed in his easy chair and studied poker videos.

I said, "Isn't your brain saturated after playing all night?"

"I'm not watching poker anymore. I'm looking at Guy Hamm's assets."

"Seriously?"

"Know thine enemy. Guy will try to play head games. He's been doing it all his life."

"How did you even get access?"

He shook his head. "Some of it's in the public record. It depends. Now that I hear how he's treated you, I have double reason to go after him."

He rubbed his eyes, and I could see his exhaustion. I thought—and almost said—he ought to quit that recliner and try stretching out here next to me.

* * *

I got called into the school.

Something rotten had happened. Em was safe but she was in trouble. Big trouble. They wouldn't discuss it over the phone.

Most kids attended Logger Elementary down in Greater Suspicion. Not the handful of children on Cable Hill. Cable Hill Elementary was a one-room schoolhouse of the Laura Ingalls Wilder ilk. It had three teachers and one principal. Children learned inside a massive classroom like a church—including steeple and bell tower, and the bell sounded for school-in and school-out. Once a week, a different sixth grader earned the exquisite privilege to ring that bell.

Children *never* raised their voices inside. Cable Hill children, from kindergarten to sixth grade, shared a great hall for their schooling and understood the taboo of a loud voice, and teachers groomed them to be little gentlefolk. Recess was a different matter. Once outside, they raised hell.

As I trotted up the steps, Dannie called. I doubled back, tried to score privacy. Parents were collecting their children, teachers directing traffic—vehicular or trail-goers. I found some tall bushes off the lawn and stuck my finger in my ear.

It sounded like Dannie was talking to me through her terrain rocket's sound system. "Hey lady, I figured it out about Judge Goshen."

"What'd you find?"

"He's dirty, all right."

"In what sense?"

She said, "Those ladies in those photos? I found out who they were through an image search. The one thing they had in common—they all stood before him in court."

I unpacked this for a moment.

She said, "When you sent me those photos, I could see the date/time stamp underneath. It looked like he was consorting with them around the time they were appearing before him in court. One was for solicitation, one was for drug charges, theft."

I said, "Have there been complaints? I mean, come on."

"So, yeah, here's the thing. Judicial Conduct is funny. If you complain about a judge, it goes to a commission—made up of judges, and overseen by a judge. If these judges find that the complaint is valid, it's public. Otherwise, it's not."

"But there's a freedom of information act."

"Not when judges are watching other judges. The FOIA has a blind spot. A judge could have a dozen complaints, and we'd never know."

I snorted. "'All animals are equal, but some animals are more equal than others.'"

"Hey, *Animal Farm*. That's pretty good."

I felt embarrassed pleasure over the compliment. Even though my reading was slow, I did enjoy it.

Dannie said, "It damn sure looks like Frieda was bribing Judge Goshen, if not extorting him."

I groaned. Familiar territory. Begin with blackmail, move on to a bribe.

I looked up at the school doors. "Thanks, Dannie. I'm late for an appointment."

“Okay, but Janey?”

“Yeah?”

“I’ve been reading more about the Red King and the Seattle set. They’re scary people. Everywhere they go, there’s carnage. This is bad, hon. You should go to the police or the FBI or something.”

“They’ve infiltrated the police and the FBI, *and* the courts. I don’t know who’s tainted and who’s not.”

“Then you have to run.”

“They’ll hunt me down.”

I frowned, pressed my lips together. At least I had a friend to share my stomach acid.

She said, “You’ve got to figure something out. They’re going to kill you.”

CHAPTER

54

The Hatch

THE SCHOOL HAD me meeting with Em's teacher, Mykayla Jansen, and Principal Zarate. He kept an office at the end of the breezeway.

Mrs. Jansen skipped the usual smile and handshake. "Miss Hendee, I'm glad you came."

"Of course."

She ushered me in the direction of Zarate's office, and just outside of it, Em sat with her school bag, her eyes pinched and red-rimmed. She rose when she saw me.

Mrs. Jansen said to her, "Wait here until we're done, Emmie."

I said, "Actually, please give us a minute."

I jerked my head to Em. Jansen's eyes bored into our backs as we strode for privacy.

I spun around and knelt before my daughter. "Spill it. Every word."

Em took a shuddering breath but spoke without weeping. "I did it again. I brought in another backpack candy store."

I blinked through fury. I'd given her permission for this—one time. But she had to know that once the school objected, she couldn't keep doing it.

Em said, "I did it knowing they were just going to steal it again like last time."

"Who?"

"Julia. Darren. And . . ."

I waited.

"Sierra."

I gasped. Her best friend. The one who lived near our little house on Cable Hill, with the mom who could make torta ricotta.

I said, "And everyone got caught?"

She said, "And Mrs. Jansen."

"What do you mean?"

"She confiscated the candy, but then she ate some."

Em saw that as stealing. She'd bought the candy from her own saved-up nickels and dimes.

Her tears flowed. "Mom, I *love* Mrs. Jansen! It was awful!"

I nodded, hugged my daughter. "Okay. I'll talk to them."

She pushed away from me. "No! You have to let me tell you. It was bad. I got so mad that first time they stole my backpack store that I did an awful thing."

I swallowed, stared at my daughter. "Tell me what you did, Em."

She rocked her shoulders, her breathing heavy. Then she looked up at me. "I mixed spider eggs in with the candy."

My jaw dropped.

She said, "I found them under the house."

"Those children ate spider eggs?"

"No. They tore open the candy inside wrappers. But—the eggs hatched!"

"Did they eat *actual* spiders?"

"No, Mom, they just got scared."

I was getting the picture. "What kind of spiders?"

"Cellar spiders. Daddy longlegs."

I exhaled. Cellar spiders were about as harmless as you could get. But they were big.

She looked away, her face defiant. "When they took my backpack, I said, 'Have fun with your spider snacks,' but they just ran off."

Em looked at me, her expression returning to horror. "I thought the kids would see those baby spiders and freak out. I couldn't believe it. They stuck their hands in there without looking."

She gazed at me with tear-filled eyes, her voice in a whisper. "But then it was Mrs. Jansen, too. I never thought she'd *eat* some."

I said, "Did your teacher eat a spider?"

"No. But they crawled on her."

CHAPTER

55

He's Back

"YOU'RE SUSPENDED," I told Em as I drove her home.

Suspended, thank God, and not bounced. I'd spent forty-five minutes lobbying her case before Mrs. Jansen, who advocated expulsion, and Mr. Zarate, who ultimately allowed her to stay.

Em's face reflected the level of mortification I would hope to see. No one at Cable Hill Elementary got suspended. If it happened in the past, they only spoke of it in whispers. When Em had told me the kids stole her backpack store and that she'd deal with it, I never dreamed she'd rain hellfire. I'd grown up in a wolf world that would have laughed off Em's deed as trivial, but on Cable Hill, she was a serial killer.

We headed toward my garage apartment to grab a few things, namely her train case. No one was home yet at Trent's—the teardown, the seed of potential in the beautiful neighborhood. My attempt at blooming our family into a different flower.

Fog swept us in such a way that a person down the valley would look up and see us swallowed by clouds. Here, the fog tripped six inches aboveground at bicycle speed. It engulfed the Subaru for a quarter mile, cleared, and then swallowed us again.

Em's brows creased. "I'm the one who's stupid. I should have just hung out with Isabelle."

I'd never heard her mention this name. "Isabelle's in your class?"

"She's the only other one in Advanced, like me. She tried to sit next to me during lunch, but I walked away. None of the kids like her, and Mrs. Jansen doesn't like her, either."

I frowned. "Why don't they like her?"

"She's just weird. Wears weird stuff. Off by herself. Sherry was right."

"Sherry?" My heart gave a skip.

Em nodded. "I told Sherry about Isabelle, and Sherry said, 'Whenever you have a chance to be generous, be generous.'"

"Sherry said that?"

My head swam. Even I, right now, hearing Sherry's words as I drove through this cloud, felt I'd learned something I could reuse for the rest of my life. "Whenever you have a chance to be generous, be generous." Sherry had told my daughter the thing you're supposed to say, at the time you should say it. For people like Sherry—not even a mother—this came at zero effort.

Em said, "I just wanted to go back to being friends with Sierra, but she stopped talking to me. Then she stole my backpack store and laughed."

I said, "Why do you think Mrs. Jansen doesn't like Isabelle?"

"I don't know, but I don't think she likes me anymore, either."

My impulse was to correct her, except she was probably right, and it didn't help to lie.

I said, "You know, I struggle with reading and writing, and you occasionally point stuff out for me. It's helpful. But have you ever corrected Mrs. Jansen in class?"

Her eyes snapped, and she looked at me. "Not like that."

I said, "Sometimes people get things wrong, and you just have to let them have their mistakes, even if it's right up there in front of everybody."

I stole a glance at her, then looked back at the road. Mist flecked the windshield and I used the fluid, but it smeared and the wipers squeaked.

Then I did a double take. The SUV two cars back looked familiar. It had its headlights on. For a moment it looked like Roman's moon buggy.

"Mom?"

"Yeah. Um, let's not go back to the apartment just yet. Let's get ice cream."

A Rosauers van switched lanes in front of the SUV, and I hoped to God I was mistaken about Roman. He wasn't due back for another four days. Fog knotted between cars and distorted my view.

Em scanned the cold landscape. "Ice cream? Don't they only serve it in summer?"

"Hot apple pie, maybe."

If that was Roman, I didn't want to lead him to my home. But above all, no way in hell would I allow him near my daughter.

I turned right down Lone Pine and watched. The SUV passed and did not turn. And yet I felt sure. It was him. It was him.

* * *

Tears sprang. What was I thinking when I'd reached out to the Red King's army? Did I really believe I'd survive this bargain?

I made conversation to cover my anxiety. "Em, what do you want to be when you grow up?"

"Teacher."

My pulse threaded. Even though he hadn't turned to follow me, I got the sense he was watching. I checked the rearview mirror, the side mirror. No SUV.

I said, "If teaching is your first choice, what would be your second?"

She said, "Um, mapmaker?"

That grabbed me. When they'd been studying Italy, Em had drawn a map of the country with an inverted V for Mount

Vesuvius, and a dog biting into a torta ricotta. I'd thought it clever. I asked her what she got for a grade, but she'd told me she did it for fun.

Maps were digitized these days. They still needed mapmakers, though—to work with geologists, like the mines they had around here. A tear trickled down my left cheek, and I was glad it happened outside her view since she sat to my right.

A large black SUV advanced up the side road.

I gasped, then recovered for Em's sake. "You should tell your dad and Sherry. That you want to be a teacher, or a mapmaker. It's important they know that."

"I did already. Sherry said a mapmaker's called a cart—a cartographer."

Of course Sherry would know the word.

"Mom? What's wrong?"

I wept on both sides of my face now. I kept tissue—actually, scavenged fast food napkins—in the console.

Em's voice became small. "Why can't I stay with you at the apartment?"

"I'll be honest with you, honey. We agreed to tell each other the truth. The apartment's not safe. Not for either of us right now. Okay? Can you not tell anyone?"

It should have made her more anxious, but she accepted this with a nod. The mist turned to drizzle, and the wipers were finally able to clear the windshield.

Roman's Q7 pulled up behind me.

* * *

Two minutes later, we pulled into Suspicious Perks.

I told her, "Go in and use the washroom. Wait for me there. If you don't see me within fifteen minutes, come out and have the cashier call your dad."

I put the Subaru in park, biting my lip. "Or Sherry."

"Mom, what's—"

"Go!"

She went. This was a wolf upbringing. Straight-up wolf life.

I hunkered in the Subaru, hands shaking, and pulled out the phone—the band phone. Like for Harvey's stage musicians, but in reality, his bandits. I didn't have Roman's number.

He pulled in, his gaze tracking my daughter entering the coffee shop. I brought up my contact info and shared it blindly via AirDrop. It had me listed as "Band Coordinator," along with a phone number. Only one other AirDrop user, RR, appeared in the vicinity. I waited.

Roman stepped out of his Q7 and walked behind my Subaru.

This man needed to evaporate. I couldn't talk to him with my daughter right there in the café. If we spoke face-to-face, publicly, that would be bad for me and terrible for Em.

He'd be angry I hadn't called. He might pull a gun, force me to come with him. Knowing Dannie's tale about the Red King's bloodthirst, I'd never escape with my life. Sweat drenched my hair as I watched Roman circle in my car mirrors.

"Come on, come on," I said, jarring my steering wheel.

One step shy of my window, Roman stopped, looked at his phone. The breath stilled in my lungs. I kept my face forward, my eyes pinned to the side mirror where I could only see him torso to neck. He typed something, and a moment later I received his contact info bundle through the same Air Drop. Then he stretched, turned, and walked back to his SUV.

CHAPTER

56

An Important Phone Call

I called Roman. We each sat in our own vehicle, a fine drizzle at our windshields. I kept the wipers going because it felt like a clear field of vision mattered, even though it only availed me to a view of shamrocks in the Suspicious Perks window.

"My phone got destroyed after we talked," I said.

"You greet me like that? I haven't seen you in a while. Heard you were hurt."

"Please, Roman, I can't talk."

A grunt. Then, "Did you learn anything about our list?"

"A little."

"You either have answers for me or you're no use."

My breath caught, my voice strained: "I have answers."

"Good. See? Let's meet."

"You told me to avoid meeting you in public."

He paused. "Are you worried I'd hurt your little girl? That's not my style. Look how independent she is there in the coffee shop."

"Later. Please."

"This afternoon."

"Not this afternoon. I have the card games. That schedule's carved in stone."

"Really," he said, a bend in his tone.

The drizzle and the windshield wipers sounded loud. As a youth I believed I could escape people who bite, that I could run away to my mountain home. I looked to my right but through the passenger window I saw only his door. He sat somewhere above.

He said, "We're having a crisis of trust. I thought we were doing well. You and I had rapport in the beginning but that's gone to shit. I haven't heard from you, and your priorities are messed up."

I wanted to dash in and snatch my daughter, then duck out the back. Abandon my Subaru, still running. Ditch my life with nothing but the clothes on our backs.

I said, "My phone was destroyed and I lost your phone number, that's why you didn't hear from me. I couldn't very well go to Frieda and ask her to put me in touch with you."

He made a noise of irritation.

I said, "We've never canceled the games before. If I cancel, it'd raise flags."

I paused, and he kept silent, so I ventured, "I could meet you tomorrow evening. And Roman, I have a lot to report."

My car chugged beneath the wipers. Somewhere beyond a field of paper shamrocks, Em hid in the washroom. I looked over at the condensation beading his door.

Roman shifted and his vehicle backed out. I jerked my gaze forward, gulping against a dry throat. His parking space now lay empty. Roman's Q7 flashed in my rearview mirror, pulling out of the lot.

He said, "Tomorrow evening," and the connection went dead.

* * *

I took two folded napkins from the console to clear my face, and several deep breaths. Two weeks ago, I'd inhaled the clean mountain breeze as I stood beneath Cinnamon Falls, not knowing my cousin might have been floating somewhere beyond. Now, the air inside the Subaru had gone steamy and each inhalation felt bottomless.

I opened the door as the band phone rang again. Harvey.

I said, "I can't talk. You still coming to the games tonight?"

His voice took on a clipped quality. "Yes, I am coming. He wants you to go back up to that *mine*."

"What?"

"What's going on between you and him?"

"I gotta go."

"Something's up, you better tell me. Why are you two so friendly?"

I ended the call and tumbled out into the drizzle as the phone dinged again. Harvey, with a map link. I didn't need the damned link. I'd been to that mine before. A hillside with an eyebrow over a gaping black hole, a sightless eye staring back. The way Roman had stepped inside, it felt like an insect crawling into a skull.

I strode into the coffee shop and stopped dead.

Em sat in the corner booth, skinny legs dangling. She ate hot apple pie á la mode, and opposite her, in the empty space, another slice waited for me. She'd had them put the ice cream in a separate dish, likely so it wouldn't melt. I sat down in front of my pie.

She said, "I'd rather spend the backpack store on this type of thing, anyway."

"I told you to wait in the washroom."

She turned, and I followed her gaze. A sign hung on the door: OUT OF ORDER.

I closed my eyes.

She said, "We really need to talk. Can we talk about stuff here?"

She gestured at the parking lot where Roman had driven away. "Stuff like that?"

I shook my head, checking my pie for cellar spider hatches.

She kept her voice low. "Okay. Don't worry, Mom, I can keep a lid on it."

CHAPTER

57

The Vote

I WAS UNLOADING MY Subaru for tonight's games at Cedar Mountain Christmas Tree Farm when Ponce, Cast Iron, and two other Strangers pulled in. They had no business here. My players were going to freak when they caught wind of a bunch of one-percenters loping around their clandestine, illegal, hard-cash-carrying poker games.

Then I realized: The Strangers had come here for me.

They parked their motorcycles at the far end of the gravel lot. How in God's silver winter did they know we'd scheduled the games here tonight, all the way down mountain at the Christmas tree farm?

My hatch gaped open, and I closed it. Cast Iron was recounting a story to the two new guys that made them choke with laughter. I strode over to Ponce, who stood a small distance from the group, smoking his American Spirit and gazing at the grid-planted saplings. His eyes spoke of ten-year-old Ponce who'd begged Santa for a Daisy BB gun, but found only magnetic darts under the Christmas tree.

He said, "We voted. We're gonna do it. Gonna find out what the fuck happened to Logan."

My heart gave a spring brookie leap. "Ponce! Seriously? Thank you!"

"Don't thank me. I voted against."

My enthusiasm waned, but only a smidge. "You think you can figure it out?"

He shrugged, took a drag. "No promises. You got the money?"

The answer was no.

I ran a quick analysis of my decision to hire bikers with funds I did not have. "Do you need money down?"

He shook his head. "Just make sure you get it."

He nodded toward where Cast Iron palavered with the others. "Those two just showed up tonight. There's more of us on the way. Clubhouse'll be full and we don't hold no debts."

One of the others—Vaughn, his name was—approached Ponce with a wide and slow, rocking-boat amble. He blinked a "How you doin', Janey" to me, then said something to Ponce about a plumbing leak at the clubhouse he could fix in exchange for relief on his dues. Ponce responded with irritation. The other guy, Rendon, joined Ponce and Vaughn.

I headed for Cast Iron.

He greeted me with a (motor-oil-stained) fist bump and a hip waggle. "We're on it, girl! I got you the vote!"

"*You* did?"

"You bet I did!" He swamped me with a spinning hug, and his pride and pleasure left me flushed.

He set me down and cocked his head toward the brotherhood. "Ponce'd never admit it, but that shit didn't sit well with him, neither, man. He's upset. Only reason he voted against is cuz he don't like to get involved with shit, ever. Drives me crazy."

Cast Iron seemed less committed to the Stranger rule about only club members being privy to club business.

Cast Iron said, "I mean, the point of a club is to ride out into the world *as a club*."

He laughed, back-kicked his boot in the dirt. "Everyone knew Logan was my buddy, but Ponce liked him, too. It meant someone else besides me'd be around to drive Ponce's drunk ass home on Saturdays, if Logan got the affiliation."

Cast Iron was making light like he always did. I appreciated that. And yet it scorched my eyes to hear endearments for my cousin, even couched the way Cast Iron had expressed them.

Cast Iron got his nickname because of his stomach—he'd eat anything—but he favored the chicken pot pies. Everyone loved comfort. Even big, tough bikers.

He said, "The thing that's got everyone hacked off is we keep our prospects on the down low. Other clubs, you wear the vest but not the colors. We don't play that way. Prospects wear street clothes. Part of the reason is because our prospects don't carry. No guns. Not even for hunting. Not until you're fully affiliated. That makes them targets if people find out."

My jaw dropped. The Saturday night special. Logan was breaking club rules. He'd been forced to carry it because he'd gotten caught up in this awful situation like me, but he had to hide it from the Strangers. That's why he'd stashed it in the ladies' room at the Hideout.

Cast Iron grabbed my shoulder in a firm Gabe-style squeeze. "We won't let you down, girl. You got friends in the Strangers."

My eyes burned dangerously hot.

He saw it. "Aw, shit, don't do that!"

I dashed away the evidence and threw back my head like I could inhale the moon. "How did you guys even know to find me here?"

He shrugged. "It's our business to know shit that goes down in our territory."

That stopped me. Roman at the coffee shop, watching my daughter. That occurred in their territory, too. The Red King's army and their vengeance on snitches. Involving the Strangers wasn't snitching. Would the Seattle set agree? Did I really want to risk this overlap?

I said, "What if I asked you to pull the plug? Maybe it's better to back off."

Cast Iron took it like I'd said something hilarious. "Ain't no such thing, girl, we voted. Train has left the station."

It hit me: the enormity of my decision to bring them in. I'd actually planned to shake down Roman for the money to pay these guys. I looked down, feeling like the mountain had revealed itself as a giant sleeping troll beneath my feet. I dragged my gaze back up to Cast Iron.

He said, "Something you wanna tell me?"

My mouth opened. I groped for the right way to say this.

He put a hand to my back. "It's all right. I got you."

How to do this without giving away something that could get somebody killed—my God, a lot of people killed.

Ponce shouted at the other three, "Let's go!"

I stepped in toward Cast Iron and he pressed my back, leaning his ear down close.

I whispered, "I need you to . . . just . . . stall."

He narrowed his eyes and shook his head. Vaughn and Rendon milled in the general direction of their motorcycles.

Cast Iron dropped to a serious tone. "Ain't no stalling, girl. It's a freight train. Don't worry about it. Strangers are a tough bunch of motherfuckers. These nuts don't crack."

He squeezed my elbow. "You need anything, just shout. You got that?"

I licked my lips and pressed them tight, not sure what might come out.

What would happen if I lit this fuse and tossed it, then vamoosed the hell out of town? Took my kid and disappeared?

Blood. A massive bloodbath. And the Seattle set would catch up with me.

I glanced at the others, and back at Cast Iron. "How'd you get the other two to vote in favor?"

"Other two?"

"Vaughn and Rendon."

He gave a throaty laugh. "They just rolled in tonight from Reno. When we voted, it was just Ponce and me. One against one."

I frowned. Ponce had seniority. I would have expected his vote would gain the balance.

Ponce revved his motor to show his vexation.

Cast Iron turned but I touched his wrist. "If it was one against one, how'd you get the winning vote?"

Cast Iron grinned. "Only way that makes sense. Coin toss."

* * *

Tonight was high-stakes, and not just at cards.

Tonight I'd introduce Jude as taking Wes Cooney's seat. That was going to light Guy Hamm's shirt on fire.

Harvey'd be playing again for the first time in ages.

Tomorrow I'd face Roman and talk about a police chief, a prosecutor, and two judges, and I'd find out whether the Seattle set would keep their end of the bargain or murder me. Right now the answer felt like another coin toss.

I needed the players to bet heavily so they'd tip heavily. To skip town tomorrow, tips reigned supreme tonight.

I set up my card table inside the tree farm storefront—a scented wooden area where they sold Christmas wreaths, swags, candles, and of course, the trees. Maycie showed up first, then Guy. Then Dannie and Jude arrived at the same time.

Guy Hamm said nothing when he laid eyes on Jude, but his arms swelled and he looked like he'd just been told to muck a stall tainted with pinworms. Then he turned his focus to me. And there it stayed.

I took my dealer's position, my fingers splayed where I leaned into the tufted rails. "I think everyone knows Dr. Jude Summers, our good dentist. He'll be joining us from here on out."

Everyone chatted with Jude as they sized him up in a fellow card player way. Everyone except Guy, who stared at me, inching closer with his chest barreled.

I regarded him from beneath my brows. "Got something to say?"

His eyes drilled mine, and as he whispered, his nose wrinkled. "He a little present for me?"

"It's not about you, Guy. We're all here to play cards."

I switched on my crumb vacuum though my red felt looked impeccable. Guy's neck stretched another inch. I'd expected friction, but this seemed a bit much.

Where the hell was Harvey?

I checked time. Two minutes late. Arriving late for the games was grounds for losing your seat. But this was Harvey, a founder and organizer.

I addressed the group. "We're waiting on Harvey. Sorry for the delay. Just a reminder, especially with new players, Big Bald Luck games always start on time. No exceptions."

"Unless your name is Harvey," Cam said.

I gritted my teeth. "Ordinarily, if you're late, you're gone. Also, and this is important, you must not talk about our locations to anyone, ever. This is for your protection and for the security of the small business owners who lend us their space."

My mind flickered to the Strangers who'd just crashed our party. Maybe one of the players spilled about it, or the tree farmers did.

I said, "There's a lot of cash changing hands on Game nights. Even a casual slip to a spouse or friend can result in that person thinking it's harmless to mention our location to someone else, and before you know it, we are no longer safe."

A murmur from my players.

I checked my phone. No messages.

I said, "We're gonna give Harvey until ten minutes after the hour and then it's—"

My lips froze around the words. The players listened, expectant, and as they waited I could see a shift on Dannie's face. Then Maycie's. Her eyes narrowed.

I licked my lips. "—it's underway. I'll be right back."

CHAPTER

58

Underway

I STALKED TO MY Subaru and wrenched open the door, grabbing the band phone from the console. No messages. Harvey's call at Suspicious Perks was last in the log, and I tapped it, listening to it ring, then again, until his automated voice mail kicked in.

I started to say, "Call me," but stopped. I held still, listening to the emptiness of his burner phone's voice mail as it waited for me to say something. Maybe I shouldn't let it record my voice.

In my other hand, I held the legitimate phone with all the nonresponsive messages I'd left.

I ended the call on the band phone. An oily sensation wound through my stomach. I should toss the burner into the irrigation pond. Instead I stuffed both phones in my pockets, breaking my own rule about putting them on silent for the games. Tonight I'd let them ring.

* * *

"We begin." I seated myself at the dealer position and unsealed a fresh pack of cards.

Guy Hamm threw his hands wide. "Not without Harvey, we don't."

"You're free to leave. There's the door."

"You're just dumping him?"

"He's not answering."

Guy whipped out his cell phone and tried Harvey.

"No bars," he said.

I checked mine. Same thing—though I'd just reached Harvey's voice mail, the network blinked out.

Guy pointed at me. "Is this really what you want? You want to go head-to-head with me?"

He hated me with the same passion Frieda did, only Guy wasn't under some delusion that I'd slept with his partner, so what the hell? Why the tantrum?

The shop owners had set the heat to low, and we all wore light coats. Guy wore a denim jacket. One with a hood and lined with fleece. I told myself not to make anything of it. Half the population here wore jackets like that, including Gary at the police station and Trent, my ex. I couldn't use that as a way to identify the fireworks stand shooter.

At the refreshment area, Maycie poured from a bottle of Jack into a whiskey tumbler. She brought it to her chair and sat.

I said, "In or out, Guy?"

Cam said, "I'd be cordial with her. She's packing heat."

The others chuckled.

Jude pulled out a flask—nothing hard in it, but only I knew that. He rocked it so we heard the slosh. He took a sip over a side glance at Guy. Great performance.

Guy slid his gaze from me to Jude, then to Jude's flask. His eyes settled there. Then Guy burst out laughing with that earthshaker of his. I felt it carry down my vagus nerve. Cam Scarver and Dannie laughed along—Cam from disquiet, Dannie at the spectacle. Then Dannie shot me WTF eyes.

Guy said, "Why not? Waitress, deal me in."

Waitress. I ground my teeth, my toes, my butt. I enjoyed my job waiting tables, so why did I feel heat creeping up my neck?

I looked at my players gathered around the red oval table—Jude, Dannie, Maycie, Cam, and Guy—and I thought:

Tonight will hurt.

* * *

Ordinarily, blackjack generates the most cash for Harvey and the least tension between players. I started with that. But they acted spooked. Guy grew more agitated. My tips were anemic.

We moved on.

After a few rounds of Texas Hold'em, Maycie and Cam ran about even. Dannie was up the most, and Guy was up by a little. Jude lost every hand. Sparks flew, but I wanted more. Em's future depended on it.

I advised we play one last round, then switch—five-card draw.

Guy's lip curled. "Why not five-card stud? You afraid to throw your boy into the fire?"

Jude shrugged. "I like stud. Why play five-card when we can play seven?"

The crimp on Guy's face cinched it for me. Seven-card stud.

Stud games required more skill than draw. Draw was like Hold'em, with the shared faceup cards. Though I rarely played, I excelled in the studs because they leveraged memory.

But the other skill lay in the betting. This came from experience. Dannie had given Jude some pointers the night she came to the fishing cabin, but that was one single night. Also, my long-timers—Guy, Maycie, and Cam—had years of betting against *one another.*

Dannie and Jude were still learning—who might fold when someone got aggressive, who called with a weak hand, who bluffed, and more importantly, who could *be* bluffed.

My phone showed three bars. I let my players have a break and I stepped outside. The only other time I'd ever taken a dealer's break in the history of the Big Bald Luck games was the night at

Cinnamon Falls when I received the voice mail from Logan. Now, I checked my phones for Harvey, hoping a message had come in.

Nothing.

I redialed—my seventh attempt—letting it ring until it clicked to voice mail.

Something had gone down with Harvey. I *had* to run.

Lucky for me the poker room smelled like wet plains before the lightning. Ordinarily that would mean trouble, but tonight I cared about one thing only: scoring tips. Whatever I earned would equal all the money Em and I would have to our names. We'd take it into the wind.

* * *

Guy got chatty. Players did that sometimes to put worms in each other's ears. With Guy, it could get nasty.

I set my phone on the shelf where all could see the timer display. "A reminder, we are on timed play."

Guy laughed. "Right. Beg pardon."

He tapped his cards, looked up. "I was just reminiscing about Kierra. We dated before she ever got with Jude over there."

Maycie and Cam glanced up from their cards. Dannie rolled her eyes. Jude sipped his flask and ran his tongue over his teeth.

As if goaded on, Guy said, "We were lovers. First year of college." He shook his head. "Damn! What a woman."

"Shut yer pie hole, Guy," Maycie said.

Guy put up a hand. "No offense, Jude. But you know, she was passionate."

Jude stared at him, his forehead taut.

Guy shrugged. "Or maybe you don't know. She was passionate with *me*, anyway."

I said, "You got five seconds, Guy, or it's a fold."

"Pass," he said.

The bet went to Cam, but Guy said, "Can you imagine if her name had been Kierra Hamm, instead of Kierra Summers? Couldn't do that to the poor girl. I tossed her back."

He leaned in and said to me, conspiratorially, "Course if I kept her with *me*, maybe that little piece of ass'd still be alive today."

Jude leaped from his chair and Maycie threw herself over his cocked fist before he could let it fly. Cam hooked Guy by his (denim) jacket collar and hauled him toward the exit. Guy hollered, "Aw, come on," and "Everybody's so pasty-faced," as Dannie slammed the door after them.

Dannie said, "What the hell just happened?"

Maycie said, "I apologize, Jude. We run wild here, but not savage. I don't know what's gotten into him."

Jude shook his head. "I don't usually let him get to me."

"That would have gotten to anyone," Maycie said.

I flung my hand at the door. "He's bounced. That was uncalled-for. I warned him."

I boiled, glaring at the door where Cam and Guy had disappeared. I should have bounced Guy ages ago.

Jude said, "I'd rather you didn't. As a favor, I prefer you kept him in the game."

I looked at Jude's dwindling pile of chips. "As a *favor*?"

Jude nodded. Maycie looked from Jude to me. Dannie stalked to the refreshments and poured herself a stiff one.

I did owe Jude. I owed him a bushel. This would have been the last favor I would have expected him to call in.

CHAPTER

59

Team Players

I DID NOT BOUNCE Guy, nor did he remove himself. He didn't even sit out a hand, though I called that last one a fold. He'd intended to fold anyway which was why he'd run his mouth.

The chips piled in the same streaks as they'd begun with Dannie holding the luck and Guy in the middle. Jude at the bottom.

Finally, one round whittled down to just Guy and Jude, except Jude ran out of chips. He asked for additional buy-in. The minimum was $5,000.

But Guy said, "No need."

He waved me off. "It's just us friends. Tell you what, Jude, I'll let you keep playing if I can ask you a question. Any question I want. You win this hand, you'll have, what, a $3,700 freebie for the hand? That's pretty good."

Jude said, "Forget it. I'll take the money."

I reached for the ledger.

Guy said, "Hold-hold-hold on. This is what the game's all about. One question. Play along with me, man."

Jude appraised him. "What's the question?"

"I would only ask if you lost. But you'd have to answer."

Jude nodded at me, and again I lifted my pencil over the ledger, but kept half an eye on Guy. I needed these tips.

Guy threw his hands to his lap. "Aw, hell. You're a goddamned buzz kill. Here's the question I'll ask you. You ready?"

Jude thumped three notes on his flask, listening.

Guy said, "I want to know how Kierra died."

Cam said, "Dammit, I told you to back off from that!"

My pencil froze over the ledger. Despite the chill, sweat had formed at my underarms. Dannie pulled her fingers through her hair.

Guy pointed at me. "You thought I'd ask if you were sleeping with *her*, didn't you? Now that would be inappropriate."

He grinned, or rather leered.

Dannie said, "One more stunt like that and I'll shoot you myself."

Maycie said, "Guy—"

Jude said, "I'll take it."

Guy's expression grew wide and predatory, his lips stretched. Tonight, everything about him clung to a slope of tumbling rocks. Sure, he'd despised Jude since childhood, but he usually kept up appearances. He had the salesman patter, the big laugh, the bankroll for carefully selected politicians. Ever since the night at the rental, his mask had not only slipped, it had shattered into pieces.

Jude threw his cards on the table and said, "Call," showing a pair of fours.

Not much.

I avoided chewing my lip because no one needed to keep a poker face like the dealer, and us dealers remained solemn beyond end of game.

Guy's snarl broke to a grin. "See how easy that was? You won a nice little pot there."

He tossed his cards at me facedown and I whisked them away. Our house rules stated that losing players need not present losing cards, only that they concede the win. Guy could have had an ace-high and we'd never know.

Guy shrugged. "There's enough in that pot, you can stay in the game and you don't have to pay big bad Harvey. Wherever he may be."

Jude left the pot untouched. "She bled out."

I crushed my hand to my heart. The pair of fours lay before Jude, the other cards back in my muck, and he leveled his gaze on Guy.

Jude said, "I was away at a conference and left her alone. She was a hemophiliac and I—I didn't know. Should have. Someone in my position. I should have known."

The heating system clicked. We watched Jude tap his flask once, pause, tap again.

Dannie placed her hand over his arm. "What happened? Did she fall?"

"Something like that. Cut herself. She was up on a chair, is what it looked like, trying to change a lightbulb, and the glass cover from the fixture slipped. Maybe she tried to catch it. Glass smashed everywhere. Police say she attempted to call for help but we were out in that cabin and cell phone service wasn't so good. We had a landline. Maybe she was too light-headed to use it. I found her in the car. Never made it out of the driveway."

Jude looked at Guy. "All you had to do was ask. I'd have told you."

Guy shrugged. "If it's true. Guess all we have is your word."

Cam said, "Christ almighty, Guy."

Sitting to my right, her cowboy hat resting over her barrel curls, Maycie said, "It's true. My team in Missoula took that case. If you don't want to take Jude's word for it anyone can order the reports. It's in the public record."

She thumbed the rim of her whiskey glass. "Kierra's meds had either run out or she'd stopped taking them. She'd told no one about her condition but her physician. Her mother didn't even know. Unclear why. It's just hemophilia."

Kierra's iron grip on privacy sounded like a quintessential Suspicioner move. Her death, Suspicion's gossip feast. And now the tide of gossip shall roll.

I said, "Let's take another break."

Jude said, "Not for me. I'm ready."

"I'm out," Maycie said, gathering her things. "Long autopsy tomorrow."

We bade her farewell for the night, and I checked the remaining players. No one else wanted to stop.

I should have hit the brakes, though, because they were all revved and luck was blitzing the walls of that little wooden Christmas store—good luck and bad.

CHAPTER

60

Revved and Flying

THE NEXT ROUND built up quickly. Within ten minutes, the pot spilled over. My ledger showed entry after entry and I'd had to twist my pencil into the sharpener more than once. I still had access to Harvey's Big Bald Luck account. That cast a shadow over the question: Did Harvey run, or was he murdered? If he ran, would he not drain that account?

I needed tips. I said nothing.

When the bet came to Cam, he added an even $10,000 in chips. That meant he had a seriously good hand because he did not bluff and everyone knew it—probably even Dannie and Jude.

Next, Dannie. She checked her cards, shook her head, and leaned back. Then she produced her terrain rocket keys and carefully slid them across the felt. A murmur rippled through the players. If everyone agreed on a value for Dannie's Land Rover and accepted the bet, she could stay in the game.

I said, "You looking to add that to the pot, or to cover?"

"For the pot."

I shifted in my seat. If Dannie were to draw against an account with money in it, it wouldn't bother me. But throwing her terrain rocket on the table felt like the very thing I'd feared—I'd triggered her gambling addiction by allowing her in, like serving drinks to an alcoholic.

Cam said, "Blue Book has it right around $44K. I guess we can call it—"

He looked from Jude to Guy. "Thirty thousand."

Dannie said, "That's serious low-balling."

"None of us wants the hassle of selling a vehicle. All the expense involved, taxes."

Guy said, "Cash is king, sweetheart. You want full value, put up cash."

Dannie said, "Thirty-five."

They settled at thirty-three. The betting came to Jude. He'd already bet his entire winnings from last round plus taken another buy. I felt sick. I wished I'd maintained emotional distance from these players. At least Maycie left early.

"Can't justify another line in Harvey's ledger," Jude said.

He moved to cast his cards on the table in a fold but Guy stayed him. "Hold on. You could put up your practice."

Jude paused.

Guy said, "I saw your For Sale sign. Is that for the building? Or your entire practice?"

"Here we go," Dannie said.

Guy said, "Is it because of Kierra?"

Cam snapped, "Off-limits!"

Jude gave a one-shoulder hitch. "I'm not looking to sell my practice."

Guy smiled. "But you could put up the deed to the building. It houses both the clinic and the barber shop, right? You'd have a chance at this nice big pot."

He pointed at the mound of chips. "I might even put up Big Copper Ridge."

Jude snorted.

Guy's fake smile dropped. "What's so funny?"

Jude chuckled, slid his thumb along the leather rail, said, "Just, uh . . . *copper*?"

Something moved inside of Guy though he sat absolutely still, his chin pointing like a bayonet. Something moved inside me, too.

Jude said, "Ever pull any copper outta that mine, Guy? Even one time? Up on Big *Copper* Ridge?"

Guy's ears turned scarlet, his blood rushing to his temples.

Jude said, "Do you even own it anymore? I don't know how you could put that sinkhole up in a poker game. What'd you tell'm when you listed it as collateral on your loan docs? Did you say the mine was full of copper?"

Guy practically had steam coming out of his ears.

Jude started chuckling. "It's been forty years since that hole gave up anything other than chalk or talc."

Jude's laughter escalated to bright-eyed body coughs. He got a kick out of his own revelation to the point I had a hard time understanding him when he said, "Maybe you should call it *Big Talc* Ridge."

Unfortunately, oh, so unluckily, Jude's laugh was infectious. "Big Talc" was just too much.

I breathed through clenched teeth to keep from snickering. But Cam Scarver was infected. He choked down his laughter with a weird sound he didn't want to unleash. He tried to backstop his tongue down his throat, but the resulting strangulation was so vaudevillian that Dannie fell victim. She covered her mouth.

Cam got out, "Guess that makes you the Big Talc-er."

The room exploded with peals of laughter. Guy turned purple.

I looked desperately at my timer, but the counter showed plenty to go.

Across the hysterics came the click of a safety being released. Guy Hamm pointed his pistol at me.

He said, "You told him. You told him about the mine."

The laughter died.

Jude said, "Slow down, Guy. I'm sitting over here. You were talking to me, not her."

The barrel loomed disproportionately large as it stared at me, striking me mute. I lifted my hands in surrender. My mouth turned to parchment. Tucked away in my boot, a million miles down my leg to my foot, the Saturday night special burned. Still jammed.

Guy said to me. "You're gonna get your boyfriend there killed, too."

Too? *Too?*

I stared at the outsized cylinder, remembering Guy's outsized temper. His behavior at the rental after overhearing the phone call. That damned denim jacket.

I found my voice. "You killed Logan."

"*You* killed him. *You* are the reason he's dead."

Click, click, click—around the table. Safeties being released.

Jude said, "Right here, Guy. Look at me."

I said, "Guy, whatever business you think I have with some copper mine, you are mistaken. I know nothing about mines."

"You're helping them take it from me. Know what happens once they no longer have any use for you? Good as dead. Nowhere to run. Can't even change my name. They'll find me."

My voice shook. "Do you mean Roman?"

Jude said, "Guy, come on. Look at me."

With his pistol trained on my heart, Guy said, "They've got a big surprise coming. It's all gone by morning. Unless I stop it."

I looked around wildly. "Can we go for a walk, please? Just talk a little?"

He said, "Yeah, sweetheart. Talk to this."

He extended his arm. I crossed my wrists over my face.

Screams. A shot rang out.

CHAPTER

61

That Guy

I'VE HEARD OF time standing still. For me, it separated.

I could have jumped up, eased around the bullet, and driven my station wagon home before the shot landed. The mortal world was mired in pine sap, but I zipped around free.

But although my *mind* accelerated to superhuman speed, it left my body behind. My body occupied the pine sap time-space continuum while my superhuman mind looked back helplessly.

My arms flew to an X across my face. Gunfire deafened me, followed by the sound of ringing.

And then, somewhere beyond, I heard the rise and fall of that wolf howling—probably the same wolf who witnessed Wes Cooney's death. The beast who'd conversed with the train on that windy night. The train's whistle had come from down the mountain, and the wolf, from the other direction, up Cinnamon Falls.

Now, as my mind levitated in its useless superhuman state, I remembered something I'd heard about those falls. The reason it got its name.

When Suspicion first became a town, the railroad had just laid tracks and two families staked claims: the Batheries and the Sherwoods. Their homesteads met along Pika Spur. They shared supplies to get through winter, and they helped raise each other's barns. The Sherwoods' son, Tom, fell in love with Catherine Batherie, and the families planned a wedding.

Until one day while picking cloudberries. Tom stabbed his younger brother to death. Then he murdered Catherine Batherie. When Mr. Batherie came upon his mutilated daughter, he shot Tom. Within minutes, the Batheries and the Sherwoods each hunted down and killed one other. Every single soul. This soon-to-be united family. These loving neighbors.

Suspicioners say the massacre began because Tom found his brother and girlfriend together, but you never know. There's no one left to tell us.

The falls got their name because cinnamon candy is red and the waters filled with blood that day. That's the story we told as teenagers sneaking into Ponderosa Lodge. But it's what they call a "mondegreen." Misheard words.

In their grief, the local congregation had named the waterfall "Sin of Man." Over time it became "Cinnamon."

Did these thoughts reflect my brain at superhuman speed, or my life passing before my eyes?

The howling wolf became Dannie screaming.

* * *

Last time I'd been shot I didn't realize it. I looked down at myself now, and found no bullet holes. My players looked safe. Except Guy. Guy's fingers were blown into the pile of poker chips like he'd bet them with the pot.

Guy threw furious eyes toward Jude. "You shot off my trigger fingers."

Jude scowled back. "I was aiming for your head."

I stuttered through my breathing. All four players had popped their safeties but only Jude had fired. Jude was a wolf, like me.

Guy made a gurgling sound. Then keeled forward.

Cam yelled, "Guy's shot!"

Like we hadn't just discussed this, but then he cried, "The bullet went straight through his fingers and into his chest!"

Dannie, who'd only just stopped screaming, shrieked afresh. She tumbled to the floor and huddled against the empty shelves. Kept screaming.

Guy hung slack from his chair. I'd been so fixated on the fingers that I hadn't noticed the hole in his chest. It streamed cardinal red syrup onto my red crumb-free felt. Drool, too. Parallel streams that melted into a unified pool.

"Call an ambulance," Cam said.

Jude shook his head. "Too late. He's dead."

I staggered over to Dannie, who continued to scream in a huddle, and I wrapped my arms around her. "It's over. You're okay."

Dannie relinquished her screaming to sobs. I gathered myself to my feet, mesmerized, and circled the table. Definitely dead.

Dannie punched numbers into her phone and pressed it to her ear. She breathed in pitching gulps, her mascara seeping toward her cheeks.

She looked at her phone, dropped it to the floor. "No signal."

Cam said, "Maybe that's a good thing."

Dannie sniffed, blinked. "What are you talking about?"

"Guy Hamm was about to shoot Janey. He might have killed us *all*. The man was not in his right mind."

"Right. It was a legal shoot. But we have to call the police."

The rancher looked at Dannie, huddled on the floor, then at Jude and me. "The law doesn't always work the way it's supposed to, see. That's the trouble."

CHAPTER

62

Tunnel Vision

DANNIE GAPED FROM where she sat sprawled, fingers to brow. "Surely you're not suggesting we don't report this."

Cam said, "I'm not suggesting a damn thing. The phones don't work, and that gives us time to think and listen."

I prayed that the lack of phone service would continue. My intentions had funneled to one goal: keep my daughter safe. Forget tip money. Guy was dead and probably Harvey, too. But I couldn't just walk off and leave this.

Dannie aimed a humorless laugh at Guy's slumped form. "Guy Hamm is a prominent member of the community. He owns copper and silver claims all the way up to the border. Folks are bound to notice his weaselly ass is missing."

Jude said, "He's got two sons and an ex-wife."

Cam waved them off. "I'm not saying don't go to the police. I'm saying less talking, more listening."

I cleared my throat. "Let's hear what Cam has to say."

Cam shot me a look of fire. "Not me, you. You're the *very* person we need to hear from."

He pushed away from the card table and stepped toward me. "Why don't you tell us what in stormy *hell* Guy was going on about because I'd damn sure like to know what's stuck to the bottom of my boots."

Dannie stood abruptly and ran to the door. She made it to the railing just in time to empty her stomach.

I dashed after her, held her hair out of her face and rubbed her back. She heaved and spat. I checked the road—no vehicles, not even a horse. Only the wind. The Christmas tree farm stood on remote property in a remote wilderness.

Dannie whispered to me, "Did you know Guy was part of this?"

"God, no. It was as big a surprise to me as it was you."

I glanced back. Behind us, inside the store, Guy still sat defiant in death. His body curved to a capital G around my card table.

I said, "He seemed to believe I'm some kind of queenpin."

She said, "Go on and tell Cam."

* * *

The cold night carried a taste of balsam. The four of us gathered—Jude, Cam, Dannie, and me. We huddled around a picnic bench overlooking the Christmas trees, away from the railing Dannie'd just puked over, out of sight of Guy's dead eyes.

I began recounting the whole rhapsodic horror.

When I got to the part about having been shot, Jude said, "I treated her gunshot wound."

Cam said, "*You* knew all about this?"

I'd wanted to leave Jude and Dannie out of it, but both spoke up anyway. Up until now, they each had separate buckets of information that didn't involve each other.

After I finished, Cam tented his fingers. "So we have Frieda, a criminal defense attorney who's an active participant in bribery and knows how to work the justice system. We have a dirty judge. Questionable law enforcement—"

"—not my brother—" Dannie said.

Cam opened his hands. "I'm not saying Quincy's in, but it sounds like we don't know. Then there's that whole FBI connection both Harvey and Guy mentioned. As a rancher in outlaw country, I've seen some things."

He pointed at Dannie. "From what you found out, this drug ring is quick to torture witnesses. Of which we all are."

Jude looked out over the perfectly spaced Christmas trees. "It's also worth noting that Harvey is unaccounted for. He might have-absconded. Or he is deceased."

He looked at me. "Have we left anything out?"

"That sums it up."

I rubbed my arms. Always hanging over me was the fear of losing Em. I wanted to do right by her, and I wanted to get right with the law. But my ongoing mistrust added texture. Even my card players viewed the legal system as flawed.

Cam said, "So one option is that we come forward and risk getting tortured and killed, and cross our fingers that the law will prevail."

Dannie said, "It's the right thing to do."

I piped up. "Why?"

Jude said, "Guy does have adult children. There are people who care about him."

Cam said, "We sympathize. That won't bring him back." He shrugged. "It's a crap sandwich, and we've all been served. Let's walk through it. We go to the police. Tell them what happened. Everything about who Guy's tangled up with, who Janey's tangled with, who we're *all* now tangled up with. Those people are not going to want to see us testify."

Jude looked grim. "Spin the bottle to find out which one of us gets picked off first."

We fell silent.

Finally, Dannie said, "From what I hear, the Seattle set would make that a drawn-out torture-kill to scare the rest of us."

Jude made a sound with his tongue, regarded me, and then looked back at the others. "Do we have an alternative?"

Cam voiced the thing that was burning in all our minds. "We clean up this mess."

Dannie wrapped her head in her hands. "Oh, my God."

* * *

No one moved. No one spoke. I looked from Dannie to Jude, my mind clicking backward to Guy's fury in the moments before he extended his pistol toward me.

I said, "I think I know why Guy believed I had more involvement than I did."

Jude said, "Has to do with the mine?"

I nodded. "Harvey told me I had to meet there with Roman. He sent me a map."

I took out my phone to show them. The map tried to load, but only got as far as blank tiles on the grid. No internet.

I gave up and pointed to a pine knot at the center of the picnic table. "Here's Suspicion."

I ran my finger along the seam between boards. "This is the border between the U.S. and Canada. See? Here's Montana, here's Alberta."

I dragged a pine cone to a position just below the seam. "Here's where Harvey and Roman wanted me to go. Right here, at the border, Montana side. They'd sent me there once before. It was a mining company—"

"—Big Copper Ridge," Dannie finished.

I nodded. "Big Copper Ridge. I didn't know Guy owned it. On the satellite map I saw another entrance here—"

I placed another pine cone on the Alberta side. Two points close together on opposite sides of the border.

Jude said, "Because it's a tunnel."

"Exactly. It *is* a mine, but I think it has more than one entrance. One on the U.S. side, one on the Canada side."

Dannie leaned forward. "If that's true, if Guy's copper mines—"

Jude said, "Really, they were chalk—"

I shot him a look.

Dannie said, "That must be how the Seattle crew smuggled their mess between the U.S. and Canada. It's their alternate route since they cracked down on the ports."

I cut my chin toward the poker table inside the store. "I think we take Guy to the mine. I've been to Big Copper Ridge with Roman. I know how to slip in where there are no cameras and no people. We lay him to rest, and if enough time goes by before he's discovered, maybe it never comes back on us."

Jude said, "The Seattle set might be around."

"I don't think so. They have a fake operation. They were working a different mine on the property, a bigger mine, and even that one didn't have many workers."

Cam said, "You'd do that, Janey?"

"I'm the only one who's been there."

Cam said, "If we can get Guy's body in the mine, even if the Seattle set finds him, they're not going to dial 911."

Jude said, "I'll go with Janey. Can the two of you take care of things here?"

Dannie, eyes wide, threw her gaze to Cam. He frowned back, silent.

Finally, she nodded. No one was protesting anymore, not even Dannie.

Cam said, "We have a plan."

I clutched Jude's fingers for volunteering to do the horrible task alongside me. He pulled his hand loose, and the rejection pierced my heart. But then he slipped his arm over my shoulders and pulled me in close.

CHAPTER

63

A Short Walk

MAYCIE HAD LEFT the game early tonight. I wondered whether things would have gone differently if she'd stayed. She carried a badge, the county coroner, so she might have shut down our cover up. Then again, you never knew with Maycie.

If you need to erase crime scene evidence, grab a crime scene tech. If you don't have one, get an ME. If no ME, snag a former medic, retired detective-cum-coroner. We came so close to having one of those.

We wrapped Guy Hamm in my card table cover. His earth-shaking laugh echoed in my mind, the best thing about him; now haunting me as we rolled, lifted, and carried him into the night. We asked ourselves, "What would Maycie do?" and realized we'd have to watch out for ways law enforcement could track our movements: phones, the vehicles' factory-installed GPS.

So Guy, may he rest in peace, rode in the back of his own truck while Jude took the wheel. I drove my Subaru—no GPS tracker in the old car—and led the way to Big Copper Ridge.

If we needed to communicate along the way we'd have to flash headlights like 1979, because neither of us brought our cell phones. Those stayed behind in Jude's Sequoia, which Dannie and Cam would drive to his clinic once they finished cleaning the Christmas tree store.

They'd do a good job with that.

I found the turn-off without effort, even in the dark. Gravel crunched beneath the tires. We parked near the gap in the chain link where Roman had greeted me weeks ago.

We carried Guy, still wrapped in the card table cover, through the woods. Even with the two of us, Guy was heavy. I was grateful I'd had practice with my 143-pound card table. But that was rigid on casters. Guy was dead weight.

The woods blocked the moonlight and twice I stumbled, but my sense of direction remained sharp. Off in the distance, no vehicles were parked at the active mine where workers previously had been milling.

With each step, my thoughts ran on hairy knuckles. This was supposed to be when I took to the wind. I should have been grabbing tip money, scooping up Em, and turning to vapor. Now Guy Hamm was dead and by the way, he'd held a key to the Seattle set's golden passage.

They'd find out we killed him.

And Harvey. They'd either murdered him, were torturing him, or he was in the wind. Any of these poisoned my fate.

I had to escape before the meeting with Roman.

* * *

The mine looked different at night. It looked like a hobbit hole. I felt both terrified of the dark but also desperate to get it over with.

We had to crouch, an excruciating demand on my already taxed muscles as we carried Guy through the opening. Once inside, we could stand. We set Guy in the dust and stretched our backs. It was pitch-black.

I pulled out my penlight and shined it, but the earth swallowed the beam. Dust motes drifted and the walls narrowed from two abreast to single file.

Jude said, "You okay?"

"I need a rest."

"Catch your breath. I'm going to move Guy's truck around to the active mine."

I nodded.

Fuck the dark. Though it was a dark night, the mine was darker. Ink in gaseous form. The passage formed a throat that exhaled. Cold air slid over my ear and down my neck. I sat next to Guy, my hands in my hair, elbows on knees, and pinned my gaze on the entrance—hungry for what meager light filtered from the woods.

I reached for a phone I didn't have. I wanted to see if Harvey showed signs of life. I wanted to know what time it was. How were Dannie and Cam managing with all that blood?

But I could do none of those things because I'd surrendered my phone to the cleanup crew. I could only sit in a pitch-black mine with a dead man and my howling thoughts—the tunnel heaving at my neck.

When Jude returned, a hint of twilight colored the sky's edges. I hated to let it go.

He said, "I'll transport him myself from here. It'll be easier."

Jude pulled Guy into a fireman's carry, and I led the way with the flashlight. Our footfalls whispered on the soft, chalky dust.

An opening appeared to my left. "Jude."

He swung heavily. The alcove veered to a side tunnel. We hadn't traveled far but in the dark with a cadaver, it felt like miles.

He said, "As good a spot as any."

While Jude released Guy from his shroud, I panned the floor and wished for a shovel. If we had to, we could bare-hand scoop the loose, chalky dirt over Guy. An odor would set in, but that couldn't be helped.

Jude tucked the card table cover under his arm and paused. "What's that?"

He took my hand and guided the beam toward the ceiling. Something winked from the supporting beam. A device with a pulsing red pinpoint.

I said, "Camera?"

My heart rate jumped. Jude sucked in his breath and I understood what we were looking at. Worse than a camera. Guy had wired the tunnel with explosives.

We left the body and made haste back to the open air. I recalled Guy's words as he'd trained the gun on me: *By morning, it'll all be gone.*

CHAPTER

64

Dusty Fingers

As we staggered back to the Subaru, dawn glowed in Saturn colors. I handed Jude my keys because I couldn't drive. We climbed into the vehicle and watched light fall up to the sky, darkness washing back. It made me dizzy.

As we turned onto the main road, I felt the boom hit my bones.

Jude's eyes flicked to the rearview mirror. "See anything?"

Treetops. A beautiful sunrise. Storm clouds rolling from the east. Then, a tiny finger of dust rose from the direction of the mine.

He said, "A transformer must have blown somewhere."

"Right," I said, "transformer."

Guy had tried to kill me twice—or does the rigged mine shaft count as the third, a posthumous attempt? My body quaked. I was dirtier than I'd ever been—talc and chalk, but also Guy's sweat, blood, and whatever else.

Jude put a gritty hand over mine. "You all right?"

I managed a groan in reply.

He said, "You're at risk for shock. Slow breath in, slow breath out."

I breathed with him, and his warm hand, dirty as it was, felt reassuring.

I had to face Roman tonight. I might be gazing into my last sunrise now—a spreading peach center with a roiling, smudged horizon.

I scanned the sunrise, the smoke from the mine, the lightning flashes on the horizon. "It's going to rain."

It had been dry in this corridor, and therefore we didn't leave behind many tire tracks, but whatever had been there would soon wash away. Same with footprints.

Jude said, "Yeah, I think you're right. Rain would be good."

He kept holding my hand.

* * *

As we turned onto Farm to Market Road in Suspicion, the rain hit. I felt that same awkwardness about parting and didn't want to drop Jude off at his place.

He touched my wrist. "Janey."

"Yes?"

He said, "It was awful."

I nodded. Nodded again.

I regarded him. He was filthy. "What time is your first patient?"

"Eleven. My dental hygienists have the early ones."

"Someone'll see you come in looking like that. You should shower at my place. We'll wash your clothes."

He blinked.

I said, "I'm just being practical."

CHAPTER

65

Shower

WE PULLED INTO my drive. Rain pelted my landlord's cabin. Mr. Traverse had left for a three-day pipeline inspection, and I'd told him I'd do rounds on the property. We ran to the garage and got soaked crossing the few feet to my outer door. Inside, we climbed the stairs to the inner door with the broken lock.

Jude said, "I can fix that lock."

"I'd like that."

"Why don't you take your shower first?"

I nodded. I pulled off my shoes and stepped into the bathroom, leaving the door ajar. I threw my socks in the hamper. Jude waited in the living room, unsure about sitting on the couch.

I twisted on the water and pulled off my jeans, then my top, and looked over at Jude again. He still hung there, only now he'd turned his back. That sweet man. I had to walk over wearing only my bra and panties and take his hand, slip it around my waist. His breath came slowly.

I said, "Is it too soon?"

It had been two years since his wife died, but grief is as private as a fingerprint.

He cupped my cheek. "The way you handle yourself in the face of all this, it's extraordinary."

That surprised me. Most people would have called my actions the opposite of extraordinary. I should have attended twice-weekly therapy since birth. Taken meds. I should have called the police at this or that precise moment. Then called the FBI, CIA, the governor, and the U.S. Senate.

I pressed myself against Jude's warmth.

"I didn't have a choice," I said.

"You had many choices. You're extraordinary."

My eyes dropped, and he lifted my chin to look at him. "The way you move, like a cat. You're lithe. I see you at the Hideout and you're beautiful. Your face, your bone structure. The things you say."

So different from what Harvey or Guy Hamm had told me, and I realized I could choose whom I believed. Jude's words softened the muscles in my shoulders. I wasn't beautiful, but in Jude's eyes, I felt attractive.

He kissed me, full and gentle. His hand caressed the back of my neck. The other rested at the curve of my back. My heart eased toward him.

He said, "I'll tell you something."

"What?"

"You make me want to figure out Carrie Grosvenor's chili recipe. I'd make you a proper—"

I pressed my lips over his and drank in another kiss. He pulled me to him, hand on my cheek, but with his other he tugged at his filthy shirt. I helped him out of it. We stole kisses and removed clothing until we were finally down to skin, and we pressed our abs together. I could feel the expanse of his middle against mine, the vulnerability of skin against skin, and heat flooded to my core. I ran my hands from the inside of his chest to his shoulders.

His erection rested against a v of my hipbone, unlocking a curling sensation between my legs. We kissed again, tender and expansive, a kiss that plunged deep into my heart and radiated toward my extremities. Outside, rain tapped the window. It seemed to tell me to hush—hush all the thoughts that had carried me away. Our hips kneaded together. Our bodies gently rocking, skin heating.

I led Jude to the bathroom. We lightly touched each other, murmuring. He pulled the shower curtain for me and I stepped inside. Steam filled my lungs. Already, it loosened what had felt unbreathable. I tilted back my head and let the warm water course through my hair. He brought me close and we rocked beneath the steaming flow, brushing dirt, our lips searching for one another. The water poured over us as though our bodies had become a single creature, heated and fervent. Hopeful.

* * *

I awoke to Jude kissing my forehead.

He said, "I have to go to clinic."

A few hours ago, we did manage to get his clothes in the laundry. He wore damp jeans from the dryer and no shirt. Now he kissed me, lingering and tender.

"I don't want to leave you, not for a second," he said.

I squeezed my eyes, remembering last night's grim events. "We should spend today like an ordinary day. Go see your patients."

"You'll be okay?"

"I'll be fine."

I hadn't told him about yesterday's encounter with Roman. That I'd planned to run. Now I had no money, nowhere to run. No plan.

He frowned. "Where's that little gun of yours?"

He found it where I'd left it by the kitchen. I got dressed.

"It's jammed," he said.

"I tried to fix it."

"I'll see what I can do."

He pulled on his own shirt and it was a pity. The dentist had quite the physique.

* * *

It'd stopped raining, but the sky promised more to come. We stood by the garage. Jude borrowed one of Mr. Traverse's tools and disassembled Logan's little Röhm.

Jude said, "It looks like you've got to get the whole cylinder out just to clear the jam."

We were dithering, nuzzling legs where we stood, extending our time.

He pointed his screwdriver. "Get this cylinder pin out. Then you can access it."

Once he removed the cylinder it looked even more like a toy. With a few grunts, he popped out the jammed bullet, then he replaced the cylinder and screwed the pin back.

He gestured at the stump where Mr. Traverse split firewood, black and rotted on one side. Coral plate mushrooms sprung from the rot.

He said, "You could take a shot at those."

"I'm used to long guns," I replied.

He nodded, and showed me how to make a tripod using my hip, elbow, and extended arm. I fired at the largest mushroom and missed, hitting the cluster next to it.

I lowered my hand. "Only two rounds left. Better not waste them."

"Do you have more ammo?"

"I can get some from Logan's place."

I drove Jude to where his Sequoia was parked by the dental clinic. To my surprise, he kissed me before getting out of the car. To hell with gossip. I told him to get to clinic before teeth started falling out. He retrieved both my phones from his Sequoia and handed them to me, then kissed me once more. I wondered if I'd ever see him again.

I drove toward the school. I would collect Em and together, broke-ass, we'd disappear on the wind. Then one of my phones rang. The band phone.

* * *

I fumbled to answer and missed. I started to call back but pulled over, wiped my face, breathed, and checked caller ID. It hadn't come from Harvey's burner. Somewhere local. It could be Roman. Or law enforcement—the good kind. Or the bad. Either was problematic.

On my normal phone, the voice mail indicator showed. I played it. Mr. Zarate's voice said, "Miss Hendee, we released Emmie to the custodial guardian as per court order, and—"

I slammed End and redialed the band phone. Frieda answered.

I shouted, "Where is she?"

A raspy chuckle. "She's fine. We made a spring Jello and it's setting up in the refrigerator."

"Let me speak to her."

Frieda drew out a breath. "I want to talk to Harvey."

"You stupid, stupid woman. What in the hell makes you think—"

I stopped, looked at the Saturday night special with its two bullets. Crystal formed in my heart and crackled my veins.

I said, "All right, Frieda, how do I do that?"

"How do you think, you imbecile? You little slut? I want my husband. And the money that goes with him."

I tugged at my hair. I'd hoped to grab Em and go on the run, but now Frieda has snatched her. Roman expected me to meet him this evening.

I thumbed the cylinder and felt a thrill of impending disaster I hadn't known since that night outside Trent's house. "Fine. Come on over to my place, lady. Come get your husband."

CHAPTER

66

The Squeeze

ROXIE ANSWERED ON the first ring. "Hey, gorgeous!"

"Hey," I said, my heart fragile.

She spoke in an excited whisper. "How you doin? You all right?"

"Not so good, actually. Frieda took Em, and I'm trying to get her back."

"Oh, God!"

"Are you . . . home?"

Roxie paused. "Uh . . . ? No . . . ?"

I said, "Are you . . . in Montana . . . ?"

"No . . . ?"

She said, "I should have given two weeks' notice at the Hideout, but it all happened so fast. Harvey came by yesterday and we just packed up and left."

"Wow. That's . . ." I swallowed. "Just so crazy, sweetie. Is Harvey there with you? Can I talk to him?"

"He won't talk to you, honey. He said not to answer if you call. In fact I'm supposed to get rid of my cell phone."

She paused and said, "I left you something."

"What sort of something?"

"I taped it to the back of that Big Foot picture at the Hideout. The 'real and actual Sasquatch' photo Tag Benson took back in 1981."

"That was sweet of you." My mind pinwheeled.

Roxie said, "It's all yours, anyway. Those meds you were taking knocked me on my ass, so I sold them."

Tires crunched on gravel in the driveway. Frieda had arrived. I looked through the garage window, scanning for Em, but they were too far.

I shoved the Röhm down the back of my jeans. "Gotta go."

She said, "Janey, I wish you all the happiness."

"You too, Rox."

I ended the call with endearing thoughts for Roxie, but also wondering if I was going to have to shoot some shitwitch lawyer in front of my child.

* * *

As Frieda's car approached, I texted Trent: Need you to pick up Em from my place. Urgent.

He'd say no. He'd be busy. He'd be working at Peak Auto and wouldn't make the time. I'd reached out to him because he was Em's father, but I should have texted Sherry. Dannie was at a meeting in Eureka. Who else?

To my surprise, Trent replied: omw.

Frieda's Audi rolled to a stop in front of me. Em sat in the back, and my spine softened with relief. She looked okay.

I stashed my phone and stalked toward the car. Em stared, eyes wide but not frightened. High alert.

Frieda, wrapped in a tweed coat and wearing massive designer sunglasses, let herself out and clicked the locks. I gave Em a jerk of the head toward the house. She tried her door but it wouldn't open. Child locks.

I said to Frieda, "You really want to try this with me? I'm not going to stand here and let you smack me around this time."

"Where's my husband?"

While Frieda stood facing me, Em crawled up through the front seat and climbed out the driver's side door. My kid was no fool.

Frieda lunged but Em easily dodged her, and I slapped Frieda across her face. "Stay away from my child. You do not touch her. Hear me? Don't you *ever* go near her again."

Frieda's designer shades had clattered to the gravel, but she left them where they lay. Now, without them, her face looked puffy, her eyes red-rimmed.

I turned to my daughter. "You all right, baby?"

"I'm fine. She made Jello but I think she put something in it. I didn't eat any."

"Get inside. Your dad's coming to pick you up."

She cut eyes to Frieda, then back to me. "Can I get my snow pants and train case? Isabelle's family invited me to go skiing."

Perfect. I wanted her well away from here. Out of town, away where no one could find her.

"Yes. Just hurry, and don't come out until I get you."

The weather had shifted to a sprinkle. Emmie dashed into the garage, and when I turned back to Frieda, she was scrutinizing my tiny log cabin garage apartment.

"It's not much," Frieda said.

"What's that supposed to mean?"

"This shrunken place of yours. I can't picture Harvey holed up here."

I said, my teeth tight, "He is not. Frieda. Absorb that. He isn't here. When was the last time you talked to Roman?"

"I haven't talked to that man. I'm not his attorney. I represent the interests of Baltazar Valencia. Harvey deals with the rest."

I snorted. The foundational criticism the Red King had with Frieda Kanjo was that she never got her hands dirty. She let her people do that.

I said, "How did you drag my cousin into this? I know he had no desire to work for you anymore than I did."

"I don't have to answer that." She swiveled back toward her Audi.

"You came here to talk, now we're going to talk. Do you want to know whether your husband's dead or alive?"

She paused, and she angled her chin toward the sky.

She said, "He's dead," and strode for her car.

I yanked out the Röhm. "Stop, Frieda. We haven't come this far just to have you walk away from me."

She turned and looked, then scoffed. "Oh, that. The pea shooter."

I fired at the biggest coral plate mushroom on the stump. Like my previous attempt, it missed, but it made an impressive explosion of black bark fireworks. Frieda went rigid.

"You're not going to shoot me."

"You willing to bet your life?"

I understood that bet well. Things change when a gun is pointed at you, whether you think the person might shoot or not. Fog drifted where only a moment ago it had been sprinkling, and a piney scent from the meadow underlay the aroma of gunpowder.

Frieda swerved back toward me and jammed her fists against her tweed jacket. "All right. It wasn't my fault. It was Harvey. You're dying to know how it happened? Fine. Don't blame me if you feel a sting."

* * *

According to Frieda: Logan had gotten interested in motorcycles, and he'd heard about a Victory Jackpot for sale out in Kalispell. Logan and Cast Iron wanted to go see it. Harvey got wind and offered to drive them in the Tundra.

The VJ was a beauty. Logan wanted the bike but when he tried to haggle, the seller held firm. The three nearly turned around and came home. But then Harvey told Logan he'd loan him the money.

"That was it," Frieda said.

"What do you mean, 'That was it'?"

"Logan owed us. I don't remember what it cost but we loaned him over $7,000. It was a hard winter and he didn't make as much money on guide trips as he expected."

My cousin. He was a good man. An outdoorsman, funny, willing to help anyone who asked. Not great with money. He'd never said anything to me about struggling, and I'm sorry to recall, he wouldn't have. Not to me, the single mom paying double rent.

Frieda was right. I felt the sting.

I said, dully, "So that put him under your thumb."

Frieda pointed at herself, then down the valley. "Not my thumb. Theirs. We brought Logan in once. Then Baltazar had him driving trucks to Seattle. I told Baltazar it was a bad idea. Logan wasn't cut out for it. Didn't have the head."

She gestured at me. "People like you and Logan are valuable because you don't have a drug or alcohol dependence, and you have established local ties. But see, Janey, Baltazar had gotten wind of Logan's parents' place out there in Idaho."

"Uncle Reggie and Margot? They rent kayaks and tiny cabins. They don't make any money. Just enough to support themselves."

"They're in a good location between here and Washington. They are humble people, well-established. They live near casinos, places to wash money."

"Oh, dear God."

Frieda shrugged. "It wouldn't be so valuable on its own. But Baltazar likes to hang onto people like Logan once he's got'm."

It made sense. Logan no longer wished to go home to Coeur d'Alene, and instead he joined the Strangers. A desperate attempt to shake off the Red King.

But why would Guy murder him?

Another vehicle approached, and I felt my shoulders loosen. Trent would collect Em and I'd get her away from all this.

But I was wrong. The vehicle turning down my driveway now was not Trent's.

Frieda grabbed my wrist, her eyes desperate. "Tell me. Is he dead? Is Harvey dead?"

I swallowed, looked down at Frieda. She appeared small standing there before me. It formed on my lips: *No, he took the money and ran off with Roxie. He left you behind.*

The vehicle was part moon buggy, part hearse. Roman. He wasn't supposed to show up until tonight.

A white truck pulled in after him: the F-150. *That* one was Trent. They squeezed in behind Frieda's Audi so she couldn't get out. Neither of us could.

CHAPTER

67

The Money

I MARCHED STRAIGHT TO Roman and whispered, "What are you doing here? I wasn't supposed to meet with you until later."

Roman stretched, scratched his side. "I got impatient."

He brought people, the same two guys from the fireworks stand. He introduced them as Dario and Fabian. Dario was older with thinning hair and the smile too taut for his face. Fabian was the younger one with no smile—straight-faced Fabian.

Roman breathed in deeply. "I do like the air up here. You mountain people are a strange breed, but I get it."

I said, "I can't talk right—"

He lifted a finger. "I keep thinking about that day you got shot, what happened with the money. A whole sack full, and everybody's pointing fingers at everybody else."

I shifted feet. According to Harvey, the Seattle set had condemned it as Harvey and Frieda's liability. They ate the loss.

Roman scanned the woods, scanned the treetops and Mr. Traverse's cabin, then my little log cabin garage apartment where Em waited.

He said, "When it comes down to it, the last person who had their hands on that money—"

His eyes fell on mine. "Is you."

I stole a glance at my window. I didn't care what happened to me. I just needed to get Em safe.

I said, "Okay. We'll talk about that. But not now. I got people here."

Trent was climbing out of his F-150.

"What people? I know her." He waved at Frieda, who stared back, morose.

Then Roman sauntered in the direction of the F-150, stepping on Frieda's sunglasses along the way.

He waved me over. "Introduce me to your friend."

I followed. Left with no alternative, feeling like my own face had pinched into a bat, I said, "Trent, this is Roman. Roman, Trent."

Roman was already shaking Trent's hand, but Trent must have picked up on my discomfort because he frowned. "What. He a friend of yours?"

I said, "Business associate."

Trent's frown deepened. "Business? What the hell kinda business?"

Roman laughed. "Business and friendship go hand in hand. We like Janey."

Trent's mouth creased.

I said to Roman, "I'll get my daughter, and then Trent's heading out. Then we can . . . talk."

Roman tapped out a Marlboro and offered it to me like he hadn't heard. I shook my head. He offered one to Trent, who accepted.

Roman extracted another cigarette for himself, then gestured at the driveway. "This road, I tried to take it at the speed limit and thought my air bag was going to deploy."

Trent said, "Yeah. They're slow getting around to paving things around here."

Roman first lit Trent's cigarette, then his own, then did his flourishing wave of the match. I turned and headed for my apartment, fast, but without running.

But Roman called, "Join us!"

I paused, looked over my shoulder. He wasn't speaking to me.

Roman said, "Frieda! It's been so long. Do you know Trent?"

Trent grinned. That fast, he was grinning. Roman, too. Dario and Fabian had eyes on me. Dario smiled his taut smile, and straight-faced Fabian just stared.

Here, as I occupied this blur between winter and spring, I longed like never before to be that person who knew how to be a good mother. Would a good mother retrieve her daughter and march her up that driveway, escort her through that gauntlet of outlaws?

Think!

We could escape behind the garage to the deer trail. Run through the woods to town. But we'd have to cross the meadow first. They'd see us.

One bullet left. I'd shot at that mushroom twice and missed both times, but I did come close.

* * *

Em had dressed for skiing and packed her train case.

"Come on, baby, let's get you into your dad's truck. Quick and quiet, understand?"

"Got it."

I led her to the door. "Hold my hand. Don't talk to anyone, just go straight to the F-150. If your dad hangs around gabbing, you wait inside the truck and play with your dolls. Okay?"

"Mom, I saw the guy from Suspicious Perks. Is everything all right?"

Things were not all right. I didn't want to scare my daughter but I didn't want to fib, either. If this should be the last time I ever saw her, I couldn't allow my final words to be lies.

"Just do as I ask, baby."

We got halfway down the steps—only to find Dario and Fabian waiting in the garage. Roman entered through the side door.

I said, "Where are the others?"

Roman nodded toward the driveway. "Oh, Trent's helping Frieda look for her car keys."

He pulled them from his pocket, tossed them in the air and caught them. "You're not the only one who grew up a street kid."

I folded Em tight against me. "What do you want?"

"We're going to find what disappeared."

He moved a step closer. "I'm going to give you some advice. I hope you'll listen."

He directed the next statement at Em: "For your daddy's sake . . ."—finger to his lips—"Shhhh . . ."

He glared at Dario and Fabian, then jerked his head toward Em.

I scooped her into my arms and ran back up the steps as Dario pursued, his footfalls like explosions in my head. His taut smile had disappeared.

He snatched the train case from Em and handed it to Fabian, then dragged me back down the steps. Neither Em nor I screamed, though neither of us could stanch our muffled whimpers. Roman pointed at the case. Em's eyes froze in horror.

Fabian opened her train case and emptied her dolls onto the oil-stained concrete, then pawed at the lining. One of the old hinges broke. I clutched Em tighter and swiveled her away from the men. She trembled in my arms.

Roman whispered something I couldn't hear, and Fabian took out a long jagged knife, and cut away the satin lining.

I shout-whispered, "What are you doing?"

How utterly stupid. I had my hands on that money. *They* had their hands on that money. The bundles were hefty inside their precious, stupid, godforsaken backpack and it never would have fit behind the frayed lining of my daughter's train case.

I said, "Go through my apartment! My car. My bank accounts. I have nothing! I am destitute. I am not stashing your idiot money."

Roman scowled. The other two stared. My heart rabbited.

Roman said, "All right, little girl. Go see your daddy."

* * *

I escorted Em to Trent's F-150 and she climbed in back—without her train case, now destroyed, alongside her dolls on the garage floor.

I stroked her hair and whispered, "I am so sorry, honey. Are you all right?"

"I'm fine, Mom. He didn't hurt me. I won't tell anyone."

"I wasn't—"

But thank God she'd keep quiet. Speaking of this would only mean more danger for her. I had made a wolf's lair.

I glanced back where Frieda sat behind the wheel of her Audi—she'd looked confused and frightened when we passed, but now I could only see her from the back.

I kissed my daughter on the forehead and walked around to Trent.

He gestured toward Frieda. "I don't know what's wrong with her. Think she's getting a little dotty."

I said, "You better go. Em's supposed to go skiing with Isabelle's family."

He took off his Peak Auto Repair hat and thwacked it on his jeans. "Listen, they're finally voting to rename Cable Hill. Wanna know what the new name's gonna be?"

"Trent, please go."

"The Balcony. As in, looking down from a balcony. I think they even considered Pedestal Hill. Isn't that crazy?"

I looked across the clearing to the darkening sky.

He said, "Thing is, I probably won't get to vote on that. You had it right. I got notice. Bank's taking back the house."

My eyes shot up to him. "But you got your job back with Roy."

"Yeah, I did. But you know, the payments were already so far behind. Felt like pissin' into the ocean."

I cast helplessly at Em in the back seat, and looked at Trent. If I didn't survive this next hour with Roman, Trent was supposed to make a decent home for Em.

I said, "What about Sherry?"

"She's not thrilled about the foreclosure, but we're good. We'll make it through."

I closed my eyes. "Thank God."

"Really? You're happy about Sherry and me?"

"She's good for you, and she's good for Em. Em likes her. You need to make a proper home for your daughter, though." My voice cracked.

I glanced over my shoulder as Roman emerged from the garage. Dario and Fabian were likely going through my car and my apartment—using that long blade.

I said, "Please, get the hell out of here."

He pointed at Roman. "That guy a problem?"

"Just go."

His brows drew together. "Listen. This is why I came right away. Roy and the boys found something when they were working on your Subaru. There was a tracker. One of the cars was making a sound while it was in the shop. They couldn't figure out which one. But as of today we cleared them all. So the only other one it could have been was yours. Any reason someone might have put a tracker on your car?"

CHAPTER

68

Raw Dog Cereal

I PROMISED TRENT WE'D talk later. He finally left—with Emmie. Em was safe. Nothing else mattered.

Roman, Dario, Fabian, Frieda, and I assembled around the gutted stuffing of my couch in my cramped living room, everyone afraid to stand in the wrong spot lest they bump their heads on the sloped ceiling.

Frieda sat in the Windsor chair, and Roman and I sat on the slashed couch while Dario and Fabian continued to ransack my apartment. It wouldn't take them long.

I glared at all the stuffing on the floor. "These couch cushions unzip. You didn't have to slash them."

Roman spread his arms along the back of the couch, crossing an ankle over his knee. The mess bothered me even knowing I may not survive the day. Mr. Traverse, who charged me fifty cents a phone call during emergencies, who rarely waved at me, was an otherwise good and fair landlord and didn't deserve to have his garage apartment ruined. I hoped they wouldn't leave it bloody. Roman with his casual executions looked prepared to kill us right here, today. Leave our bodies in the dissected living room. How mortifying. No, I didn't believe a dead person like Cable Gross cared about a name like Cable Hill after his bones stopped pumping marrow. But I, Janey Hendee, was still alive, and I didn't want Mr. Traverse to have to deal with the mess.

I didn't dare think about Em.

Canned goods flew from the pantry. I closed my eyes.

Frieda said, "I am needed at the office. I have clients."

Roman ignored her. He walked to the kitchenette where Fabian was elbow deep, raw-dogging my bulk sale bag of cereal.

Roman said to me, "Where's all your food?"

"What are you talking about? Right there, that's our food."

He opened the fridge, scanned, let twenty-six cents in kilowatt hours leak into the already drafty living space, slammed it shut. Rubbed the back of his head.

"This is all the food you have?"

I shrugged. I sometimes clipped coupons but found them to be 95 percent rabbit hole and 5 percent payoff. I bought everything in bulk, on sale, off brand. My little kitchenette was lean.

I said, "Oh, I get it. If you didn't find wads of cash, you thought you'd find signs I blew money on high-dollar coffee and yogurt smoothies. Like I'm some big spender."

He said, "You've at least been making the money from the drops. You can't buy the little girl some Cinnamon Toast Crunch?"

I looked at Frieda. "Do you want to tell him or should I?"

On the Windsor chair, Frieda massaged her knees. "I've been making sure Janey's pay goes straight to her medication. It's in her best interest."

Roman scowled, then waved off Dario and Fabian, terminating my apartment's strip search. They joined us in the living area.

Roman drew a pistol from its holster and placed it on the coffee table. The barrel was three times the length of Logan's Saturday night special. Frieda stared at it as though assessing whether she could snatch it with any beneficial outcome.

Dario and Fabian did not sit. They bookended Frieda and me.

Next to me, Roman resumed his position of spread arms and figure-four legs on the couch. Beautiful smile. "Let's talk."

* * *

Roman gestured between Frieda and me. "It feels like neither one of you wants to be my friend."

I said, "I've had more sincere friend requests from Nigerian princes on Facebook."

"We've lost rapport."

"You just terrorized my daughter. You're worse than her"—I nodded toward Frieda.

Frieda kept still.

Roman said, "All right. You have completely fallen out of contact. People are disappearing. I want to know what's going on."

He pointed at Frieda. "Where is your husband?"

Frieda glanced at me with a flash of vulnerability, a woman who'd lost the man she loved. Hard to think of Frieda and Harvey that way, but you never know what goes on inside a marriage.

She looked at Roman. "I haven't heard from him."

She could out me as knowing something about Harvey's fate. In the moments before Roman showed up, I'd said I could tell her whether Harvey was dead or alive.

Roman pointed at me. "You? What do you know about Harvey?"

I felt no more loyalty for Roman than I did Harvey, but I would *not* give up my girl Rox. If they hunted down Harv they'd find Roxie, too, and that wasn't okay.

Odds were that I'd go down in flames today anyway. So fuck 'em.

I said to Roman, "After you and I spoke, Harvey called me. He said you wanted to meet me at the mine tonight."

I flung my arm at my apartment. "As in not here. Not like this."

My body did not feel the indignation my words pulled off.

I drew in my breath and took it down a peg. "That was the last I heard from him. He was supposed to attend the Big Bald Luck games, but he never showed."

Roman said, "If he's missing, we'll find him. No one stays missing for long. Not from us."

I didn't like the sound of that.

Roman said, "He's not the only one missing."

I pushed on one of my cuticles. "You mean Guy Hamm? We had to kill him."

Frieda startled in her chair.

Roman lurched forward. "Fucking mountain people. Who is *we*?"

"Everyone. He shot off his mouth and blew up the mine. And you, Roman, with your *bullshit*, you damn near got me killed *twice*."

* * *

Roman glanced at his guys, then made a rolling motion at me. "Back up. Tell me about the money."

"I don't have your money. It was stolen out of my station wagon. Look at my apartment door—the lock's torn out. The garage window's broken."

"Seven hundred fifty-thousand dollars doesn't just vanish."

My stomach pitched. I had no idea I'd been hauling around that much money. I was thinking tens of thousands. The entire game board reconfigured itself in my mind.

He turned to Frieda. "Where has our money been going?"

She straightened in her Windsor chair. "Are you talking about Baltazar's legal defense?"

Roman rose from the couch, which caused me to seesaw lower into my half.

He retrieved his pistol and cocked it. "I am not talking about Baltazar's legal defense. I am talking about our bribes."

Frieda threw a hand toward me. "I don't want to talk about sensitive matters in front of her. Tell her to leave the room."

"She stays."

Frieda closed her eyes, folded her hands. "It takes time. The case has drawn media attention, so we can't just spring Mr. Valencia out the back door."

Roman muttered something to Dario, and Dario set down a pen and notepad in front of Frieda.

"Write down the names," Roman said.

Frieda shook her head. "I can't just—"

"We are done playing. Write them down. A police chief. A prosecutor. Two judges."

Frieda drew herself into her tweed coat and wrote a list. Watching her scratch notes infuriated me. I'd seen her do that in her office, when she tried to get me to sign away my rights to my daughter.

When she finished, Roman tore off the paper and handed me the notepad. "Now you."

I glanced at him, then Frieda. As much as I hated her, I understood that this could end her life. She was a sad, sick woman and she needed to be locked up—with a psych eval—but I had no desire to see her tortured and killed.

"Write it down," said Roman.

There was no way around it. Doug Barkling would soon make his announcement, and then it would be too late. I began to write.

CHAPTER

69

A Police Chief, a Prosecutor, and Two Judges

ROMAN SCANNED MY list, then nodded. "I knew you could do it."

Frieda's brows knit, forming a new shape other than her bat.

Roman read aloud from Frieda's list: "Police Chief Quincy Tigner," then from my list, "Police Chief Quincy Tigner—likely no bribe."

He regarded me. *"Likely?"*

"You can't prove a negative," I said.

Frieda took affront. "She doesn't know! Why are you elevating that little gutter trash?"

I looked at her. "Prove me wrong. Call up Quincy right now."

Frieda's expression went flat. Roman had confiscated both our phones and keys, but Frieda didn't ask to place the call.

Roman said, "Frieda's list says, 'Doug Barkling,' and Janey's list says, 'County Attorney Doug Barkling'—that one's too easy, by the way. There's only one prosecutor."

He turned to Frieda. "You want to know what Janey put on her list?"

Frieda's coloring receded to parchment.

Roman said, "Actually, I'm not sure I understand myself. I think it's a No. Janey, please explain what you wrote."

I did not enjoy this. "Doug Barkling has not been receiving any bribes. He is going to seek capital punishment against Baltazar Valencia."

I swallowed and darted my eyes toward Frieda. It looked like she already knew this.

I said, "There'll be a public announcement."

Roman's expression turned from sobriety to shock. And folded into rage. Clearly he'd expected confirmation that Frieda and Harvey had been swindling them. This, however, was an embarrassment.

No one in the Red King's army or elsewhere would respect him again. And here's me, the messenger. We all know what happens to the messenger. Dario started to speak, and Roman barked him down.

He said, "The death penalty."

I nodded.

Red heat crept to his face. "We've been paying a man who was supposed to make this go away, and instead he wants to put Baltazar to death."

Roman swung his pistol up to Frieda. She whimpered.

I said, "Roman, you need her."

He kept the gun leveled at her head. Frieda's eyes streamed. I saw the space in the forehead where the bullet would land. Her hair framed it. A forehead is a part of the face we rarely notice—we look at the eyes, the mouth—but when someone points a gun in someone else's face, the forehead becomes everything. The creases come out. The skin becomes dewy. I watched Frieda's terror, and I saw the lifeforce behind that space, the brain; the wickedness, her memories of pain, and whatever was left of her that was worthy of pity.

I said, "Roman. There are two more names on that list. Two judges. One's a No. But the other, the other one's a Yes. Judge Mitch Goshen."

Roman didn't budge.

I said, "Frieda, is Mitch Goshen one of the names you wrote down?"

She gulped, her eyes fluttering. "Yes."

"Roman, listen. Of all the bribes to have banked, the judge would be the one. You need Frieda to work with Judge Goshen. If she dies or goes missing, he'll spook. You won't be able to touch him."

Roman said, "He can work with somebody else in our network."

"I doubt he'll do that."

The pistol formed its vector on Frieda. I saw Guy Hamm pointing his gun at me in the same way. The horror of his remains forming a G while we wondered what to do with him—not even twenty-four hours ago. His laugh still echoed in my brain. Frieda was my enemy, but I didn't need her haunting me, too.

I said, "Roman, you need that judge."

He lowered the pistol.

He gestured to his men. They hoisted Frieda—she had trouble standing—then they hustled her out of my apartment. She cast me a plaintive look before the door closed behind them.

Roman sat back down next to me on the gutted couch.

I said, "Where are they taking her?"

He waved his pistol, then rubbed his forehead like he had a headache. "They'll wait for us by the car."

Us. They waited for *us*. I didn't want to think where they'd take *us* after such humiliating news. At least they wouldn't leave corpses all over Mr. Traverse's place.

Roman said, "Let's have a quiet chat before we join them. Just you and me."

CHAPTER

70

The Tangled Web I Weave

ROMAN HELD HIS pistol, and my tiny snub nose remained in my boot—with its one shot left.

He said, "Tell me about Guy Hamm. Is he really dead? Did you really shoot him?"

I nodded, leaned back on the couch. "We all did."

I did not shoot him—Jude did that while I'd crossed my wrists over my face in terror. It felt like we'd all pulled the trigger because everyone participated in the cleanup work.

I was crap at lying. But perhaps if I hovered just over the surface of truth, maybe I could get away with it, just this once.

Roman said, "Tell me."

"We were at the Big Bald Luck games. Harvey was supposed to join us but never showed. I didn't know Guy Hamm was mixed up in your nightmare, but he and I got into some friction."

I scowled at Roman. "It would have helped if you told me things like that. You're always popping off about trust. You know what, I need some water. You want water?"

"Got anything stronger?"

"I don't drink. I can offer you mountain spring water, straight from the tap."

He snorted. "I will take your *highly regarded* mountain water. Do you have aspirin?"

I went to the tap and filled two glasses. "I don't do pain killers."

"Aye aye aye."

From down below in the driveway, screaming erupted. I dashed to the window and pulled the sheers. Frieda struggled against Dario, her tweed coat discarded in the mud. Fabian hovered over them both with an ax. I tried to turn away. I didn't want to see them kill her. And yet my body betrayed me and I stood paralyzed.

Fabian swung the ax, severing her hand.

It lay on the stump Mr. Traverse used to chop firewood. Frieda's arm now ended at the wrist and was leaking blood. She broke away from Dario and sank to her knees with her one hand dug into the earth.

"Hey, hey, hey," Roman said. "It's over, just one clean chop. I don't know, maybe it took two. Come on."

I collapsed to the linoleum, the childproof tumbler bouncing from my hands. Water splashed everywhere.

Roman dragged me back to the couch and hunted for a towel. He returned to the window, opened it, whistled to the trio below. He tossed the towel.

He sat down next to me and handed me a fresh glass of water. "See? They're wrapping the arm. She can last like that a long time."

I gulped the water and spilled it down my shirt.

He said, "Please continue. Guy Hamm."

* * *

People make like compartmentalization is bad. It's coping. The hinge word is "mental." When people endure horrors, compart-*mental*-ization enables them to function until they can deal with the trauma one inch at a time. Street kids get good at this.

I tucked what I'd witnessed back into the invisible space where I'd once had a molar, and I continued, voice shaking. "Guy Hamm was furious with you guys. Enough to go down in a blaze of glory, and I mean that both literally and figuratively. Guy started picking fights at the card game. Next thing I know, he pulled a gun on me and was hurling accusations. He thought I was some kind of a queenpin. Like I was taking over his business with this big master plan."

Roman's eyes lit. "Queenpin? You . . . ?"

He rubbed his hand over his mouth. "Ohhh."

"What do you mean, 'Ohhh'?"

For the first time since I'd spoken of the death penalty, Roman set his gun back on the table. "I may have contributed to that misapprehension."

"Misappre*hension*?"

"We use that mine for transport. I tried to show you, but you refused to enter. I probably would have filled you in about Guy Hamm's involvement then."

He shook his finger at me. "You accuse me of not telling you things. But you were being difficult."

"Because I wouldn't enter a dark cave with some stranger!"

He said, "Guy Hamm's a pain in the ass. I felt no rapport with him."

I appraised Roman, recalling how he'd once spoken of having rapport with me. Probably this meant he believed he enjoyed dominion over me.

He said, "Guy didn't think we'd continue to use the mine. We might not. The heat's off the ports, and coming all this way is a grind. But that doesn't mean we'll abandon it. If you have a good resource, you keep it, even if you don't always use it. Guy Hamm wanted to finance other mining ventures, and he put up Big Copper Ridge as collateral. We caught wind and financed the loan, but as a third party. He didn't know it was us. We called in the note, and he figured it out."

"I don't understand."

Roman smiled his beatific smile. "I had Frieda draw it up as Hendee Interests LLC. We knew Frieda didn't like you, and we wanted to put her off balance."

I recalled Harvey referring to my spectacularly timed, precision fuck-up. I'd believed it had to do with Logan, and maybe that was indeed what he meant. But I saw now that the Seattle set had already decided to use me to antagonize Frieda.

I said, "Well, that's just brilliant, Roman. Maybe before you go poking sticks into hives, you should think about consequences. Frieda going mad with jealousy. And Guy Hamm losing his mind, trying to kill me. It doesn't exactly make for a smooth operation."

I waved toward the garage. "You'd think since he stole that bank bag from my Subaru after shooting me, he could come up with the cash to pay off his note."

It was the wrong thing to say.

Roman's face darkened. He still harbored some belief I'd taken that money. I had no idea how far three-quarters of a million dollars went toward mining properties—whether Guy could pay off his loan, pay it down, or what. And if he did pay with a sudden blob of cash, wouldn't that raise flags?

To me, 750,000 might as well be 10,000 or 40 million. I had no concept of such money other than it scared me.

Trying to regain footing, I said, "Do you realize what you've set off? In the end we *all* killed Guy, and *everyone's* a witness."

"You are referring to the people at the games."

"Everyone. Before we shot him, Guy was raging over losing Big Copper Ridge, and so he ran his mouth to people around town: at Suspicious Perks, the Hideout, Jemma's Finds. Told everyone that Seattle drug runners had taken over his mine. They were going to blow it up. Do you have any idea how something like that gets around?"

The lies scorched my lips.

Roman frowned. "Blow it up?"

"I guess because he thought my name was on the note. He told me I'd never get the mine. It'd all be gone by morning. After he tried to shoot me and we all killed him, we decided to bury him in the mine because we didn't know where else to stash the body. But he'd already set explosives on a timer. He blew it up."

Roman frowned, eyes wide. "Did you call the police?"

"That's not how we do things around here."

"Don't you have a county coroner at your games?"

"Did Harvey tell you that? He should learn to keep still. Our attendees change, and we keep them secret." My breath heaved from the exertion of navigating lies so close to the truth.

I said, "Our problem is"—*our* problem, I specified, not *his*—"everyone at the games knows about the cartel now. They all witnessed Guy's meltdown. Same with everyone in town that Guy mouthed off to yesterday. I don't even know how many dandelion seeds he blew into the wind. They'll have been talking about it all last night, and it'll have spread."

"You should have called me."

"I was busy with dead body cleanup and if you haven't noticed, phone service out here is crap."

His gaze swung to the window. "It's crap, all right."

I said, "The mine rubble is unstable. I wouldn't walk six feet inside. I don't know how soon anyone'll find out."

Roman thought it over. "They might not. I can shut it down."

I nodded. His eyes dropped to his pistol.

I licked my lips, hoping he couldn't see my pounding heart. "Good. And I can do some damage control on my end."

He looked into my eyes. It seemed he still hadn't made up his mind yet what to do with me.

I said, "Since the gossip machine is already churning, I could give it a little fuel. Today's Thursday and I'll be the only waitress on shift at the Hideout. Thursdays are gossip nights. I can shape it to our favor. Put some spin on it."

Two fingers over his mouth, Roman drew his brows tight, shifted, then finally nodded. "Hmm."

I said, "Are you done with Frieda?"

He shrugged. I didn't know what that meant.

He got to his feet and stepped toward the door. I rose with him.

He said, "A death penalty defense is costly. She's our attorney and we gave her a substantial sum, not just the $750,000. One option is to recover part of that money in legal services."

He gave me a pointed look. "It doesn't mean we stop searching for it."

"I don't know what in the hell happened to your money. Back at Ponderosa Lodge, *you* lectured *me* about the money-obsessed culture."

He scoffed. "Well. We owe you, what, fifteen thousand dollars and a new home? And a different car."

"I don't need to relocate anymore."

"No? What about the money? Fifteen thousand."

In any other situation, I'd jump on it. But not from these guys, not under these circumstances.

He laughed. "Come on, real Cinnamon Toast Crunch for the kid. I have your envelope in the car."

I shook my head and backed away, feeling a shift I didn't want to acknowledge. The room had taken on a hard vibration.

He waved his gun toward the door. "Don't make this difficult."

* * *

"No, Roman, please." I staggered backward, the Saturday night special—the Suicide Special—molten inside my boot. One bullet left.

I'd used up ten minutes convincing myself he'd bought into my plan. That he'd spare me.

If I lunged for my snub nose, he'd shoot me in the head before I even reached my boot. There was nowhere to run.

I offered pleading hands. "I'm a mother. I cannot leave my child without a mother."

"Baltazar doesn't care about that."

"Will you shut up with your bullshit! There is no Baltazar! He stopped existing when they threw him in jail. Did he murder your parents? Took you in, the little card-dealing street kid? I'll bet he pretended to be a father figure, just to extract some kind of Pavlovian loyalty out of you. I had one of those, too."

I flung a finger toward his gun. "You want to shoot me because I'm inconvenient. You'd turn my daughter into another street kid like you and me. Don't put that off on Baltazar. It's you making that decision."

He scowled, red fury returning to his cheeks. "I would have taken you somewhere quiet. Give me one reason why I shouldn't shoot you right here for your daughter to find."

I licked my lips, my hands trembling. I racked my brain. I'd already given every argument in my bag of tricks.

Except—

"Rawhide."

He frowned. "What the hell is that?"

"Rawhide is the name of Harvey's FBI agent."

His face went blank.

I gathered my breath and pressed forward. "On the first day this started for me, Harvey called Rawhide at three in the morning and woke him up. It was a way to show me that he had a connection with the FBI."

Roman's brow furrowed.

I said, "Your payroll had a police chief, a prosecutor, and two judges—but you never asked me about an FBI agent. Harvey's got something going that he hid from you."

"Are you telling me the truth?"

I thought it over. Harvey might have simply beat that FBI agent at cards somewhere and won the privilege to call him up in the middle of the night, and Rawhide played along with the masquerade. Or maybe Harvey knew him from school. Or Rawhide was dirty—but not directly known to the Red King's army.

And of course, there was the possibility that Harvey was cooperating with the FBI.

I said, "Read into it what you will. Harvey disappeared knowing full well you Seattle guys would come looking. If he's working with the feds, they might have pulled him out. Frieda seems to have known nothing about it."

Roman searched my eyes. He made a clicking noise with his tongue, fingers tapping his thigh.

He stepped forward and took my hand, put it to his face, and breathed in.

He said, "Gun powder. You fired that tiny weapon of yours recently. You really did shoot Guy Hamm."

I jerked my hand away.

He added, "You might be telling the truth about the FBI."

Then he gave me a flat-eyed smile. "Weave your little gossip web at the roadhouse."

Blood pounded in my ears. I waited.

His eyes dropped to my throat and slowly climbed up again. "This has nothing to do with whether or not I am willing to kill you. I have no problem leaving orphans behind."

He turned his back to me and hesitated, hand on the doorknob. The Saturday night special throbbed heartbeats inside my boot.

He looked back at me. "Baltazar didn't have my parents killed. He did get them embroiled in the mess that ended their lives."

He walked out and closed the door behind him, his footfalls descending the garage steps. I sank to my knees.

The outer door slammed. Their voices called to one another. The sounds of engines turning over. Quiet, luxury vehicle engines—nothing like the Subaru. Gravel scraping the driveway.

I pulled Logan's gun from my boot and set it before me on the couch-fuzzed floor.

My fingers did smell like gunpowder. I'd shot mushrooms off the tree stump where Frieda's severed hand now lay in the rain. I had receipts for the entire line of bullshit I'd just fed Roman. Everything in my tale would check out. I was a wolf among wolves.

I could tell myself I was clever. I'd talked my way out of a death sentence. I'd cleansed Suspicion of these criminals.

But I knew better. My fingers just *happened* to smell like gunpowder. What were the chances?

It stemmed from that flip of a coin all those nights ago. My winding road to luck.

CHAPTER

71

Lending a Hand to Frieda

I SCANNED THE MUSIC storage area of the Hideout. Harvey had come here before he'd bugged out. He'd left it in disarray. I knew it was him and not someone from the Red King's army, or even Frieda; I knew it was Harvey because he'd taken his vibraslap.

It fell to me to put things in order, and putting things in order was how I rolled—going manic helped but was not required. Gabe and I would serve the usual Thursday dinner crowd. My eyes were bloodshot, my face puffy, but no one would give it a second thought. They'd be thinking of Gabe's steak fries and tonight's lip-smacking gossip about Guy Hamm, who just left. (*Did you see him? Yeah, think so. Isn't that his truck out there?*)

Roxie had said she'd stashed something for me.

I went to Tag Benson's "real and actual Sasquatch" photo, pulled the upside-down chair off the table, and stepped up onto it. Taped to the back of the photo, an envelope bulged with mucho dinero. I whistled. Eight hundred dollars. Lucky for me old Tag Benson wasn't using one of those instant Polaroids back in 1981, or all this cash would never have fit.

Also inside the envelope I found a lip color: American Woman by NARS. Similar to the one Dannie had been wearing the night she'd told me about Logan, only a different shade. Dannie's had been called Somebody to Love. It had given me a catch in my throat then, and thinking about it had the same effect now.

Rox had left a note:

Hey girl,

This is your money anyway. You should match your lip color to your nips, and I took a guess on yours. You already got somebody to love. Before putting it on, go watch a how-to video or you'll look like a blow-up sex doll.

xo
Rox

I read it through twice and praised my decision to give up being a beauty influencer.

My phone rang. At the same moment, the growl of motorcycles rose from down the Hideout road. Frieda's name displayed on my caller ID. I gasped.

"Frieda?"

"Janey, it's me, Quincy."

I licked my lips. The police chief calling from Frieda's cell phone sounded like bad news for Frieda.

He said, "We're over here on South Farm to Market. I just sent Frieda's Audi over the cliff. Make it look like an accident. She wants me to check on you, see if—"

My stomach dropped. I didn't say anything, didn't bail him out. Let him flounder through what he was trying to get across.

"You know. If you made it or—"

I said, "Frieda doesn't care if you check on me, Quince. This is her proving to me that you were on the take."

"What? No, it's not like that. They threatened—"

"Forget it."

"I thought Harvey told you."

"Please, Quincy. I know." I was the last person who should judge him.

I recalled Frieda's face turning to paper when Roman had read my list aloud, and I'd put down Quincy Tigner as a probable No. Frieda had pushed back, but only a little. Likely because she'd already marched three steps into the future, and she knew the rest of the list would prove disastrous.

I said, "But Logan—what about his murder?"

Because I didn't understand why Guy Hamm wanted him dead. To inflame the Seattle set? It wasn't Logan Chasse's name on some bogus lending agreement.

"It's like I said, Janey. You kiddin' me? I wouldn't lie to you about that. He slipped, he fell, he drowned. Ask Maycie. She'll tell you—"

"All right. All right. Are you taking Frieda to the hospital?"

"Ambulance is on the way. They might air lift her."

"I still have her—"

I paused, swallowed. "Frieda's hand is still over there at my place. I don't know if they can reattach it or if it's too late. She was wearing rings. Does she want it?"

"Oh, God." He made a gurgle like this one question took him out, even though this whole time, he'd been standing next to a woman with a bloody towel wrapped around her freshly severed appendage.

He murmured to Frieda, then got back on the phone. "She wants it."

I said, "Go to my apartment. The lock's broken. I didn't want to just leave it on that stump so I put her hand in the refrigerator. You'll find it folded inside some flour sacks."

Cheap by the dozen, but nice enough for embroidery.

I said, "It looks like a neat white triangle bound with twine."

I could hear bike motors pouring into the Hideout parking lot. The Strangers had arrived.

* * *

Ponce stepped through the double doors as though he'd never been here before, taking in the great rustic chandelier, still missing a light; the wooden chairs upside-down atop wooden tables; the scuffed wooden floor. Tag Benson's framed photo still lay face-down before me.

I wrapped my arms around my ribs. "This time I won't ask how you guys knew I was here. Trent told me there's a tracker on my car."

Ponce said, "You can come with me for this, or stay behind and I'll get with you tonight. I recommend you do not come."

"I'm coming."

"Then you ride with me."

CHAPTER

72

The Murder of Logan Chasse

We gathered beneath the shelter of sassafras trees. Rain turned to sleet up here with the higher elevation of the falls. Snow lay in the forest's deeper shadows. The cinnamon-scented forest. I could *taste* it. Especially now with the sleet drawing essence from the timber.

That cinnamon scent came from a combination of sassafras and duff, and wood and bark and shale. How had I never before closed my eyes and breathed in this forest, this scent, and noticed that it smelled like cinnamon? The woodland creatures drew it out, sharpening tooth and claw on the bark. Now the sassafras bloomed in yellow-green flower clusters. Spring had taken hold, despite the sleet.

I had never looked up the story of the murderous families, the Sin of Man legend, to see if it was true. My little mountain town had fostered a tall tale, I felt sure of it now.

The Strangers and I stood by the silent water. Several feet down creek, Cinnamon Falls tumbled its dizzying vertical drop.

A flow rate of 16,000 cubic feet per second. Nowhere near the force of the larger waterfalls in this wilderness, but enough to kill.

From where I stood, I could not hear the falls. A strange auditory phenomenon. Here, the only sound came from sleet and wind and any noises we made ourselves. And yet if I walked twenty feet along the creek, I'd come to the weir, and I'd have to shout over the torrent.

I could see the ghosts from here. The spray billowed above the fall-off. Shifting, swaying, perfectly formed entities at the creek's end. Each seemed to watch us for the ephemeral moment of its existence before it disappeared and another entity formed.

At first I couldn't look at him. And then I couldn't take my eyes off him.

He was laughing with the others—Vaughn and Rendon, and two new guys. One called Carro and the other I didn't know. They weren't laughing along. They looked nervous. What did Cast Iron think? Did he believe they'd all come here to take me out? He seemed energized.

Perhaps I should be nervous. Me, with my snub nose in my leather jacket pocket, my one last shot, walking among Strangers.

Tracks led through the snow. Solitary tracks.

Cast Iron must have been watching from the corner of his eye because he said, "Look at that. Must have been a wolf up here. Or a coyote or something."

It was a wolf. Coyotes leave small ovals that hook inward. Wolf tracks are round and symmetrical, twice the size of coyote tracks. I knew because of Logan.

Carro said, "If I see a wolf, I'm shooting it."

Ponce said, "I'm out of smokes. You got one?"

Cast Iron reached into his vest. "Yeah, man, I got—"

As Cast Iron plunged his pocket for the cigarettes, Rendon snatched his piece and Vaughn grabbed his arm. The other two drew down on him.

Ponce said, "Never mind. Turns out I had a whole pack. Don't like your kind anyway."

* * *

Cast Iron scoffed. "What the fuck? You set me up?"

Rendon patted him down and found a Buck folding knife. He walked him toward the falls, Cast Iron laughing like it struck him funny. No different from any other day. Cast Iron enjoyed a smoke and a drink. He enjoyed backing me up bouncing people from the Hideout for a pot pie.

He enjoyed the hour of his destruction.

I followed to the exposed area of the ridge where the sleet took my cheek on one side, and a grassy shelf, devoid of snow, jutted into the creek. Here, the cascades rumbled up through my boots. The scent of mist mingled with sleet.

I said, "This is how you killed my cousin."

For once, Cast Iron wouldn't meet my eyes.

Ponce lit an American Spirit and took a deep drag, glanced at me as he blew it out. "We knew Logan had a thing going with Frieda. He wanted out but Cast Iron here wanted in. He thought there'd be a lot of money in it for the Strangers."

Ponce pointed his cigarette at Cast Iron. "But we voted on it and the vote was No. It should have ended there. But it sounds like one of our own kept the heat on Logan. You need to take a walk there, brother."

Cast Iron said, "Seriously? Logan was just a prospect. I *am* your brother."

"No point in arguing. It'll only mean a bullet for you. At least this way you got a fighting chance."

Ponce turned to the group. "Who's gonna keep time?"

I said, "I'll keep time."

I had no idea what Ponce was talking about but this centered around my cousin's murder. I wasn't just some leering observer from the balcony.

Ponce nodded at me. "He gets three minutes."

I pulled out the timer app I used for my card games. It gives warning tones along the way.

Ponce turned back to Cast Iron but instead of speaking, he delayed with another pull from his cigarette.

Finally, he said, "Cast Iron, if you can cross the falls in three minutes, then you win the prize of getting the fuck out of Montana by sundown, and we'll leave you the fuck alone. If you try anything then Rendon here gets to shoot you. I think you know, Rendon never misses. But if he does, Carro'll back him up."

Ponce continued. "If by some miracle you do make it across the falls in under three minutes, but fail to leave the state by sundown, you're a dead man. If you should ever come back to Montana again, you're a dead man."

I panned the shelf spilling to the falls and couldn't imagine anyone surviving that crossing. Only two rocks rose above the surface. Most sat just below it, disappearing to dark, roiling pools. I didn't know which were worse—the shallow flat surfaces or the mysterious black pools. The former would ride slick with algae. The latter would mean a heavy drag toward the falls with nothing to latch on to.

The way Ponce conveyed the rules, it sounded as if the Strangers had done this before.

Cast Iron said, "Can I have a smoke?"

Ponce said, "I got no problem with that so long as you smoke with your boots wet. Do it fast or your feet'll freeze up. You wanna be nimble."

Cast Iron splashed into the water like he intended to grab a few extra feet into the shelf before the timer started running, but stopped when his boots slipped. His arms swung out and he gave a hard grunt. Then he cackled for us like a contestant on a TV game show. I pressed my lips tight and watched. He clutched his pack of cigarettes but he'd crushed them, and he tossed them onto the bank.

He pointed at Vaughn. "That's for you, man. Sorry they're fucked up."

Vaughn retrieved the derelict pack.

Cast Iron took out a joint and lit it—three tries—inhaled slowly, held, released.

I recalled his friendship with Logan. How Cast Iron had ignited Logan's interest in motorcycles, traveled with him to look at that Victory Jackpot. How they both had the ever-present crinkle around the eyes like they'd just heard a joke. Logan had taken Cast Iron at face value. Just a simple guy who loved the steel horse, the outdoors. A joker—neither of them from around here.

Cast Iron teetered against a storming sky and twelve inches of creek bed before the drop-off to falls. Leaves, froth, and wave formation all sluiced around him in the same direction—over that shelf into nothingness.

He looked down and cried out, "Woooo! Look at that! The view from here is like, I feel like a fuckin' bird!"

He guffawed and took another toke, staring down the falls from a vantage point most only see from drone footage.

I shouted, "I hope that view's worth it!"

I gripped my phone with the timer and gritted my teeth.

Cast Iron looked at me, spread his hands like a drunken boyfriend caught flirting. "Aw, Janey, don't be that way. It was dark, I was drunk. Just wanted to scare him, but he ended up seeing my face. He slipped and—"

He shrugged. "Shit."

"Is that how it was when you shot me? You slipped?"

He laughed, took another drag, made a jump of his brows. "Look, it's nothing personal. I love both of you. Like family. Just tired of living tight on some shitty auto shop job."

Peak Auto Repair. I remembered seeing the motor oil beneath Cast Iron's fingernails. He had access to my car, and that's how he slipped in the tracker.

A golden leaf drifted past Cast Iron's boots and vanished into stormy sky.

Cast Iron said, "I wanted that Red King to see it was stupid to fuck around with civilians. They need a reliable soldier."

I shook my head. No point in telling him that Baltazar and Roman would never have brought him in. The drinking, the drugs, the affiliation with an outlaw motorcycle gang. The Seattle set wanted long-term anchors in the community, at least on paper. They pursued and cultivated people like Logan and me *because* we were teetotalers with no criminal records—ironically, mine was sealed as a juvenile. Logan and I were the kind of people who got weirded out by three-quarters of a million dollars in a backpack. Cast Iron was not.

Cast Iron looked down at his boots. "Damn, this water's cold."

He pulled from his joint, the end flaring red against the sleet.

I said, "Did you have fun with the money? Get a new bike? Did you hide it from your brothers here?"

Another laugh. His was not a Guy Hamm laugh. Cast Iron's was earthy and rolling.

He pointed his joint at me. "Girl, you owe me."

And then the joint rode the water's surface and disappeared over the negative edge, and Cast Iron splashed toward the opposite bank.

He pulled off a one-second advantage before I started the timer.

CHAPTER

73

Cast Iron's Run

CAST IRON SPRANG, practically flew, to the first rock, and in that motion had crossed almost half the stream. But it cost him. He landed in a crouch and cried out, his ankle turning sideways. I felt a bizarre thrill—not knowing whether I wanted him to succeed or fail.

Ponce had it right about numb feet. It probably made Cast Iron less nimble but it might have rendered him less susceptible to pain. He held the crouch, shuddering, then rose. The second jutting rock was an easy step from the first one, and he crab-walked to it, which put him at the halfway mark.

My timer dinged.

"Thirty seconds," I shouted.

He lunged into a pool and his body ballooned with the force. It looked like he'd sunk hip- or chest-deep. He turned his back to the fall-off, and that was a mistake. The full power of the creek hit him broadside. He nearly went over the edge.

But at the last instant of mad scrabble, he grabbed a shelf of rock which slipped through his hands and cracked him in the face. I cringed. But he'd turned at a good yaw to the creek flow.

He came up bloody but stable, and at a favorable angle.

He stationed there for a spell, a post in the flow, and I held my breath. Even if the Strangers hadn't imposed the deadly time limit, he'd have to keep going. He was crossing snow melt on a sleeting day at the edge of a waterfall. He'd freeze.

My timer dinged. "One minute!"

He moved up creek at the same angle to the flow, pivoted, lost his yaw, and lunged. He grabbed for shale but it only tumbled into his pool. But that at least gave a foothold that wasn't covered with algae. He scrabbled atop it.

Another chime. "Ninety seconds!"

Cast Iron had only a third the distance to cross. He belly-slid forward. The shelf upon which he'd landed spread long and singular, as opposed to the brittle, smaller rocks he'd contended with earlier.

"Come on, man," Vaughn said.

I blew out my breath, my eyes glued to my cousin's killer. I was both pulling for him and hoping he'd slide over the edge. It looked like Cast Iron had lost a tooth when he'd taken that rock to the face, and maybe crushed his nose. I recalled how Jude said Logan had sustained a cracked jawbone. That some unknown assailant had cold-cocked him. Cast Iron, trying to make him look weak to impress the cartel.

I wondered how well Cast Iron could breathe with his broken nose amid all that spray.

He crabbed over the algae-slicked rock, his butt in the air. It worked well. Until he moved too fast and reached a welter flowing over the slab. Then the water lifted him like a paper boat down a storm drain.

He vanished over the edge without a sound.

We froze, all of us, not speaking. It felt unreal. The water flowed over the rock into the sleeting sky. He'd gone so silently. It was as if Cast Iron had never been there.

* * *

The five Strangers and I crowded around the rim and peered into the cascades, each of us falling back almost immediately from vertigo. Carro sat down. I caught my timer at one minute, forty-three seconds, stopping it before it chimed. None of us saw Cast Iron's body. He was gone. Cinnamon Falls heaved with great spills of water, bursts of mist.

Ponce took a flask and poured whiskey over the churn, then took a swig. "Vaya con Dios, brother."

A few of the others did the same.

I staggered away and up the hill to the sassafras grove. Back to where snow still lay in patches of shadow. Back to the scent of cinnamon.

I crumpled into a squat and breathed between my knees, my hands at the back of my neck.

I had felt nothing watching Cast Iron die. No sorrow, no sympathy, not even satisfaction. The only thing: I couldn't breathe.

Before me, on the other side of a fir tree, came a puff of mist. Just like one from the waterfall, only small and on the wrong end of the creek.

It stepped out to look at me. A wolf.

The creature was bold. I should have been terrified. It had impossibly long front legs, golden eyes, and it emitted clouds as it breathed. It held my stare.

I said, "I heard you talking to the train."

A tear slid down my cheek.

I said, "You need to find a pack."

Snapping twigs advanced in my direction. The others were coming, their voices strengthening now that the shock had passed. The wolf gave a low growl.

I pulled out the little Saturday night special, Logan's revolver, the Röhm.

I aimed, and I shot.

The bullet landed true. I'd been sitting close enough that the pine bough tore loose and swept down between the wolf and me.

It worked. The creature turned and bolted up the slope. It couldn't expect to keep this mountain to itself forever.

From behind me, Carro said, "Shit, you scared it off. If I'd have seen that fucking thing, I'd have shot it."

Vaughn said, "The head'd look good mounted in the clubhouse."

Rendon said, "Shut up, assholes. Show some respect."

Ponce barked at them, "All of you. Give us the room."

* * *

I worked to catch my breath. Ponce was down to the butt of the same American Spirit he'd lit when he'd handed Cast Iron his sentence. Hard to believe the whole thing went down in the space of one cigarette.

Ponce lit a fresh one off the end. "I told you I didn't recommend coming."

I said, "The job I hired you for was to find out who killed my cousin. It didn't have to be an execution."

Ponce shrugged. "What we did just now wasn't for your benefit. It's club business."

I rummaged in my pocket, handed him Roxie's envelope. "There's about eight hundred of it. I'll get you the rest."

"Don't fuck around. Those guys lost a brother."

I nodded, then said, "How *did* you find out? How did you know it was Cast Iron?"

"He told me. Yeah, he was actin' weird. Mysterious errands in the night. So I asked him straight up. It's why he wanted to take you up on your offer. He wanted to resurrect all this bullshit. He thought he could convince the club to vote to take you down so he could get in with the Seattle set."

"*Did* the club vote? I mean, did anyone down there vote to have me killed?"

His face pinched. "Gettin' tired of all this shit, Janey. Club business is club business, and you're already in deeper than you got any right to be. I don't see you wearin' a fuckin' patch."

He started toward the trail, then turned. "Don't worry about the body. Ain't gonna be no floater showin' up in Cloudberry Creek. We'll find him and pull him out before it gets to that. So no clever stories. Got it? No nothing. The last time you saw Cast Iron was whenever you saw him at the Hideout."

I nodded.

Ponce took another drag from his cigarette and looked upslope to where the wolf had disappeared. "Probably won't be no questions anyway. People are used to Strangers driftin' in and out. It's why we're called Strangers."

Hearing the loneliness in that statement, I clutched the flannel over my heart, eyes toward the water. Joining them had been Logan's last desire.

Ponce continued down the trail.

CHAPTER

74

The Little Fox

JUDE RANG MY phone as I climbed into my Subaru.

He said, "Hi, pretty lady. I picked up some parts to replace your door lock."

"Thank you. Locks are probably overkill. It's a quiet town."

He chuckled, but I was only half-kidding. Unbeknownst to Jude, I'd driven off a dangerous ring of criminals. If that meant Suspicion went back to its old ways, crime here got pretty lazy. Nobody wanted to knock over a single mom who bought oat cereal in bulk and refused to spring for k-cups. One whose job at Harvey's Hideout ran on borrowed legs. With Harvey gone, I didn't know how long the roadhouse would stay open.

I'd called Dannie's new doctor, who started me on a minimal dose of medication, and I was supposed to start therapy—the kind where you talk out your woes. I wondered if it would stop me from wanting to shoot, smash, or jab. Seemed unlikely.

Jude said, "You still all right with me coming by to fix that lock?"

"Yeah, my shift won't run too late."

"I can get it done while you're on the clock. I'll make you something to eat afterward."

My belly filled with butterflies. Jude was A Good Man. With enough tarnish to shoot antlers off the ceiling every now and then. It sent a flood to my cheeks.

I said, "I'd like that. But let's take a rain check on dinner. I might not be able to hold down much more than tea and crackers. If you can stand that, it would be good to see you."

"I make a mean pot of tea, and you should see my flair when I open a sleeve of crackers."

I smiled to myself. "I drove by earlier. Your window looked empty."

"How's that?"

"No For Sale sign."

He chuckled. "Oh, that. I put that away. Town's gotten interesting."

A tone sounded, and I recognized the caller ID for Isabelle's mother.

I said, "That's Em on the other line. I've got to take this."

* * *

Em had opted out of skiing after all. I was glad because I wanted to see how she was dealing with all this. She asked me to come get her and even though I couldn't spend the night with her because of my shift, I went straight to Isabelle's place. Em came trotting down the walk, still wearing her sweater and ski pants though the rainstorm had broken to bright afternoon sun. An end to winter.

I pulled my daughter close and held tight. Em locked her arms around my neck. Tears sprang to my eyes, remembering that moment on the stairs when Roman's guys destroyed her train case.

"Are you all right, baby? I was so worried."

"I'm fine, Mom. Are those people coming back?"

"Never. It's over."

I repeated those words, letting them sink into our bones: *It's over.*

* * *

When Em was buckled up and I'd pulled onto the road, I said, "You have to stay the night with your dad, kiddo. I have to open the Hideout in forty-five minutes. But I'm glad we can grab a little time to talk."

"Yeah, Mom. We need to talk. I keep saying."

"Sorry. It's been rough on you but things are about to change."

I turned onto the lonely road toward Cable Hill where Trent awaited foreclosure. A tear-down that now would actually get torn down. Trent and Sherry would find someplace new in Suspicion, and Em would go to Logger Elementary, where (I hoped) she'd feel less inclined to terrorize classmates.

I said, "How do you feel about attending a new school?"

"I'm glad. I asked Dad if I could move a week ago. But Mom, you gotta listen. That's not what I want to tell you. It's been so long since we've been alone—"

I glanced at the rearview mirror and saw her face turning red. She was working herself up.

She said, "It's hot in here!"

"You're wearing your snow bib, honey. Let me kill the heat."

I switched it off and cracked the windows a few inches. The scent of woodlands filled the Subaru. Not like cinnamon, not like up by the falls. This smelled like heady pine and spring shoots.

Em screamed.

My eyes flew to the rearview mirror. Papers were blowing into her face and streaming out the window. She shrieked and tried to catch them. I tapped the brakes and pulled over, looked in my side mirror. They drifted along the road. A few of them had danced into the front seat.

Money. Hundred-dollar bills.

"That's what I've been trying to tell you, Mom!"

"All right, all right. Let's just—" I turned on my hazard lights.

Cold cash, all over the otherwise tidy, vacuumed, rusted-out, ancient car. I stuffed every bill I could find into the ever-accommodating Subaru console. Em did the same.

I said, "Does anyone know about this?"

She shook her head.

"Your dad?" Head shake. "Sherry?" Head shake. "Isabelle?"

"Mom, I have told no one. I've been waiting to get you alone."

I unbuckled myself and twisted to face her in the back seat. "Tell me what happened."

She took a breath. "When Dannie took us all out for hot chocolate, I wasn't supposed to stay the night with her. But I guess then something bad happened, right? You had an accident."

I nodded. The night of the fireworks stand, when Cast Iron shot me and I chased him into the woods.

She swallowed and looked into my eyes. "So Dannie took me back to the apartment to get some overnight clothes."

My heart stopped. Of course she would. I can't believe it hadn't occurred to me.

Emmie said, "And as I was going upstairs, I saw a bloody handprint on your car. So I waited until Dannie was on the phone in the kitchen, and I snuck back to get a better look.

"I got down in there and flipped on the light. And I saw a man going through the back of the Subaru. He was cutting open a backpack with a huge knife. So I screamed. Like, over and over."

My throat shrank to sand. That would have been Cast Iron, slicing open the locked backpack from the drop, staring at my daughter with his Buck folding knife in hand.

Em said, "Dannie threw open the door and ran down the steps with her gun. I thought she was going to shoot him. But he was gone. That's when we both saw the broken window. Dannie told me to run back upstairs.

"So I ran up and hid, but I could hear her. She kept saying, 'Come on out,' and 'Who wants to die,' and she was dropping the f-bomb. Then she went outside to look for him. I came back down and saw the bag he'd cut. The hole was barely big enough. I stuffed the crap ton of money into my overnight bag, and then we left. I told her I didn't need my train case after all."

I asked, "Did the guy know you'd taken the money?"

Em shook her head. "Maybe? I don't know if he got outside or what."

My pulse skipped. After Dannie scared him off, Cast Iron must have returned later to break into my apartment. He probably thought Em had hidden the money in there.

In the moment he made his run, Cast Iron's last words were, *Girl, you owe me.* He could have told everyone Em had the money. Instead he took the secret with him over the falls.

Em said, "It's not stealing if you're taking back what was yours to begin with."

I felt ill.

Em watched my face, searching for confirmation. "You made a crap ton of money for us, Mom."

I said, "It wasn't mine. I was holding it for someone else."

Now *she* looked ill.

I said, "That's why we talk about these things. You were right to tell me. I'm sorry you had to wait so long. We're going to work it out."

"Give it back?"

"Sort of. But we'll definitely keep it quiet. Never tell anyone. Not a soul. Got it?"

"You all right?" someone shouted to my left.

Em and I both screamed. We'd been so deep in conversation we hadn't noticed a woman had rolled up alongside the Subaru.

I said, "We're fine. Just pulled over. To . . . pee."

The woman looked shocked, nodded. She gave a pained smile, then drove away.

I checked my rearview mirror, saw hundred-dollar bills dancing in the vortex left by the vehicle's departure. The other driver hadn't noticed, or maybe she saw it as highway litter. We'd been lucky.

I said, "We'll have to collect the money that went out the window. A trail of Benjies is a little too high profile at a time when we're trying to melt back to normal life."

Em nodded, big-eyed and pointy-chinned, and for the zillionth time I felt the bittersweet kiss of memory in how much she reminded me of my mother.

* * *

I told Em to keep to the wooded area while I worked the road. My part went quickly—only a few bills there—and then I joined her on the shoulder and into the meadow, where we collected hundred-dollar bills we could not keep: a weird Easter hunt. The sky stretched clear and blue, and my mind tilted after what Em had told me.

Em said, "I have an idea."

"What's that, baby?"

"If we bury the money, maybe it would undo the Hendee curse."

I turned and looked her full in the face. "Where did you hear about that?"

"Dad told me."

I shook my head, scraping my lip. "I lost my mom and my aunt and grandma due to a disaster that hit a lot of people in this area. There's no such thing as the Hendee curse."

Saying it aloud made it true.

Patches of grass emerged, and spring flowers pushed toward the sun—florid green blades and yellow crocuses.

What were we going to do with three-quarters of a million dollars? We couldn't spend it because the Seattle set would find out. The money was radioactive. We couldn't even donate it.

Actually, maybe Em was right. The only thing I could think to do—it felt like a superstitious thing—was to bury it. And as it happened, I knew of an abandoned, caved-in mineshaft, a tunnel really, near the Canadian border.

Beyond, where snow still lingered under a grove of fir and hemlock, I saw tracks. Large hind feet, tiny forefeet. The snowshoe hare would change its colors to brown for summer, because it no longer needed to disappear into the snow. I added this moment to each time I'd come across those tracks—that first time with Logan, the last time with Em. Each day added another clue in how to be a mother to her.

I'd blundered through mistakes before her very eyes. By the time I, her wolf mom, got it right, she'd be full-grown.

The sun's warmth spilled across my shoulders. I noticed Em had left her own tracks in the damp earth. Hers looked different from mine—she walked in a straight line. One foot in front of the other. Like a little fox.

How startling, how pleasing, to discover my daughter was her own creature.

ACKNOWLEDGMENTS

It is with great pleasure that I sing out my gratitude to those who have helped with this book journey. First and foremost, thank you, readers, for accompanying me on this thrill ride. I'm a reader, too, a proud member of the tribe.

Great heaping wheelbarrows of thanks to Sandy Lu of Book Wyrm Literary Agency. You make me think twice. Your advice, expertise, (patience!), and friendship are so valuable to me. You are the jewel that turns the puzzle box.

Thank you to the wise and wonderful Tara Gavin at Crooked Lane. It felt like an instant connection to a kindred spirit, and how lucky I am that we could collaborate. It's been a delight to work with an editor of your experience, especially one with a love of the genre.

Thank you to my colleagues of Café Writing. Your dedication to the craft and love of the written word inspire me tremendously, as I've told you a hundred times during our daily Zoom check-ins. I probably learn more from you than from any writing classes I've taken—your challenges, your insights and discussions, and all those tiny, delectable epiphanies.

A special thanks to Thaisheemarie Fantauzzi Perez, who kept this clockwork ticking. Your capable management is a godsend. Also, much gratitude to Julia Abbott, Elizabeth Oliver, Dulce

Botello, Mikaela Bender, Megan Matti, Rebecca Nelson, Stephanie Manova, Lexi Baker, and our fearless leader, Matt Martz. Many thanks to Ian Koviak at theBookDesigners, who worked with Crooked Lane to design the cover. You have alchemized metal into gold.

To my family, especially my parents Richard Burns and Jacinta Burns: You are my rock. Also Jacquelyn McCann and Peggy Burns, my beloved aunts and lifelong advisers—and book club buddies! Deepest love to you all. The party never stops.

Thank you to Joanna Folger and Marc Folger, tellers of tales and practitioners of animal husbandry. I love you, Delf and Iota, nut and nut.

A deep, rolling, echoing thanks to Elizabeth Crook of noFilter-Editing.com. I toast a Dr. Pepper to the lack of filters—what every good book needs in a developmental editor.

Thank you to my Candlelight buddies, David Liss, Robert Jackson Bennett, Ronald Malfi, and Hank Schwaeble. It's been an honor to roll up my sleeves with writers of your caliber.

Thank you to the special people who have acted as mentors and guiding lights in my career, especially F. Paul Wilson, who gave me my first real red pen experience, and Harlan Coben, for the advice and wisdom. Eric Raab and Whitney Ross, I appreciate your professional support through major challenges.

Above all, from the bottom of my heart, thank you, Hank Schwaeble. What a treat to be married to a fellow author with amazing skill and a love of the craft. I get to bandy literary ideas with you, talk shop, and explore good reads. I am the luckiest kid.